A Girl among the Anarchists

A GIRL AMONG THE ANARCHISTS

By Isabel Meredith

*Introduction to the Bison Book Edition
by Jennifer Shaddock*

University of Nebraska Press
Lincoln and London

Introduction copyright © 1992 by the University of Nebraska
Press
Manufactured in the United States of America

First Bison Book printing: 1992
Most recent printing indicated by the last digit below:
10   9   8   7   6   5   4   3   2   1

Library of Congress Cataloging-in-Publication Data
Meredith, Isabel.
A girl among the anarchists / by Isabel Meredith.
p.   cm.
ISBN 0-8032-3168-7
ISBN 0-8032-8190-0 (paper)
I. Title.
PR6025.E58G57   1993
823'.912—dc20
92-12212   CIP

Reprinted from the original 1903 edition published by Duckworth & Co., London

INTRODUCTION

By Jennifer Shaddock

A Girl among the Anarchists, an obscure and as yet critically untreated early twentieth-century novel, is fascinating, and historically rare in its explicit focus on politics and gender and the relationship between the two, from the perspective of two bourgeois women deeply immersed in radical politics. Written in 1903 under the pseudonym Isabel Meredith by Helen and Olivia Rossetti—daughters of William Michael Rossetti, nieces of Christina and Dante Gabriel Rossetti, and cousins of Ford Madox Ford—the book gives a fictionalized account of the their actual experience as adolescent editors of the anarchist newspaper, *The Torch: A Revolutionary Journal of International Socialism.*

The initial excitement and appeal of this novel reside in its entertaining account of an innocent, middle-class Victorian girl provocatively committing herself to an apparently fanatical, even dangerous group of subversives. The heroine's unchaperoned idealism enables an emancipatory narrative that provides a marvelously sustained vision of the New Woman. Indeed, the novel's central, implicit assumption that a woman can, in fact, be politically effective challenges powerful nineteenth-century injunctions confining the middle-class woman to the privacy of the home. Even the novel's abrupt and curious retreat from its initial emancipatory optimism raises compelling questions about the work, the two sisters who wrote it, and the political climate of turn-of-the-century Britain.

The history behind the novel is as fascinating as the novel itself. The Rossetti sisters, along with their brother Arthur, founded *The Torch* in 1891 after reading anarchist Peter Kropotkin's famous essay "Appeal to the Young." So inspired were the youths by Kropotkin's call to action that they developed an editorial, "Statement of Principles," and began duplicating the journal out of their basement at St Edmunds Terrace. At the time of the journal's inception, Olivia, the eldest child, would have been an astonishing sixteen years old, Arthur fourteen, and Helen thirteen! According to David Garnett, the Rossettis' next-door neighbor, when Kropotkin first visited William Michael, he was immediately directed to the nursery: "He bustled off, full of benevolence, and was considerably surprised when a girl of 14 handed him a sheet of paper and said drily: 'Will you sign a statement to say that you agree with the political platform of *The Torch?*' The eminent man was delighted to do so."[1] While this story has an apocryphal ring to it, the Rossetti children actually proceeded to publish a serious journal that included such eminent anarchist writers as Emma Goldman, Sebastien Faure, Louise Michel, Malato and Malatesta. On the literary side, the paper also carried "Why I Am an Anarchist" by George Bernard Shaw, a translation of a story by Emile Zola, an article by Octave Mirbeau, and poetry by Ford Madox Ford. Lucien Pissarro contributed an illustration entitled "Misery," which ran in a January 1895 issue.

The journal's "Statement of Principles," published in October 1891, proclaimed that "the present division of society into rich and poor, oppression and oppressed" was unjust and provided the foundation for society's sociopolitical malaise. The journal strongly advocated social revolution by the masses themselves since "revolutionizing from above had been so often tried and failed that it had proved its insufficiency." Although the journal did run articles advocating violence, it nonetheless considered education as the primary tool by which the masses could discover a "true understanding of their wrongs, their duties and their rights," and the journal itself functioned as part of the larger educational groundswell the editors hoped to produce in order to catalyze the revolution. Moreover, the journal pronounced that the revolution must be waged on an international front, to abolish "all petty race-hatred and race-pride." The propaganda most useful in inspiring revolution, according to the journal, included translations of foreign books and accounts of previous attempts to effect a revolution.

In his *Return to Yesterday,* Ford Madox Ford, cousin to the Rossettis and occasional contributor to the journal, provides a colorful picture of the Rossetti basement where for a time the journal was actually printed:

> Until my aunt's death, the Rossettis' house being her property, my juvenile relatives carried on their activities at home. Why my aunt permitted them to run in her basement a printing press that produced militant Anarchist propaganda I never quite knew. She no doubt would have approved of any activities of her children, so long as they were active in a spirited and precocious way. But I imagine she would have preferred their energies to continue to be devoted to the productions of the Greek plays which caused me so much suffering. In any case the world was presented with the extraordinary spectacle of the abode of Her Majesty's Secretary to the Inland Revenue, so beset with English detectives, French police spies and Russian *agents provocateurs* that to go along the sidewalk of that respectable terrace was to feel that one ran the gauntlet of innumerable gimlets.[2]

Ford, as an apologist of the school of Imaginative Reminiscences, is notorious for his hyperbolic autobiographical accounts, and indeed William Michael was not Her Majesty's Secretary to the Inland Revenue but rather a clerk in the Excise Office. Still, the passage successfully portrays the whimsical scenario of a staunchly bourgeois household serving as London's center for anarchist activity.

While decidedly middle-class, William Michael Rossetti and his wife, Lucy Madox Brown Rossetti, did provide intellectual role models for their children's radical practice. William Michael, for example, proudly describes in *Reminiscences* his family's long-standing commitment to political freedom. He himself advocated theoretic republicanism in his "Democratic Sonnets." Lucy Rossetti held progressive views of her own. Early in her life, she was a highly ambitious painter, daring to aspire to fame in an artistic field dominated by men and actually, for a time before her marriage, enjoying professional success. Later, she gave up the paintbrush and took up the pen, demonstrating an interest in the emancipation of women by writing the *Life of Mary Wollstonecraft Shelley* for a series entitled *Eminent Women*.

Despite their politically advanced ideas, however, William Michael and Lucy Rossetti both viewed their children's "overstrained ideas" about anarchism as an adolescent stage that necessitated, as William Michael recounts, a "restraining influence and sympathetic guidance."[3] Much later, in hindsight, William Michael defended such a liberal course by reporting that his children did indeed negotiate the turbid waters of anarchism to land safely on the bank of maturity. "The plan which we followed with our children has succeeded; for some years past the excesses and fantasticalities of anarchism have shredded away from them, while they remain free-minded, open to new impressions, and exempt from class prejudices."[4] In the end, as I will comment on later, the Rossetti sisters seem to have assimilated their parent's view of their anarchist activities as a symptom of immaturity.

After Mrs. Rossetti's death in 1894, the *Torch* was moved to Ossulston Street, and the Rossettis resigned their positions with the journal two years later. There are differing accounts as to why the Rossettis left. As historian John Quail and Ford Madox Ford would have it, the sisters felt victimized and exploited by members of the *Torch* group.[5] Historian Hermia Oliver, however, accounts for the Rossettis' departure from the journal in much more pragmatic terms, and William Michael's *Reminiscences* generally support her reading. In 1896, Olivia went to Florence to join her future husband Antonio Agresti. At the same time, Helen became ill and departed with her father on a recuperative journey abroad. And Arthur left for Salford to become an electrical engineer. As Oliver concludes, "the connection of the three Rossettis with the *Torch* ended simultaneously."[6] Whatever the reason for their abandonment of the journal, the *Torch* managed to survive for only a year after their departure. The Rossettis left the journal to four remaining members of the *Torch* group, and the journal subsequently collapsed in 1897.

Both Olivia and Helen went on to minor publishing careers. Their "joint performance," as their father called *A Girl among the Anarchists,* was published in 1903 by Duckworth Press. In 1904, Olivia also published the *Life of Giovanni Costa,* a friend and celebrated Italian landscape painter. In 1902, Helen published a monograph on *Dante Gabriel Rossetti* for *The Art Journal* and, much later, a biography of Charles Augustus Howell, *Pre-Raphaelite Twilight* (1954).

A Girl among the Anarchists[7] was mildly received at the time of its publication and in subsequent years was buried in oblivion, vaguely acknowledged by only a handful of historians of anarchism. The novel, however, is perhaps more provocative and useful now than at the time of its debut. *A Girl among the Anarchists* provides a rare perspective of fin-de-siècle anarchism as experienced by two highly literate and politically active women. With the current demand for the recuperation and reevaluation of women's literature and a sustained interest in the political novel, the value of *A Girl among the Anarchists* lies not with its aesthetic merit, though it is competently written and entertaining, but with its ideological revelations, with its unself-conscious portrayal of anarchism as the political domain of adolescent excess and its exploitation of this trope initially to challenge and then, paradoxically, to reinforce conventional notions of the "mature" woman as nonpolitical.

With the death of her last surviving parent, Isabel Meredith, the novel's seventeen-year-old protagonist, embarks upon a harrowing, but necessary journey into the space of the Other—a political and sexual "heart of darkness." In this domesticated version of Joseph Conrad's story (published a year earlier), the space of the Other is not the feminized, dark continent Africa but instead the ungoverned, masculine dominion of working-class anarchist haunts in London backstreets. This space is masculine not because of any inherent symbolic signification it possesses but strictly because in reality these spaces were virtually inaccessible to a middle-class girl.

Isabel abandons the traditionally feminine, protected, and private world of home and family to embrace an unknown world, the conventionally masculine and public world of politics. Isabel describes herself as a youth passing through a "phase of mental evolution" wherein she "felt a strong desire to free [herself] from all the ideas, customs, and prejudices which usually influence my class, to throw myself into the life and work of the masses" (see page 56). In acting upon such desires, Isabel defies class boundaries, thus implicitly and forcefully defying gender boundaries as well.

Within their narrative, the Rossetti sisters create a domain that gives Isabel, not to mention the contemporary female reader and the authors themselves, free rein to explore a masculine space that allows for a range of political and sexual freedoms unimaginable to a late Victorian bourgeois girl. Within a world where the bourgeois woman is worshipped as an angel of self-abnegation, Isabel begins to assimilate and live by the radical libertarian ideals of anarchism, ideals that implicitly emancipate woman as well as man.

Isabel's rebellion against traditional feminine codes of regulation which confined the woman to the home and promoted her subservience and obedience to others begins with her outings to the gatherings of politically radical intellects. These excursions often involved solitary travel at very late hours to deserted and squalid destinations. Though she is on at least one occasion escorted home by the benign and avuncular Dr. Armitage, the existence of a thirty-seven-year-old single man on her arm at such an hour is in and of itself a shocking display for a woman within the cultural milieu of bourgeois England and gently hints at the risque possibility that Isabel might practice the free-love principles advocated by the anarchists. After deciding to go in "the whole length" with the anarchists, Isabel begins to flaunt social codes in earnest, working long days for the cause, venturing out unescorted to disreputable locales, and spending many of her nights asleep in the grimy offices of the *Tocsin* where she edits the journal. The image created within the novel of a transient and independent bourgeois adolescent girl powerfully challenges the traditional home-bound image prescribed for moral girls by the bourgeois status quo.

Isabel's unregulated behavior is encouraged within the anarchist circle that she adopts as her new family. Within this familial setting, Isabel learns not only to reject certain social codes of behavior but also to rebel against the law. On several occasions she challenges the paternalistic symbol of the Victorian law, the British policeman. She defies his courteous endeavors to protect her, a lady, from improper influences and scandalous scenes, and she participates with the anarchists in a plan to outsmart "those heavy-witted, pudding-eating police" and in the process spring the outlaw anarchist Jean Mattieu from the house in which he is trapped.

Meanwhile, Isabel's rejection of the traditional domestic, feminine role in lieu of a masculine, public role also allows her access to the dark and grim realities of the underbelly of urban London. She begins her eye-opening experience by journeying to "places which were new and strange" to her— Holloway Jail, the Old Jewry, and the Middle Temple (p. 61). Isabel is struck on visiting Holloway Jail with "the illogical nature of the law that treats the unconvicted men, who in its eyes are consequently innocent, like convicted criminals" (p. 63).

Similar lessons of suffering and social injustice are the stuff of such classic bildungsromane as *Tom Jones, David Copperfield,* and *Villette,* but the Rossettis' sustained trope of anarchism as the embodiment of adolescent rebellion provides a more exaggerated and threatening social and political backdrop for these lessons. Isabel's intense involvement with anarchism allows her intimate communion with the most abject of the poor, with political assassins, advocates of free love, alcoholics, lazy social parasites, political martyrs, and with comrades driven mad by both the frustration of their utopian ideals and the constant paranoia about the infiltration of their small circles by spies.

Isabel's confrontation with social and political issues of abject suffering and injustice, her physical transience and independence, her intellectual autonomy from bourgeois ideals, and her rebellion against and ridicule of the law all suggest a narrative composite of a New Woman, a woman emancipated from the shackles of bourgeois expectation. Moreover, Isabel's daily interchange and fast-growing friendships with "exotic" foreign anarchists as they found temporary domicile at the *Tocsin* office challenges the anglocentrism and xenophobia so oppressively pervasive in nine-teenth-century Britain. Thus, within a society where women are abandoned to the home, where the national home is an isolated island, further alienated from mutually respectful interchange with the world by an imperialist ideology, Isabel represents an explosive model for emancipation.

Unfortunately, however, the Rossettis could not sustain such a narrative of female emancipation. In the conclusion to their novel, Isabel retracts her belief in anarchism and in-stead forcefully reinscribes the traditional feminine myth of hearth and home. This reversal may be partially accounted for by the historical relationship of women to auto-biographical fiction. Sidonie Smith argues in *A Poetics of Women's Autobiography* that women have been acculturated to devalue the legitimacy of and public interest in their voices and personal experience, thereby relegating women's auto-biography to the silent spaces of history. "For women," she says, "rebellious pursuit [of individuality] is potentially cata-strophic. To call attention to her distinctiveness is to become 'unfeminine.' To take a voice and to authorize a public life are to risk loss of reputation."[8] Have the Rossetti sisters, then, ultimately sacrificed their own audaciously public lives to appease pervasive class and gender codes? Are their re-bellions only acceptable when confined to adolescence?

The rather uneven narrative tone of the novel suggests so. For, although the Rossettis preface the novel with their in-tention to investigate objectively and understand anar-chism, throughout the novel they frequently treat their an-archist exploits with a distinctively "camp" sense of humor, a point of view that parodies and exaggerates their subject in a self-consciously stylized manner. This tone permits the Rossettis to assume a safe, because superior, position from which to explore the socially disreputable subject of anar-chism. Such a tone allows for an imaginative examination of the subject while at the same time it insures that the reader will not affiliate the novel's authors with a delegitimized movement that the Rossettis now reject as an adolescent phase in their lives. More importantly, the tone regulates the readers' response to anarchism by ridiculing the movement and anyone who identifies with it. This derision, in turn, reinforces the reader's identification with Isabel's elevated moral and spiritual position at the end of the novel when she rejects the public life of anarchism for the private life of home.

Isabel understands her steady disillusionment with the anarchist movement as a coming of age. She explains her disaffection, saying, "I seemed to have lived ages, my character was developing, a sense of humor was gradually modifying my views of many matters" (251). In effect, Isabel sees herself outgrowing anarchism, which she relates to the excesses of adolescence. In growing from girl to woman and in the process shedding her idealism, Isabel begins to align anarchism with a masculine code of value. She realizes that her anarchist colleagues—all men—wilfully sacrifice love, family, and home for an abstract principle of freedom for the individual. When Ivan Kosinski rejects Isabel's love, asserting that "an Anarchist's life is not his own. Friendship, comradeship may be helpful, but family ties are fatal" (p. 268), Isabel rejects anarchism. She considers such a sacrifice as more dehumanizing than a life of compromised freedom in the name of love. Within the moral terms of the novel, Isabel's choice for home and family raises her own moral and spiritual status and initiates her into adult life.

The novel's concluding vision for woman's self-fulfillment and self-determination is astonishingly bleak given its earlier development of a defiantly expansive space for woman's emancipation. For example, Isabel's moral superiority at the conclusion of the novel is achieved in part through the contrast of her integrity, beauty, and love with its absence in the other—mostly working-class—female characters. The depictions of these women throughout the novel reify persistent stereotypes of women as either so self-centered as to be incapable of political awareness or, in the tradition of Dickens's Mrs. Jellyby ("all devoted to public objects only"), so politically driven as to be virtual monsters. Not only are these female characters predetermined and static, but the novel's denouement decidedly constricts even Isabel's emancipatory potential. For once Isabel determines against anarchism, where else can she go but home; and once at home, how can an autobiographical novel, by definition a publicly defined genre, sustain interest in this now privately defined character?

Isabel's moral and spiritual triumph over the anarchist world of abstraction and idealism unfortunately instigates a definitive closure to the novel. Everything of public significance has now already happened to Isabel. In Virginia Woolf's early novel *A Voyage Out* (published by Duckworth Press in 1915—the same press that published *A Girl among the Anarchists* some twelve years earlier), the heroine's exploration of self ends in literal death at the moment when she chooses marriage and home. The narrative comes to an abrupt halt, unable to figure a character who is at once self-defined and married. Though *A Girl among the Anarchists* has developed a sustained and expansive imaginative ground for an adolescent girl, it too concludes in paralysis as the heroine enters adulthood. The novel's conclusion has a sudden and slightly claustrophobic feel of an Eve who has bitten the apple turning back to live again in the timeless, static garden of Eden. The Rossettis' heroine must retreat, however, since to go forward would require an imaginative vision capable of positing an anarchist as an adult woman, a vision not yet imaginable even to such radical women as the Rossettis. Instead, Isabel is engulfed by the ubiquitous bourgeois metaphor of Home.

Unlike Virginia Woolf, who ultimately strangled the bourgeois angel-woman, freeing herself from its shackles to write visionary narratives where both ordinary married women and single women without romantic prospects could constitute complete subjects, the Rossettis, despite their radical affiliations, never fully understood the political stakes for women at hand. Through the representation of anarchism as the discrete space of adolescence, *A Girl among the Anarchists*, like Henry James's *The Princess Casamassima* (1886) and Robert Louis and Fanny Van de Grift Stevenson's *The Dynamiters* (1885), explicitly appeases a cultural fascination with anarchism and the related excess of adolescence. The representation functions, moreover, both to make the unsettled years of adolescence unsafe by characterizing them as anarchic and to domesticate the political threat of anarchism by characterizing it as adolescent.

The Rossettis' novel plots a map to freedom for women, providing a rare turn-of-the-century vision of woman as independent, sexually progressive and politically effective. At the same time, however, the novel seems to warn us that the freedoms of anarchism, when applied to women, engender chaos. *A Girl among the Anarchists* ironically envisions the New Woman coming of age in Britain only to condemn her to perpetual adolescence within the paternalistic ideology of the Home.

Notes

1. David Garnett, *The Golden Echo* (London: Chatto and Windus, 1954), p. 12.

2. Ford Madox Ford, *Return to Yesterday* (New York: Liveright, 1932), pp. 111–12.

3. William Michael Rossetti, *Reminiscences* (New York: AMS Press, 1970), p. 452.

4. See *Reminiscences*, p. 453.

5. See John Quail's *The Slow Burning Fuse: The Lost History of the British Anarchists* (New York: Granada Publishing, Ltd., 1978), p. 204; and Ford Madox Ford, p. 113.

6. Hermia Oliver, *The International Anarchist Movement in Late Victorian London* (New York: St. Martin's Press, 1983), p. 124.

7. See Isabel Meredith, *A Girl among the Anarchists* (London: Duckworth & Co., 1903) for all subsequent citations to the novel.

8. Sidonie Smith, *A Poetics of Women's Autobiography: Marginality and the Fictions of Self-Representation* (Bloomington: Indiana UP, 1987), pp. 9–10.

PREFACE

IN spite of the fact that there are certain highly respectable individualists of a rabid type who prefer to call themselves Anarchists, it must be owned that it requires some courage to write about Anarchism even with the sympathy befitting a clinical physician or the scientific detachment of a pathologist. And yet it is certain that Anarchists are curiously interesting, and not the less in need of observation from the fact that apparently none of the social quacks who prescribe seriously in leading articles has the faintest insight into them as a phenomenon, a portent, or a disease. This book, if it is read with understanding, will, I feel assured, do not a little to show how it comes about that Anarchism is as truly endemic in Western Civilisations as cholera is in India. Isabel Meredith, whom I had the pleasure of knowing when she was a more humble member of the staff of the *Tocsin* than the editor, occupies, to my knowledge, a very curious and unique position in the history of English Anarchism. There is nothing whatever in "A Girl among the Anarchists" which is invented, the whole thing is an experience told very simply, but I think convincingly. Nevertheless as such a human document must seem incredible to the ordinary reader, I have no little pleasure in saying that I know what she has written to be true. I was myself a contributor to the paper which is here known as the *Tocsin*. I have handled the press and have discussed details (which did not include bombs) with the editor. I knew "Kosinski" and still have an admiration for "Nekrovitch." And even now I do not mind avowing that I am philosophically as much an Anarchist as the late Dr. H. G. Sutton, who would no doubt have been astounded to learn that he belonged to the brotherhood.

Curiously enough I have found most Anarchists of the mildest dispositions. I have met meek Germans (there are meek Germans still extant) who even in their wildest Anarchic indignation seemed as little capable of hurting a living soul as of setting the Elbe on fire. For it must be understood that the "red wing" of the Anarchists is a very small section of the body of philosophers known as Anarchists. There is no doubt that those of the dynamite section are practically insane. They are "impulsives"; they were outraged and they revolted before birth. Most of the proletariat take their thrashing lying down. There are some who cannot do that. It is out of these who are not meek and do not inherit even standing-room on the earth that such as " Matthieu " comes. Perhaps it may not be out of place to suggest that a little investigation might be better than denunciation, which is always wide of the mark, and that, as Anarchism is created by the social system of repression, more repression will only create more Anarchism. However, I am perfectly aware that the next time a wild-eyed philosopher, who ought to be under restraint in an asylum, throws a bomb, all the newspapers in Europe will advocate measures for turning all the meeker Anarchists into outrage-mongers. For of the Anarchists it is certainly true that repression does not repress. Anarchism is a creed and a philosophy, but neither as creed nor philosophy does it advocate violence. It only justifies resistance to violence. So much, I think, will be discovered in this book even by a leader-writer.

In conclusion I cannot do better than quote from Spinoza's *Tractatus Politicus*:—

" In order that I might inquire better into the matter of this science with the same freedom of mind with which we are wont to treat lines and surfaces in mathematics, I determined not to laugh or weep over the actions of men but simply to understand them, and to contemplate their affections and passions such as love, hate, anger, envy, arrogance, pity, and all other disturbances of soul not as vices of human nature, but as properties pertaining to it in the same way as heat, cold, storm, thunder pertain to the nature of the atmosphere. For these, though troublesome, are yet necessary and have certain causes through which we may come to understand them, and thus by contemplating them in their truth, gain for our minds as much joy as by the knowledge of things which are pleasing to the senses."

I think that Isabel Meredith, so far as the outlook of her book extends, is a disciple of Spinoza. But she can speak for herself.

MORLEY ROBERTS.

CONTENTS

A GIRL AMONG THE ANARCHISTS

CHAPTER I

A STRANGE CHILDHOOD

In the small hours of a bitter January morning I sat in my room gazing into the fire, and thinking over many things. I was alone in the house, except for the servants, but this circumstance did not affect me. My childhood and upbringing had been of no ordinary nature, and I was used to looking after myself and depending on my own resources for amusement and occupation.

My mother had died when I was yet a small child and, with my elder sister and brother, I had grown up under our father's eye. He was a chemist and a man of advanced ideas on most things. He had never sent us to school, preferring to watch in person over our education, procuring for us private tuition in many subjects, and himself instructing us in physical science and

A

history, his two favourite studies. We rapidly
gained knowledge under his system and were
decidedly precocious children, but we had none
of the ordinary school society and routine. Our
childhood was by no means dull or mopish, for
there were three of us and we got on very well
together, but we mixed hardly at all with children
of our own age, our interests were not theirs, and
their boisterous ways were somewhat repellent
to us.

Our father was a great believer in liberty, and,
strange to say, he put his ideas into practice in
his own household. He was a devoted and enthusiastic student, and for days, nay, weeks together, we would see but little of him. He had
fitted himself up a small laboratory at the top of
our house on which he spent all his available
money, and here he passed nearly all the time he
could dispose of over and beyond that necessary
for the preparation and delivery of his scientific
lectures. As we grew out of childhood he made
no difference in his mode of life. He gave us
full liberty to follow our various bents, assisting
us with his advice when requested, ever ready to
provide the money necessary for any special
studies or books; taking an interest in our readings and intellectual pursuits. The idea of providing us with suitable society, of launching us
out into the world, of troubling to see that we

conformed to the ordinary conventions of society, never occurred to him. Occasionally some old friend of his would drop in, or some young admirer who had followed his scientific work in the press would write asking permission to call and consult him on some point. They were always received with cordiality, and my father would take much trouble to be of any assistance he could to them. We children used generally to be present on such occasions, and frequently would join in the conversation, and thus we got to know various people, among whom foreigners and various types of cranks were fairly in evidence.

We lived in a large old-fashioned house in Fitzroy Square where our father had settled down somewhere in the seventies soon after his marriage to a South American Spaniard, whom he had met during a scientific research expedition in Brazil. She was a girl of seventeen, his junior by some twenty years. During his journeys into the interior of Brazil he had fallen seriously ill with malarial fever, and had been most kindly taken in and nursed by a coffee-planter and his family. Here he had met his future wife who was acting as governess. She was of Spanish descent, and combined the passionate enthusiasm of a Southerner with the independence and self-reliance which life in a new and only partially civilised country breeds. She was an orphan and penniless, but our father fell in love with her, attracted doubtless by her beauty and vivaciousness in such striking contrast with his bookish way of life, and he married her and brought her home to London. He truly loved her and was a good husband in all essential respects, but the uncongenial climate and monotonous life told on her health, and she died three years after my birth, much mourned by her husband, who plunged all the more deeply into scientific research, his only other thought being a care for our education. He had lived on in the same old house which grew somewhat dingier and shabbier each year, whilst the neighbourhood fell from its pristine respectability to become the resort of foreigners of somewhat doubtful character, of Bohemian artists and musicians.

As I sat gazing into the fire many pictures of those old days rose before me. I saw our large drawing-room with its old-fashioned furniture, handsome, often beautiful, but ill-kept ; its sombre hangings and fine pictures. I recalled a typical scene there with a large fire burning cheerily in the big grate, relieving the gloom of a late winter afternoon with the bright flickering of its flames. Ensconced in a roomy arm-chair, our father is seated by the fire in a skullcap and list slippers, with his favourite cat perched on his knee. Opposite him sit two ladies, the elder of whom—a quaint, nice-looking old lady, dressed neatly in black, but whose innate eccentricity succeeded in imparting something odd to the simplest and quietest of attires—is leaning eagerly forward, pouring forth a long tale of woe into my father's sympathetic ear. She is denouncing the London roughs, land-lords, and police, who, apparently, are all in league to ruin her and turn her cats astray upon an unkind world. The brutality of the English poor, who consider their duty towards the feline race fully performed when they have fed them, and who pay no more attention to their morals and higher feel-ings than if they were stocks and stones, arouses her ire; sympathy is what she needs, sympathy to help her to face the world and continue her crusade against cruelty. She says all this in a scattered and disconnected style, jumping from one point to another, turning occasionally to her friend for support or confirmation. This friend is a meek, subdued-looking person of uncertain age, some-what washed-out and bedraggled in appearance. Her attire is nondescript, and seems to consist of oddments bought solely because they were cheap and bearing no relation whatever one to the other. Mrs. Smuts, growing more and more absorbed in the course of her harangue on the great cat question, states that she believes in marrying cats young in life and looking strictly after their morals; and as she appeals to Miss

Meggs whilst voicing this sentiment, the latter timidly interjects, "But do you think, my dear Maria, that cats can maintain themselves chaste on a meat diet ?   I never give mine anything more exciting than cold potatoes and rice pudding, and I find that they thrive on it, Mr. Meredith !"

At this point we children, stifling our laughter, rush headlong from the room, to vent our mirth in safety in the kitchen.

Another frequent visitor whom my imagination summoned from the grave in which he had lain now for several years past, was a tall, thin, delicate-looking man of some thirty years of age.   He was by birth a Frenchman, but had lived mostly in England, his parents having come over as political exiles from the tyranny of Louis Napoleon, afterwards settling permanently in this country.   He was an engineer by profession, but a poet at heart, and all his spare time and thought he devoted to tackling the problem of aerial navigation.   His day was spent earning a scanty living in a shipbuilding yard, but his evenings and nights were passed in constructing a model of a flying-machine.   He would bring his drawings round to our father for discussion and advice ; and although he never attained success, he was always hopeful, trusting that some one of the ever fresh improvements and additions which his fertile brain was always busy conceiving would solve the difficulty which had

hitherto beset him. His sallow face with its large
dreamy eyes and his spare figure, clad in an old
bluish suit, rusty with age and threadbare with
brushing, stand out clear in my memory. There
was also an old professor, a chemist like my father,
who often assisted him in his experiments. He
was somewhat formidable in appearance, wearing
gold spectacles, and helping himself freely to the
contents of a snuff-box, but he was one of the most
kind-hearted of men. Children were great favourites
with him, and his affection was returned with interest as soon as the shyness consequent on his
somewhat gruff manner was overcome. He used
to enjoy drawing us out, and would laugh heartily
at our somewhat old-fashioned remarks and observations, at which we used to grow very indignant,
for we were decidedly touchy when our dignity
was at stake. He had nicknamed me Charlotte
Corday, for, after a course of Greek and Roman
history, studied in Plutarch and Shakespeare's
" Julius Cæsar," I had plunged into the French Revolution, glorying in its heroisms and audacity, and
it had become a favourite amusement with all three
of us to enact scenes drawn from its history, and to
recite aloud, with great emphasis if little art, revolutionary poetry. The old professor loved to tease
me by abusing my favourite heroes ; and when he
had at last roused me to a vigorous assertion of
revolutionary sentiments, he would turn to my

father and say, "There's a little spitfire for you;
you will have to keep a look-out or she will be
making bombs soon and blowing us all up," at
which my father would smile complacently.

Our father was very charitable. He did not like
to be bothered or disturbed, but he would willingly
give a little assistance when asked, and the result
was that our door was always besieged by beggars
of various nationalities, Spaniards and Italians form-
ing the chief contingent. Generally they confined
themselves to sending in notes, which used to be
returned with a shilling or half-crown as the case
might be, but sometimes one would insist on a
personal interview. I remember one wild-looking
Hungarian, whose flowing locks were crowned by
a sort of horse's sun-bonnet, who used to rush
round on one of those obsolete bicycles, consisting
of an enormously high wheel on the top of which
he was perched, and a tiny little back one. He was
generally pursued by a crowd of hooting boys,
advising him to "get 'is 'air cut," and inquiring,
"Where did you get that 'at?" He used to insist
on seeing my father; but the help he solicited was
not for himself but for various political refugees
in whom he was interested. One day the professor
happened to meet this wild-looking creature at our
door, and inquired of my father who that maniac
might be. "Oh, he is a Hungarian refugee; a good
fellow, I believe. I have noticed something rather

odd in his appearance, but I do not consider him mad," replied his friend.

Amid such surroundings we grew up. My elder sister, Caroline, had a notable musical gift, and even as a small child had a fine voice, which developed into a rich contralto. Our father, always anxious to do his duty by us, gave her a first-rate musical education, sending her abroad to study under famous Continental teachers, and at eighteen she made her first appearance in public, exciting much attention by the powerful dramatic qualities of her voice. It was evident that her right course was to go in for operatic singing, and this she did. She continued on the most affectionate terms with her family, but naturally her pursuit took her into quite another path of life, and we saw less and less of her as time went on. This threw my brother and myself more together. There was only a year's difference between us, and we studied together, walked, talked, played, and read together—in fact, were inseparable. Raymond was no ordinary boy. In character and in manners he was very like my father. His favourite study was physical science in its various branches; mine, history and sociological subjects. He saw things from the scientific standpoint, I from the poetical and artistic; but we were both by nature enthusiastic and dreamers, and sympathised heartily with each other's views. His ambition was to become a famous explorer;

mine, to die on a scaffold or a barricade, shouting Liberty, Equality, Fraternity.

Our father took a great pride in Raymond, and carefully supervised his studies. He passed various brilliant examinations, and at eighteen, having decided to go in for medicine, was already walking a hospital. Shortly after this our father died suddenly. He was at work as usual in his laboratory when he was seized by a paralytic stroke, and in three days he was dead.

This blow quite stunned us for a time. Our father was everything to us; and the possibility of his death we had never contemplated. Though, as I have explained, he had always left us free to follow our own devices, still he was the centre round which our family life circled; we were passionately attached to him, and now that he was gone we felt at a loss indeed. We had no relatives living of our father's; our mother's family we had never known, and they were too distant to be practically available. Our father's friends were not such as to be of much help to us. Cat enthusiasts and scientific dreamers are all very well in their way, but they almost always take far more than they give in the mart of friendship. The old professor had preceded my father to his grave.

Our father left us comfortably off. The house was our own, and property yielding a comfortable income was divided equally between us. Our home seemed desolate indeed without our father, and very gloomily did the first months of his absence pass; but in time hope and youth reasserted themselves and we gradually settled down to much our old way of life. Caroline obtained several engagements and was still studying enthusiastically. Raymond passed most of his time at the hospital, where he had rooms, though he frequently came home; I was the only one who had not a definite occupation. I read a great deal and wrote a little also, chiefly studies on historical subjects which interested me, but I had printed nothing. In fact I had never been in the way of the literary world, and did not know how to set about it. Time used often to hang rather heavily on my hands in the big house where I was generally alone. I was the housekeeper, but such cares did not take up much of my time. The result of so much solitude and lack of occupation was that I became restless and dissatisfied. Mere reading without any definite object did not and could not suffice me; to write when there seemed no prospect of ever being read, and keenly alive as I was to my own deficiencies, did not attract me; friends I might say I had none, for the few people my father knew were interested in him and not in us children, and ceased to frequent our house after his death. Caroline's musical friends did not appeal to me, so that the whole interest of my life was centred round my brother. When he came home we used always to be together, and conversation never flagged. Never having been to school he had none of the schoolboy's patronising contempt for a sister. We had always been chums and companions, and so we continued, but whereas, as children, it was I, with my more passionate and enterprising nature, who took the lead, now it was he who, mixing with the outer world, provided the stimulus of new ideas and fresh activities for which I craved. Brought suddenly face to face, after the studious seclusion of home, with the hard facts of life as seen in a London hospital, he had begun to take a deep interest in social questions. The frightful havoc of life and happiness necessitated by the economic conditions of nineteenth-century society, impressed him deeply, and he felt that any doctor who looked upon his profession as other than a mere means to make money must tackle such problems. Following up this line of thought he became interested in economics and labour questions. His views were the result of no mere surface impression, but the logical outcome of thought and study, and he arrived at socialism by mental processes of his own, uninfluenced by the ordinary channels of propaganda. I shared his interests and read on parallel lines. We had no friends in Socialist circles, no personal interest of any kind balanced our judgment. The whole trend of our education had been to make independent thinkers of us. What we saw in the whole problem was a question of justice, and for this we were ready and anxious to work. A new interest was thus brought into our lives, which, in my case, soon became all-absorbing. I was always begging my brother to bring me home fresh books. The driest volumes of political economy, the most indigestible of philosophical treatises, nothing came amiss. From these I passed on to more modern works. Raymond had made friends with a student who was a professed socialist and through him he came into possession of a number of pamphlets and papers, all of which I devoured eagerly, and some of which made a lasting impression on my mind. Krapotkin's "Appeal to the Young" was of this number. I remember in my enthusiasm reading it aloud to my sister Caroline, who, however, took scant interest in such matters, and who tried, but in vain, to put a damper on my enthusiasm.

I was always fond of scribbling, and the outcome of all this reading was that I, too, flew to pen and paper. I used to read my papers to Raymond on those rare occasions when I fancied I had not done so much amiss. They would provide the material for an evening's conversation, then I would toss them aside and think no more about them. One day, however, Raymond brought his Socialist friend home with him. It seems they had talked about me and my all-absorbing interest in social subjects. Hughes, my brother's friend, had been surprised to hear from Raymond that I knew no socialists in the flesh, and that all my hero-worship was laid before the altar of mental abstractions, of my own creation for the most part.

Great was my excitement when Raymond told me that I might expect him and his friend, of whom I had heard so much, to turn up together one Sunday evening. So great was my ignorance of the world, so wild my enthusiasm, that I imagined every socialist as a hero, willing to throw away his life at a moment's notice on behalf of the "Cause." I had had no experience of the petty internal strifes, of the jealousies and human frailties which a closer knowledge of all political parties reveals. I remember how ashamed I felt of the quite unostentatious comfort of our home, how anxious I was to dissemble the presence of servants, how necessary I thought it to dress myself in my oldest and least becoming clothes for the occasion, and how indignant I felt when Caroline, who was going off to sing at a concert that evening, said, on coming in to wish me good-bye, "Why, surely, Isabel, you're not going to receive that gentleman looking such a fright as this?" As if a Socialist could care for dress! How I felt he would despise me for all the outward signs which proved that I was living on the results of "unearned increment" (*vide* Karl Marx) and that I was a mere social parasite !

When at last the longed-for, yet dreaded moment came, I was surprised, relieved, and I must add somewhat disappointed, at seeing a young man looking much like any other gentleman, except that he wore a red tie, and that his clothes were of a looser and easier fit than is usual. "What a jolly place you have !" he exclaimed after my brother had introduced us and he had given a look round. I felt considerably relieved, as I had quite expected him to scowl disapproval, and my brother, after saying, "Yes, it is a nice old house ; we are very fond of it," suggested that we should adjourn to supper.

During this repast I took an animated part in the conversation, which turned on recent books and plays. At last reference was made to a book, "The Ethics of Egoism," which had excited much attention. It was a work advocating the most rabid individualism, denying the Socialist standpoint of the right to live, and saying that the best safeguard for the development and amelioration of the race lay in that relentless law of nature which sent the mentally and morally weak to the wall. I had read the book with interest, and had even written a rather long criticism of it, of which I felt distinctly proud. In the course of the discussion to which this book gave rise among us, my brother mentioned that I had written something on it, and

Hughes begged me to read my performance. Though I felt somewhat diffident, I acceded, after some persuasion, to his request, and was elated beyond measure at earning his good opinion of my effort.

"By George, that's about the best criticism I've read of the work. Where do you intend publishing it, Miss Meredith ?"

"Oh, I had never thought of publishing it," I replied ; "I have never published anything."

"But we cannot afford to lose such good stuff," he insisted. "Come, Raymond, now, don't you think your sister ought to get that into print ?"

"I think you should publish it, Isabel, if you could," he replied.

"Could ! Why any of our papers would be only too delighted to have it. Let me take it down to the *Democrat,*" he said, mentioning the name of a paper which Raymond often brought home with him.

"Oh, if you really think it worth while, I shall be only too pleased," I replied.

Thus was effected my first introduction to the actual Socialist party. My article was printed and I was asked for others. I made the acquaintance of the editor, who, I must confess, spite of my enthusiasm, soon struck me as a rather weak-kneed and altogether unadmirable character. He thought it necessary to get himself up to look like an artist, though he had not the soul of a counter-jumper, and the result was long hair, a velvet coat, a red tie, bumptious bearing, and an altogether scatter-brained and fly-away manner. In figure he was long and willowy, and reminded me irresistibly of an unhealthy cellar-grown potato plant. My circle of acquaintances rapidly enlarged, and soon, instead of having too much time on my hands for reading and study, I had too little. At one of the Sunday evening lectures of the Democratic Club, at which I had become a regular attendant, I made the acquaintance of Nekrovitch, the famous Nihilist, and his wife. I took to him instinctively, drawn by the utter absence of sham or " side " which characterised the man. I had never understood why Socialism need imply the arraying of oneself in a green curtain or a terra-cotta rug, or the cultivation of flowing locks, blue shirts, and a peculiar cut of clothes : and the complete absence of all such outward " trade marks " pleased me in the Russian. He invited me to his house, and I soon became a constant visitor. In the little Chiswick house I met a class of people who stimulated me intellectually, and once more aroused my rather waning enthusiasm for the " Cause." The habit of taking nothing for granted, of boldly inquiring into the origin of all accepted precepts of morality, of intellectual speculation unbiassed by prejudice and untrammelled by all those petty personal and party

B

questions and interests which I had seen occupy
so much time and thought at the Democratic Club,
permeated the intellectual atmosphere. Quite a
new side of the problem—that of its moral bearings
and abstract rights as opposed to the merely
material right to daily bread which had first
appealed to my sense of justice and humanity—
now opened before me. The right to complete
liberty of action, the conviction that morality is
relative and personal and can never be imposed
from without, that men are not responsible, or
only very partially so, for their surroundings, by
which their actions are determined, and that consequently no man has a right to judge his fellow ;
such and similar doctrines which I heard frequently upheld, impressed me deeply. I was
morally convinced of their truth, and consequently
more than half an Anarchist. The bold thought
and lofty ideal which made of each man a law
unto himself, answerable for his own actions only
to his own conscience, acting righteously towards
others as the result of his feeling of solidarity and
not because of any external compulsion, captivated
my mind.

The Anarchists who frequented Nekrovitch's
house were men of bold and original thought, the
intellectual part of the movement, and I was never
tired of listening to their arguments. Meantime
the more I saw of the Social Democrats the less

I felt satisfied with them. A wider experience
would have told me that all political parties, irre-
spective of opinion, are subject to much the same
criticism, and that Socialist ideas are no protection
against human weaknesses ; but extreme youth is
not compromising where its ideals are concerned,
and I expected and insisted on a certain approach
to perfection in my heroes. True, Nekrovitch
made me hesitate some time before taking the
final step. His attitude in such discussions was
one of sound common sense, and he never ceased
reminding his Anarchist friends, though all in vain,
that we must live in our own times, and that it
is no use trying to forestall human evolution by
some thousand years.

At home I had become more and more my own
mistress. I was now full eighteen years of age,
and had always been accustomed to think and act
for myself. Caroline, with whom I was on most
affectionate terms, despite our frequent differences
on politics, had accepted an engagement as *prima
donna* with a travelling opera company which was
to visit the United States and the principal cities
of South America ; her engagement was to last
two years, and she had left just three weeks before
the opening of my first chapter.

Raymond slept at home, but as the date of his
final examination drew near he was more and
more occupied, and frequently whole weeks passed

in which I only caught a glimpse of him. He knew and sympathised with my new line of thought; he had accompanied me more than once to the Nekrovitchs', whom he liked much, but he had no longer the time to devote much thought to such matters. Of money I always had a considerable command; ever since our father's death I had kept house, and now that Caroline was away I had full control of the household purse.

Turning over all these thoughts in my mind as I sat toasting my feet before the fire, I felt more and more inclined to throw in my lot with the Anarchists. At the same time I felt that if I did take this step it must be as a worker and in no half-hearted spirit. The small hours of the morning were rapidly slipping by as I turned at last into bed to dream of Anarchist meetings, melting into a confused jumble with the rights of cats and the claims of the proletariat.

CHAPTER II

A GATHERING IN CHISWICK

As my first actual acquaintance with Anarchists was effected in Nekrovitch's house, it will not be out of place for me to give a slight sketch of the gatherings held there and of my host himself.

An interminably dreary journey by tram and rail, omnibus and foot, the latter end of which lay along a monotonous suburban road, brought you to the humble dwelling of the famous Nihilist. Here from time to time on Sunday evenings it was my wont to put in an appearance towards ten or eleven, for the journey was deceptively long from Fitzroy Square, and Nekrovitch, like most Russians, was himself of so unpunctual and irregular a nature, that he seemed to foster the like habits in all his friends. The nominal hour for these social gatherings to commence was eight, but not till past nine did the guests begin to assemble, and till midnight and later they would come dribbling in. Only one conscientiously punctual German was ever known to arrive at the appointed hour, but the only reward of the Teuton's mistaken zeal was to wait for hours in solitary state in an unwarmed, unlighted room till his host and fellow-guests saw fit to assemble.

The meeting-room, or parlour, or drawing-room in Nekrovitch's house was by no means a palatial apartment. Small and even stuffy to the notions of a hygienic Englishman, and very bare, scanty in furniture, and yet poorer in decoration, this room bore evidence to its owners' contempt for such impedimenta, and their entire freedom from slavery to household gods. It was evidently the home of people used to pitching their tent often, and to whom a feeling of settled security was unknown. But its occupants usually made up for any deficiencies in their surroundings.

The company was always of a very mixed cosmopolitan character—Russian Nihilists and exiles, English Liberals who sympathised with the Russian constitutional movement, Socialists and Fabians, Anarchists of all nationalities, journalists and literary men whose political views were immaterial, the pseudo-Bohemian who professes interest in the "queer side of life," all manner of faddists, rising and impecunious musicians and artists—all were made welcome, and all were irresistibly attracted towards the great Russian Nihilist.

The most notable figure in this assembly, and he certainly would have been in most assemblies, was Nekrovitch himself. Nekrovitch was essentially a great man; one of those men whom to know was to admire and to love; a man of strong intellect, and of the strong personal magnetism which is so frequently an adjunct of genius. Physically he was a huge powerful man, so massive and striking in appearance that he suggested comparison rather with some fact of nature—a rock, a vigorous forest tree—than with another man. He was one of those rare men who, like mountains in a landscape, suffice in themselves to relieve their environments, whatever these may be, from all taint of meanness. He stood out from among his guests the centre of conversation, of feeling, and of interest. He was almost invariably engaged in eager conversation, pitched in a loud tone of voice, broken at intervals when he listened to the other disputants, while puffing the cigarettes which he was constantly rolling, and looking intently out of his deep-set penetrating eyes.

Nekrovitch's wife, a Russian like himself, had been a student of medicine at the Russian University until, along with her husband, she had been compelled to take flight from the attentions of the Russian police. She was a curly-headed brunette, with bright hazel eyes and a vivacious manner; a very intelligent and highly "simpatica" woman, as the Italians would put it.

Round Nekrovitch there always clustered an eager crowd of admirers and intimates, discussing, disputing, listening, arguing. They were mostly foreigners, of the shaggy though not unwashed persuasion, but two English faces especially attracted notice. One belonged to a young woman, still on the right side of thirty, dressed without exaggeration in the æsthetic style, with a small but singularly intellectual head and an argumentative manner, whom I knew as Miss Cooper. The other was a man of some thirty-seven years, with auburn hair, which displayed a distinct tendency to develop into a flowing mane ; tall, slim, and lithe of limb, with a splendid set of teeth, which showed under his bushy moustache whenever his frank, benevolent smile parted his lips. He was somewhat taciturn, but evidently tenacious ; a glance at his spacious forehead and finely-shaped head revealed a man of mind, and the friendly, fearless glance of his eyes betokened a lovable nature, though, as he listened to his opponents or answered in his low distinct voice, there was an intensity and fixedness in their depth not incompatible with the fanatic.

This Dr. Armitage was one of the most noticeable figures in the English Anarchist movement, and it was with him that I first discussed Anarchist principles as opposed to those of legal Socialism. Nekrovitch and others often joined in the discussion, and very animated we all grew in the course of debate. Nekrovitch smiled sympathetically at my wholehearted and ingenuous enthusiasm. He never

made any attempt to scoff at it or to discourage
me, though he vainly attempted to persuade me
that Anarchism was too distant and unpractical an
ideal, and that my energies and enthusiasm might
be more advantageously expended in other directions. "Anyway," he once said to me, "it is very
agreeable to a Russian to see young people
interested in politics and political ideals. It re-
minds him of his own country."

Among the other Anarchists who frequented
Nekrovitch's house was the Anarchist and scientist,
Count Voratin, a man who had sacrificed wealth
and high position and family ties for his principles with less fuss than another rich man would
make in giving a donation to an hospital. He
seemed always absolutely oblivious of his own
great qualities, as simple and kindly in manners
as a *moujik* but with a certain innate dignity
and courtliness of demeanour which lifted him
above most of those with whom he came in
contact. I nourished an almost passionate admiration for Voratin as a thinker and a man,
and his writings had gone far to influence me
in my Anarchist leanings. Never shall I forget
the excitement I felt when first I met him at
Nekrovitch's house. I reverenced him as only a
youthful disciple can reverence a great leader.

From Armitage and Nekrovitch I heard much
from time to time of another Russian Anarchist,

Ivan Kosinski, a man actively engaged in the
Anarchist propaganda all over Europe. He was
much admired by them for his absolute unswerving devotion to his ideas. A student and a man
of means, he had never hesitated between his
interests and his convictions. He had come into
collision with the Russian authorities by refusing
to perform military service. In prison he would
not recognise the right of judges and jailers,
and had consequently spent most of his time in
a strait waistcoat and a dark cell. His forte
was silence and dogged unyielding obstinacy.
On escaping from Russian prisons he had gone
to America : he had starved and tramped, but
he had never accepted any sort of help. How
he lived was a mystery to all. He was known
to be an ascetic and a woman-hater, and had
been seen at one time selling fly-papers in the
streets of New York. In revolutionary circles
he was looked up to as an original thinker,
and it was rumoured that he played a leading
part in most of the revolutionary movements
of recent years. He was also engaged on a
life of Bakounine which was to be the standard
work on the famous revolutionist, for which purpose he was always reading and travelling in
search of material.

And at last one evening Nekrovitch announced
that Kosinski was expected. I had heard so much

about this man that I spent my whole evening
in a state of suppressed excitement at the news.
For many months past I had sympathised with the
Anarchist principles, but I had taken no particular steps towards joining the party or exerting
myself on its behalf.   I was waiting for some
special stimulus to action.   Half unconsciously I
found myself wondering whether Kosinski would
prove this.

I had passed a pleasant evening in the little
Chiswick house between the usual political and
ethical discussions and the usual interesting or
entertaining company.   I had assisted at a long
discussion between Miss Cooper and Dr. Armitage,
which, commencing on the question of Socialism,
had gradually deviated into one on food and dress
reform, a matter upon which that lady held very
strong views.   I had felt a little irritated at the
conversation, for I entertained scant sympathy
for what I regarded as hygienic fads; and the
emphasis with which the lady averred that she
touched neither flesh nor alcohol, and felt that
by this abstinence she was not "besotting her
brain nor befouling her soul," amused me much.
Dr. Armitage, to my surprise, expressed some
sympathy with her views, and treated the question
with what I considered undue importance.   This
discussion was brought at last to a termination
by Miss Cooper breaking off for a meal (she

always ate at regular intervals), and retiring into a
corner to consume monkey-nuts out of a hanging pocket or pouch which she carried with
her.

The evening advanced, and I began to despair
of Kosinski's ever arriving. Every time there
was a knock at the door, I wondered whether
it was the much - expected Anarchist, but I was
repeatedly disappointed. Once it was the musical
infant prodigy of the season whose talents had
taken London by storm, another time it was a
Nihilist, yet another a wild-looking Czech poet.
One loud rat-tat made me feel certain that Kosinski
had arrived, but I was again disillusioned, as an
æsthetic, fascinating little lady made her entry,
dragging triumphantly in tow a reluctant, unen-
gaging and green-haired husband. Nekrovitch
gave me a significant glance. "So sorry to be
so late," the little lady began in a high-pitched
voice, "but I had to attend a meeting of our
society for the distribution of sanitary dust-bins;
and Humphry got quite disagreeable waiting for
me outside, although he was well wrapped up in
comforters and mits. My dear Anna (this to
Madame Nekrovitch), *do* tell him that he is most
absurd and egoistic, and that it is his duty to
think less of personal comfort and more of
humanity."

At this last word the injured Humphry, who

had approached the fire, and was attempting to thaw his nose and toes, gave utterance to a suppressed groan ; but a cup of steaming tea and some appetising buttered toast diverted his spouse's thoughts, and she was soon deep in a confidential chat with Anna.

At last, long after eleven, appeared the new-comer of whom I had heard so much. I must confess that my preconceived notions (one always has a preconceived notion of the appearance of a person one has heard much spoken of) fell to the ground. 1 had imagined him dark and audacious, and I saw before me a tall, big, well-built man, with a slight stoop in his shoulders, fair of skin, with a blonde beard and moustache, lank long hair, a finely-cut, firm-set mouth, and blue dreamy eyes, altogether a somewhat Christ-like face. He was clad in a thick, heavy, old-fashioned blue overcoat with a velvet collar, which he refused to remove, baggy nondescript trousers, and uncouth-looking boots. He saluted his host and hostess in an undemonstrative style, bowed awkwardly to the other guests, and settled down to crouch over the fire, and look unostentatiously miserable.

From the first moment Kosinski interested me. His manners were not engaging ; towards women especially he was decidedly hostile. But the marked indifference to opinion which his bearing indicated, his sincerity, his unmistakable moral courage, perhaps his evident aversion to my sex, all had for me a certain fascination.

I felt attracted towards the man, and was pleased that a discussion on Anarchism with Armitage at last afforded me an opportunity of exchanging a few words with him—even though on his side the conversation was not altogether flattering to myself.   It happened in this way.

Nekrovitch, Armitage, and myself had, according to our wont, been discussing the great Anarchist question.   For the hundredth time the Russian had endeavoured to persuade us of the truth and the reason of his point of view.

"So long as men are men," he maintained, "there must be some sort of government, some fixed recognised law—organisation, if you will, to control them."

"All governments are equally bad," answered the doctor.   "All law is coercion, and coercion is immoral.   Immoral conditions breed immoral people.   In a free and enlightened society there would be no room for coercive law.   Crime will disappear when healthy and natural conditions prevail."

And Nekrovitch, perceiving for the hundredth time that his arguments were vain, and that Armitage was not to be moved, had left us to ourselves and gone across to his other guests. Doctor Armitage, always eager for converts, turned his undivided attention to me.

"I hope yet to be able to claim you for a comrade," he said : "you are intelligent and open-minded, and cannot fail to see the futility of attempting to tinker up our worn-out society. You must see that our Socialist friends have only seized on half-truths, and they stop short where true reform should begin."

"I can quite see your point of view," I replied ; "in fact I am more than half a convert already. But I should like to know what I can do. I have been interested now in these problems for a year or two, and must confess that the electioneering and drawing-room politics of Fabians and Social Democrats are not much to my taste ; in fact I may say that I am sick of them. A few men like our friend Nekrovitch, who ennoble any opinions they may hold, are of course exceptions, but I cannot blind myself to the fact that ambition, wire-pulling, and faddism play a prominent part in the general proceedings. On the other hand you seem to me to sin in the opposite direction. No organisation, no definite programme, no specific object!—what practical good could any one like myself do in such a party?"

The doctor smiled a quiet smile of triumph as he proceeded to overthrow my objections : "Why, the very strength of our party lies in the fact that it has not what you are pleased to call an organisation. Organisations are only a means for intriguers and rogues to climb to power on the shoulders of their fellow-men; and at best only serve to trammel initiative and enterprise. With us every individual enjoys complete liberty of action. This of course does not mean to say that several individuals may not unite to attain some common object, as is shown by our groups which are scattered all over the globe. But each group is autonomous, and within the group each individual is his own law. Such an arrangement, besides being right in principle, offers great practical advantages in our war against society, and renders it impossible for governments to stamp us out. Again, as to our lack of programme, if a clear grasp of principle and of the ultimate aim to be attained is meant, it is wrong to say we have no programme, but, if you mean a set of rules and formulas, why, what are they after all but a means of sterilising ideas? Men and their surroundings are unceasingly undergoing modification and change, and one of the chief defects of all governments and parties hitherto has been that men have had to adapt themselves to their programmes, instead of their programmes to themselves. We make no statement as to specific object: each comrade has his own, and goes for it without considering it necessary to proclaim the fact to the whole world. Now you ask me how you could help this movement or what you could do, and I have no hesitation in saying, much. Every revolution requires revolutionists, we need propagandists, we need workers, we need brains and money, and you have both."

"So you think that one ought to place one's property at the service of the Cause, and that thus one is doing more good than by helping in the ordinary way?"

"Why, of course, the revolutionist aims at eradicating the causes of poverty and vice, whereas benevolence, by making it just possible for people to put up with their circumstances, only strengthens the chains which hold mankind in slavery."

We had unconsciously raised our voices in the heat of discussion, and Kosinski, who had caught our last observations, broke in unexpectedly. It was the first time he had opened his mouth to any purpose, and he went straight to the point: "It is you bourgeois Socialists, with your talk of helping us, and your anxiety about using your property 'to the best advantage,' who are the ruin of every movement," he said, addressing me in an uncompromising spirit. "What is wanted to accomplish any great change is enthusiasm, whole-hearted labour, and where that is, no thought is taken as to whether everything is being used to the best advantage. If you are prepared to enter the movement in this spirit, without any backward notion

C

that you are conferring a favour upon any one—for indeed the contrary is the case—well and good : your work will be willingly accepted for what it is worth, and your money, if you have any, will be made good use of ; but if not, you had better side with your own class and enjoy your privileges so long as the workers put up with you."

These outspoken remarks were followed by a momentary silence. Mrs. Trevillian looked dismayed ; Miss Cooper evidently concluded that Kosinski must have dined on steak ; Dr. Armitage agreed, but seemed to consider that more amenity of language might be compatible with the situation. Nekrovitch laughed heartily, enjoying this psychological sidelight, and I, who ought to have felt crushed, was perhaps the only one who thoroughly endorsed the sentiment expressed, finding therein the solution of many moral difficulties which had beset me. Kosinksi was right. I felt one must go the whole length or altogether refrain from dabbling in such matters. And as to property I again knew that he was right ; it was what I had all along instinctively felt. Private property was, after all, but the outcome of theft, and there can be no virtue in restoring what we have come by unrighteously.

Small things are often the turning-point in a career ; and, looking back, I clearly see that that evening's discussion played no small part in determining my future conduct. I was already disposed towards Anarchist doctrines, and my disposition was more inclined towards action of any order than towards mere speculation. I was the first to speak. "Kosinski is quite right; I am the first to recognise it. Only I think it a little unfair to assume me to be a mere bourgeois, attempting to play the part of lady patroness to the revolution. I am sure none who know me can accuse me of such an attitude."

Kosinski grumbled out a reply: "Well, of course I may be mistaken; but I have seen so many movements ruined by women that I am rather distrustful; they are so rarely prepared to forgo what they consider the privileges of the sex —which is but another phrase for bossing every one and everything and expecting much in return for nothing; but of course there may be exceptions. Perhaps you are one."

Nekrovitch laughed aloud: "Bravo, bravo, you are always true to yourself, Kosinski. I have always known you as a confirmed misogynist, and I see you still resist all temptations to reform. You carry boorishness to the verge of heroism."

The hours had slipped by rapidly, and Mrs. Trevillian took the hint which her spouse had long tried to give by shuffling restlessly in his seat and casting side glances at the clock which pointed to half-past one. She rose to go. "We really must

be leaving—it is quite late, and Humphry is never
fit for anything unless he gets at least six hours'
sleep. Good-bye ; thanks for such a pleasant evening," and she bustled out, followed by her husband.
I rose to follow her example and, turning a deaf ear
to Nekrovitch, who remarked, "Oh, Isabel, do stay
on ; it is not yet late, and as you have lost your last
train it is no use being in a hurry," I shook hands
with my friends, including Kosinski, who had once
more subsided into a corner, and left, accompanied by Dr. Armitage, who offered to walk home
with me.

We walked rapidly on through the keen night
air. I felt excited and resolute with the feeling that
a new phase of existence was opening before me.
Dr. Armitage at last spoke. " I hope, Isabel "—it
was usual in this circle to eschew surnames, and
most of my friends and acquaintances called me
Isabel in preference to Miss Meredith—"I hope,
Isabel, that you will come to our meetings. I should
like you to know some of our comrades ; there are
many very interesting men, quite original thinkers,
some of them. And I think human beings so often
throw light on matters which one otherwise fails to
grasp."

" I should much like to," I replied, "if you can
tell me how and when; for I suppose one requires
some sort of introduction even to Anarchist
circles."

"Oh, that is easy enough," he replied. "I have often mentioned your name, and the comrades will be very glad to see you; we make no sort of mystery about our meetings. There will be a meeting at the office of our paper, the *Bomb*, next Saturday. Do come. The business on hand will perhaps not interest you much, but it will be an opportunity for meeting some of our men, and I shall be there."

"Oh, I shall be so glad to come!" I exclaimed. "What will you be discussing?"

"Well, to tell the truth, it is a somewhat unpleasant matter," replied the doctor with some hesitation in his voice. "There have been some strange reports circulating about the Myers case, and we are anxious to get at the truth of the business. It may strike you as a rather unsuitable introduction, but come nevertheless. The movement is always in need of new blood and fresh energies to keep it from narrowing its sphere of activity, and it is well that you should know us as we are."

"Very well, I will come if you will give me the direction."

"Let us say nine o'clock at the office of the *Bomb* in Slater's Mews, —— Street; you will find me there."

"Agreed," I replied, and conversation dropped as we walked rapidly along. I was much occupied with my own thoughts and Dr. Armitage was noted for his long periods of silence. At last we reached my doorstep. I fumbled for my latch-key, found it, and wished my friend good-night. We shook hands and parted.

CHAPTER III

AN ABORTIVE GROUP-MEETING

BEFORE describing the strange committee or group-meeting about to be dealt with, it is necessary to say a few words concerning the mysterious affair which gave rise to it.

On the 17th of December 189– the posters of the evening papers had announced in striking characters :—

"DEATH OF AN ANARCHIST :
ATTEMPTED OUTRAGE IN A LONDON PARK."

That same afternoon a loud explosion had aroused the inhabitants of a quiet suburban district, and on reaching the corner of —— Park whence the report emanated, the police had found, amid a motley débris of trees, bushes, and railings, the charred and shattered remains of a man. These, at the inquest, proved to have belonged to Augustin Myers, an obscure little French Anarchist, but despite the usual lengthy and unsatisfactory routine of police inquiries, searches, and arrests, practically nothing could be ascertained concerning him or the cir-

cumstances attending his death. All that was
certain was that the deceased man had in his possession an explosive machine, evidently destined for
some deadly work, and that, while traversing the
park, it had exploded, thus putting an end both to
its owner and his projects.

Various conflicting theories were mooted as to
the motive which prompted the conduct of the
deceased Anarchist, but no confirmation could be
obtained to any of these. Some held that Myers
was traversing London on his way to some incon-
spicuous country railway station, whence to take
train for the Continent where a wider and more
propitious field for Anarchist outrage lay before him.
Others opined that he had contemplated committing
an outrage in the immediate vicinity of the spot
which witnessed his own death ; and others, again,
that, having manufactured his infernal machine for
some nefarious purpose either at home or abroad,
he was suddenly seized either with fear or remorse,
and had journeyed to this unobserved spot in order
to bury it. The papers hinted at accomplices and
talked about the usual "widespread conspiracy";
the police opened wide their eyes, but saw very
little. The whole matter, in short, remained, and
must always remain, a mystery to the public.

Behind the scenes, however, the Anarchists talked
of a very different order of "conspiracy." The
funeral rites of the poor little Augustin were per-

formed with as much ceremony and sympathy as an indignant London mob would allow, and he was followed to his grave by a goodly *cortège* of "comrades," red and black flags and revolutionary song. Among the chief mourners was the deceased man's brother Jacob, who wept copiously into the open grave and sung his "Carmagnole" with inimitable zeal. It was this brother whose conduct had given rise to suspicion among his companions, and "spies" and "police plots" were in every one's mouth. The office of the *Bomb*, as being the centre of English anarchy, had been selected as the scene for an inquiry *en group* into the matter.

Thus on a wet and chilling January evening —one of those evenings when London, and more especially squalid London, is at the height of its unattractiveness—I set out towards my first Anarchist "group-meeting." And certainly the spirit which moved me from within must have been strong that the flesh quailed not at the foul scenery amid which my destination lay.

Half-way down one of the busiest, grimiest, and most depressing streets in the W.C. district stands a squalid public-house, the type of many hundreds and thousands of similar dens in the metropolis. The "Myrtle Grove Tavern," pastoral as the name sounds, was not precisely the abode of peace and goodwill. From four A.M., when the first of her *habitués* began to muster round the yet unopened

doors, till half-past twelve P.M., when the last of them
was expelled by the sturdy " chucker-out," the atmosphere was dense with the foul breath and still
fouler language of drunken and besotted men and
women. Every phase of the lower order of British
drinker and drunkard was represented here. The
coarse oaths of the men, mingled with the shriller
voices of their female companions, and the eternal
" 'e saids " and " she saids " of the latter's complaints
and disputes were interrupted by the plaintive
wailings of the puny, gin-nourished infants at their
breasts. Here, too, sat the taciturn man, clay pipe
in mouth, on his accustomed bench day after day,
year in year out, gazing with stony and blear-eyed
indifference on all that went on around him ; deaf,
dumb, and unseeing ; only spitting deliberately at
intervals, and with apparently no other vocation in
life than the consumption of fermented liquor.

The side-door for " jugs and bottles " gave on to
a dirty and odoriferous mews, down which my
destination lay. The unbridled enthusiasm of
eighteen years can do much to harden or deaden
the nervous system, but certainly it required all my
fortitude to withstand the sickening combination of
beer and damp horsy hay which greeted my nos-
trils. Neither could the cabmen and stablemen,
hanging round the public-house doors and the
mews generally, be calculated to increase one's
democratic aspirations, but I walked resolutely on,

and turning to my left, dexterously avoiding an unsavoury heap of horse manure, straw, and other offal, I clambered up a break-neck ladder, at the top of which loomed the office of the *Bomb*.

The door was furtively opened in response to my kick by a lean, hungry-looking little man of very circumspect appearance. He cast me a surly and suspicious glance, accompanied by a not very encouraging snarl, but on my mentioning Dr. Armitage he opened the door a few inches wider and I passed in.

It took me some seconds before I could accustom my eyes to the fetid atmosphere of this den, which was laden with the smoke of divers specimens of the worst shag and cheapest tobacco in the metropolis. But various objects, human and inanimate, became gradually more distinct, and I found myself in a long, ill-lighted wooden shed, where type and dust and unwashed human beings had left their mark, and where soap and sanitation were unknown. Past the type racks and cases, which occupied the first half of this apartment, were grouped benches, stools, packing-cases, and a few maimed and deformed chairs for the accommodation of the assembly. Then came a hand printing-press, on which were spread the remains of some comrade's repast : the vertebral column of a bloater and an empty condensed-milk can, among other relics. The floor, from one extremity to the

other of the "office," was littered with heaps of
unsold revolutionary literature, the approximate
date of which could be gauged by the thickness of
dust in which it was smothered. On the walls and
from beams and rafters hung foils and boxing-
gloves; artistic posters and cartoons, the relics of
a great artist who had founded the *Bomb*, and
the effigies of divers comrades to whom a pathway
to a better world had been opened through the
hangman's drop. But what most riveted my attention was an indistinct animate *something* enveloped
in a red flag, rolled up in a heap on the frouziest
and most forbidding old sofa it had ever been my
lot to behold. That this *something* was animate
could be gathered from the occasional twitchings
of the red bundle, and from the dark mop of black
greasy hair which emerged from one end. But to
what section of the animal kingdom *it* belonged I
was quite at a loss to decide. Other stray objects
which I noted about this apartment were an osten-
tatious-looking old revolver of obsolete make, and
some chemical bottles, which, however, contained
no substance more dangerous than Epsom salts.

The human occupants were not less noticeable
than the inanimate, and some of them are deserving of our attention.

The man Myers, round whom the interest of the
meeting was principally centred this evening, was
to all appearances a mean enough type of the

East End sartorial Jew. His physiognomy was not that of a fool, but indicated rather that low order of intelligence, cunning and intriguing, which goes to make a good swindler. The low forehead, wideawake, shifty little eyes, the nose of his forefathers, and insolent lock of black hair plastered low on his brow—all these characteristics may frequently be met with in the dock of the "Old Bailey" when some case of petty swindling is being tried.

Next Myers I noticed Dr. Armitage, who stood out in striking contrast from the rest of his companions. The smile with which he welcomed me was eloquent of the satisfaction with which he noted this my first entrance into an Anarchist circle.

The short bench on which he sat was shared by a man in corduroys of the navvy type, a large honest-looking fellow whose views of the Social question appeared to be limited to a not very definite idea of the injustice of third-class railway travelling and the payment of rent, and he expressed his opinions on these knotty problems with more freedom and warmth of language than was perhaps altogether warranted by the occasion.

Gracefully poised on one leg against an adjoining type-rack leaned a tall youth with fair curling hair, a weak tremulous mouth, and an almost girlish physiognomy. This youth had been drummed out of the army, the discipline of which he had found too severe, for feigning illness, since when he had passed his time between the bosom of his family, the workhouse, and the Anarchist party. He paid very little attention to the proceedings of the meeting, but discoursed eloquently, in a low voice, of the brutality of his parents who refused to keep him any longer unless he made some attempt to find employment. I remember wondering, *en passant*, why this fair-haired, weak-kneed youth had ever entered the Anarchist party ; but the explanation, had I but known, was close at hand.

This explanation was a square-built, sturdy-looking man of some forty years. His appearance was the reverse of engaging, but by no means lacking in intelligence. He was ill-satisfied and annoyed with the universe, and habitually defied it from the stronghold of a double bed. Thither he had retired after the death of his father, an old market-porter, who had been crushed by the fall of a basket of potatoes. The son saw in this tragic circumstance the outcome and the reward of labour, swore a solemn oath never to do a stroke of work again, threw up his job, and from that day became a confirmed loafer in the Anarchist party. Some months previously, while propagandising in the workhouse, he found the youth there, and learned from his own lips how, being disinclined to become a burden on his poor old parents

after his exit from the army, he had seen no other
alternative but to become a pauper, and make the
best he could of the opportunities afforded him
by the poor-rates. From the workhouse he was
dragged triumphantly forth by his new friend, and
became an easy convert to anarchic and communistic principles.

The only feminine element in this assembly was
a fair, earnest-looking Russian girl, whose slight
knowledge of English did not allow her to follow
the proceedings very accurately. She was an almost
pathetic figure in her naïve enthusiasm, and evidently regarded her present companions as seriously as those she had left behind her in Russia,
and seemed to imagine they played as dangerous
a rôle, and ran the same risk as they did.

There were several others present among whom
the loafer type was perhaps in the ascendant.
But there were also many of the more intelligent
artisan class, discontented with their lot ; labourers
and dockers who had tramped up after a hard
day's work, a young artist who looked rather of the
Social Democratic type, a cabman, a few stray
gentlemen, a clever but never-sober tanner, a
labour agitator, a professional stump-orator, and
one or two fishy and nondescript characters
of the Hebraic race. O'Flynn, the printer of
the *Bomb*, was a cantankerous Irishman with a
taste for discoursing on abstract questions, con-

cerning which he grew frightfully muddled and
confused. He had a rather mad look in his eye
and a disputatious manner.

When at last inquiry was made whether all companions expected were present, the red flag began
to quiver and writhe most noticeably and finally
to unfurl, and there emerged from its depths the
dirtiest and most slovenly man I had ever seen,
and the frouziest and most repulsive of dogs. This
man, if man I may call him, was bony and ill-
built, and appeared to consist largely of hands and
feet. His arms were abnormally long and his
chest narrow and hollow, and altogether he seemed
to hang together by a mere fluke. His ill-assorted
limbs were surmounted by a sallow, yellowish face,
large repulsive lips, and a shapeless nose, and to
him belonged the long, black greasy hair which
I had already noted amid the folds of the red
banner. Large gristly ears emerged from his un-
combed mop of hair, and the only redeeming
feature about the abject creature was his large,
brown, dog-like eyes. He crept forward, grinding
his teeth and rubbing his bony hands, and subsided into a waste-paper basket which was the
only available seat left unoccupied.

And now at last, after much talking and shifting
about, and not before a young German hairdresser
had been stationed with one eye glued to a hole
in the outer wall of the shed, in order to make

sure that no detective was listening outside, the proceedings commenced.

Banter, the little man who had opened the door to me, rose to his feet, cleared his throat, and said "*Com*rades" in a stentorian voice. Then followed a long and rambling statement which he read out, from amid the grammatical inaccuracies and continual digressions of which I was enabled to gather that he had noticed of late something very peculiar about the conduct of Jacob Myers, who had appeared to exercise undue influence and power over his brother Augustin; that, moreover, Jacob had been seen by a third party drinking a glass of rum in the "Nag and Beetle" in company with a well-known detective, and that, in final and conclusive proof of some very fishy transactions on his part, three undeniable half-crowns had been distinctly observed in his overcoat pocket the previous week. "And how should he come by these by honest means?" indignantly inquired Banter. "He says he's out of work, and he's not got the courage to steal!"

"'Ear, 'ear! Why pay rent to robber landlords?" the navvy, Armitage's neighbour, ejaculated at this juncture, after which irrelevant inquiry he spat defiance at Society.

Then followed the speeches for the prosecution, if the use of such a word may be permitted in connection with an Anarchist transaction. The chief

D

accusations made against Myers were his violent
blood-and-thunder speeches which he had in no
wise carried out in action, but which he had delivered under the eyes and in the hearing of the
police who had listened and seen it all with quite
commendable Christian forbearance. Besides this
several sensational articles had appeared in the
daily press in connection with Augustin's death,
exaggerating the importance of the affair and hinting at dark plots; of which articles he was suspected of being the author. Jacob was in fact
accused of having egged on his unfortunate brother
to his doom in order that he might turn a little
money out of the transaction between newspaper
reports and police fees. It apparently mattered little
to this modern Shylock whence came his pound of
flesh or what blood ran or congealed in its veins.

Through all these statements and questions Myers
sat in stolid and insolent silence — occasionally
whistling snatches of some music-hall air. At last
when reference was made to some chemicals which
he was alleged to have procured and handed on to
his brother, he roused up from his affected indifference and appealed to Armitage for assistance. "Dr.
Armitage knows," he exclaimed indignantly, "that
I only procured the sulphuric acid from him for
domestic purposes."

My eyes were riveted on the doctor's face, and
only to one who knew him well could the expres-

sion be at all decipherable. To me it distinctly denoted disappointment—that humiliating sense of
disappointment and disillusion which must invariably come upon a man of strong and fanatical
convictions when brought into contact with the
meanness and cowardice of his fellows.

Dr. Armitage was a fanatic and an idealist, and
two convictions were paramount in his mind at this
time : the necessity and the justice of the "propaganda by force" doctrine preached by the more
advanced Anarchists, and the absolute good faith
and devotion to principle of the men with whom he
was associated. A man of the Myers type was quite
incomprehensible to him. Not for a single instant
had Armitage hesitated to throw open the doors of
his Harley Street establishment to the Anarchists :
to him the cause was everything, and interests,
prudence, prospects, all had to give way before it.
And here was this man who had professed the same
principles as himself, with whom he had discoursed
freely on the necessity of force, who had openly
advocated dynamite in his presence—this man who
had spoken of the revolution and the regeneration
of Society with the same warmth as himself—talking
of "domestic purposes," and ready to recant all that
he had preached and said. And what lay behind
this reticence and these denials ? Treachery of the
basest kind, and the most sordid, abominable calcu-
lations which it was possible to conceive.

These thoughts I read in the doctor's face, and turning my eyes from him to the abject Jacob I could only wonder at the naïve sincerity of Armitage, which could ever have laid him open to such illusions and disillusions.

After some seconds' hesitation Armitage replied : "I do not desire or intend to go into any details here concerning my past conversations or relations with Jacob Myers, neither do I consider myself in any way bound to discuss here the motives which prompted, or which I thought prompted his actions, and the requests he made of me. As Anarchists we have not the right to judge him, and all we can do is to refuse to associate ourselves any further with him, which I, for one, shall henceforth do. The knowledge of his own abominable meanness should be punishment enough for Myers."

The doctor's words were received with very general approval.

"Armitage is perfectly right," said Carter. "We Anarchists cannot pretend to judge our fellows, but we can form our own opinions and act accordingly. Myers' conduct proves him to be no better than a spy; we of the *Bomb* can have no further relations with him."

"Damn about judging and not judging," exclaimed a sturdy-looking docker. "All I know is that if Myers does not quickly clear out of

the *Bomb* I'll kick him out. He ought to be
shot. I don't pretend to understand none of
these nice distinctions. I call a spade a spade,
and if. . . ."

" 'Ear, 'ear ! Down with . . ." commenced Elliot
again, and Jacob opened his mouth to speak, but
he was saved from any further need of self-defence
or explanation, for at this moment the door of
the office was broken rudely open and there
entered like a hurricane a veritable fury in female
form — a whirlwind, a tornado, a ravening wolf
into a fold of lambs. This formidable apparition, which proved to be none other than the
wife of the suspected Myers, amid a volley of
abuse and oaths delivered in the choicest Bil-
lingsgate, pounced down on her ill-used husband,
denounced Anarchy and the Anarchists — their
morals, their creeds, their hellish machinations ;
she called on Jehovah to chastise, nay, utterly
to destroy them, and soundly rated her consort
for ever having associated with such scoundrels.
And thus this formidable preacher of dynamite
and disaster was borne off in mingled triumph
and disgrace by his indignant spouse.

CHAPTER IV

A POLICE SCARE

I LEFT the office of the *Bomb* towards 1 A.M., undecided whether to weep or to laugh at what I had witnessed there. This, my first introduction into an English Anarchist circle had certainly not been very encouraging, but I was too deeply persuaded of the truth and justice of the Anarchist doctrines to be deterred by such a beginning, and I did not for one instant waver from my resolve to enter and take part in the "movement." That some insincere and dishonest men and some fools should also play their part in it I from the first recognised as inevitable, but I could not see that this affected the Anarchist principles or rendered it less necessary for those believing in them to advocate and spread them. Dr. Armitage accompanied me part of my way home and we talked the matter over *en route*. "Why trouble ourselves," he exclaimed, "about a few unprincipled men in such a wide, such a universal movement? Our objects and ideals are too far above such considerations to allow us to be influenced by them. Men like Myers are but the outcome of unnatural and vitiated conditions; they are produced by the very society which it is our object to abolish—as all manner of disease is produced by vitiated air. With better conditions such men will disappear; nay, the very possibility of their existence will be gone."

"But in the meantime," I rejoined, "they are surely damaging our Cause, and scenes like the one we have just witnessed would, if known to the public, bring our party into ridicule and discredit."

"The Cause is too great and too high to be influenced by such men or such scenes," answered the doctor with conviction. "Moreover it is our duty to bring fresh blood and life into the party, so that no place will be left to renegades of the Myers type."

And in face of Armitage's unswerving faith and optimism my moment of disgust and perplexity passed, and I felt more than ever determined to bring my quota of time and strength to the propagation of the Anarchist ideals. "I have only seen a very limited and narrow circle," I said to myself; "the field is wide, and I only know one obscure and unclean corner of it. I cannot judge from this night's experience."

As far as the squalor of the men and their surroundings was concerned, although it was at first something of a shock to me, I did not allow myself to be disconcerted on its account. I had no desire or ambition to be a mere dilettante Socialist, and as dirt and squalor had to be faced, well, I was ready to face them. A famous Russian writer has described a strange phase through which the Russian youth passed not many years since, the "V. Narod" ("To the People!") movement, when young men and girls by the thousands, some belonging to the highest classes in society, fled from their families, tore themselves free from all domestic and conventional yokes, persuaded that it was their duty to serve the cause of the masses, and that in no way could they better accomplish this object than by settling in the people's midst, living their life, taking part in their work. I was passing through a similar phase of mental evolution.

I felt a strong desire to free myself from all the ideas, customs, and prejudices which usually influence my class, to throw myself into the life and the work of the masses. Thus it was that I worked hard to learn how to compose and print, that I might be of use to the Cause in the most practical manner of all—the actual production of its literature. Thus it was also that I resolutely hardened myself against any instinctive sentiments of repulsion which the unclean and squalid surroundings of the people might raise in me. I remember reading an article by Tolstoi which appeared in the English press, dealing with the conditions of the Russian *moujïk*, in which he clearly and uncompromisingly stated that in order to tackle the social problem, it is necessary to tackle dirt and vermin with it. If you desire to reach your *moujik* you must reach him *à travers* his dirt and his parasites : if you are disinclined to face these, then leave your *moujik* alone. It was in fact a case of "take me, take my squalor." I determined to take both.

Dr. Armitage left me at the corner of Oxford Circus, but before I had taken many steps farther, I heard him suddenly turn round, and in an instant he had come up with me again.

"By the way, Isabel," he exclaimed, "I was quite forgetting to mention something I had done, to which I trust you will not object. You know how full up my place is just now with hard-up comrades. Well I took the liberty to send on to you a young Scotchman, I forget his name, who has just tramped up from the North ; a most interesting fellow, rather taciturn, but with doubtless a good deal in him. He had nowhere to pass the night, poor chap, and no money, so I told him that if he waited on your doorstep some time after midnight you would be certain to give him a night's lodgings when you returned. Did I do right ? " and the doctor's kindly face beamed with the look of a man who expected approbation.

"Ye-es," I gasped out, somewhat taken aback, "quite right, of course ; " for I felt that any hesitation would be feeble, a mere relic of bourgeois prejudice.

And, sure enough, on reaching my domicile, I found installed on the doorstep a most uncouth and villainous-looking tramp. Taciturn he certainly was, for he scarcely opened his mouth to say "Good-evening," and indeed during the three days of his residence with me he hardly ever articulated a sound. As I was getting out my latch-key the local policeman chanced to pass : "That fellow has been hanging about for the last hours, miss," he said to me. "Shall I remove him for you ?"

"Certainly not," I replied firmly, and opening the door, I requested my unknown comrade to enter. I can still see in my mind's eye that constable's face. It looked unutterable things.

After conducting the tramp to the pantry, and letting him loose on a cold pigeon-pie and other viands, and finally installing him on the study sofa, I retired to my own apartment, well prepared to enjoy a good night's rest.

This was destined, however, to be of short duration. Towards 6.30 I was roused from sleep by a loud rat-tat at the front door and, the servants not being up at such an hour, and suspecting that this early visit was in some way connected with the Anarchists, I hastily slipped on a wrapper and ran downstairs.

On opening the door I found one of the members of the previous night's meeting, the taciturn hero of the potato tragedy.

"It's rather early to disturb you," he began, "but I came to let you know that last night, after you had all gone, Comrades Banter and O'Flynn were arrested."

"Arrested!" I exclaimed, as yet unused to such incidents; "why, what on earth are they charged with?"

"Well," answered Carter, "the charge is not yet very clear, but so far as we can understand, it is in some way connected with the Myers business. They are charged with manufacturing explosives, or something of the sort. The fact is, the police and Jacob Myers are at the bottom of the whole matter, and Banter, O'Flynn, and Augustin have all played into their hands."

"Come in here," I interrupted, leading the way to the dining-room. "Let us sit down and talk the matter over together;" and we entered, Carter casting a distinctly disapprobatory glance at the "bourgeois luxury" of this apartment.

As soon as we were seated my companion returned to the question of the moment. "I fear."

he said, "that it is rather a serious affair for the comrades. That Myers is a police emissary there can no longer be any reasonable doubt, and the death of his brother is clear proof that he has not been wasting his time lately. And it is only too likely that the same hand which provided Augustin with explosives may have placed similar material in the possession of Banter and O'Flynn."

"How abominable!" I exclaimed indignantly.

"Yes, but Anarchists should not be stupid enough to take any one into their confidence in such matters," returned Carter. "It is merely encouraging *mouchards* and police plots. However, the question now is—What can be done to help the comrades out of the mess?"

"I am willing to do my best," I answered; "only tell me how I can be of use."

"You can be of great use, if you care to be," answered Carter. "A barrister must be procured to defend them, witnesses must be found, money procured (and here he cast a side-glance at my plate), and some one ought to interview the comrades in Holloway, and take some food to the poor fellows."

"I am quite willing to do my best in all these matters," I answered enthusiastically.

Carter stayed some little while longer instructing me in the various things I was to do, and then left me, retiring presumably to his double bed again, for I saw no more of him till long after the trial was over. He had handed the work over to me, and doubtless felt that so far as he was personally concerned his responsibilities were at an end.

As soon as the morning papers arrived I scanned them eagerly and from them learned further particulars of the arrest. A widespread conspiracy was suspected, the object of which was to blow up the West End of London, and leaders were devoted to the denunciation of the Anarchists and their infamous teachings. Explosives, it was alleged, had been found in the possession of the arrested men, "evidently destined to carry into effect the deadly work which was only stopped by the hand of God in Queen's Park three weeks ago."

Having disposed of a hasty breakfast, I left the house, and my morning was spent in places which were new and strange to me—Holloway Jail, the Old Jewry, and the Middle Temple. Holloway Prison was my first destination, for before any other steps could be taken it was necessary to ascertain what views the prisoners themselves held as to the course to be adopted in their defence.

I awaited my turn in the prison waiting-room along with a motley crowd of other visitors—burglars' and forgers' wives, pickpockets' mates, and the mother of a notorious murderer among

others. Their language was not very choice when
addressing the jailers, but sympathetic enough
when talking among themselves and inquiring of
one another, "What's your man up for?" or,
"How did your mate get copped?" I felt painfully
conscious of the tameness of my reply: "It's a
friend: incitement to murder." How far more
respectable murder itself would have sounded in
the midst of such superior crime!

One burglar's spouse confided to me that her
husband had been "at it for years, but this was
the first time he'd been copped:" which latter
incident she seemed to consider an unpardonable
infringement of the privileges and rights of citizen-
ship. She was a bright buxom little woman and
had evidently flourished on his plunder.

In striking contrast to the burglar's wife, I
noticed the daughter of a would-be suicide, a tall,
beautiful girl, who formed a pathetic contrast to
her surroundings. Her unfortunate father — an
unsuccessful musician — had succumbed in the
struggle for an honest life, and the cares of a large
family had driven him to desperation. As I gazed
at the poor girl with her tear-swollen eyes and noted
her extreme thinness and the shabbiness of her
well-worn clothes, and as, from her, my eyes turned
to the cheerful burglar's wife, I meditated on the
superiority of virtue over dishonesty—especially in
the reward accorded to it.

At last, having stated my name, the name of my prisoner, the relationship or lack of relationship between us, and declared my non-connection with the case, and having received a tin number in return for this information, I was ushered through various passages and apartments into a kind of dark cage, separated by a narrow passage from a still darker one, in the depths of which I perceived my Anarchist, O'Flynn, as soon as my eyes had grown accustomed to the darkness. I had several questions to ask him during the few minutes at our disposal, and conversation was anything but easy; for on all sides of me other prisoners and their relatives were talking, weeping, arguing, disputing, and shouting one another down with all their might and lungs.

Two things struck me in Holloway Prison on this my first visit to such a place. Firstly, the outward cleanliness, and I might almost say pleasantness, of the place; and secondly, the illogical nature of the law which treats the unconvicted men, who in its eyes are consequently innocent, like convicted criminals. Nothing could be more uncomfortable and unattractive than the conditions under which the detained men are allowed to see their relatives; no privacy of any sort is allowed them, the time allotted is of the briefest, and only one visitor a day is permitted to pass. The censorship over books allowed is very strict and hopelessly stupid, and altogether everything is made as uncomfortable as possible for those under detention.

Later in the course of my Anarchist career I had occasion to visit Newgate on a similar errand, and was struck by the same incongruity in the system. The external impression made by Newgate was very different, however.

There is no suggestion of pleasantness about Newgate. It strikes you indeed as the threshold of the gallows, and is calculated to arouse qualms in the most strenuous upholder of capital punishment. A constant sense of gloom is settled like a pall over the whole building, blacker even than the soot and grime which encrust it. Inside, the dreary atmosphere is ominous of the constant vicinity of the hangman's drop, doors seem for ever to be swinging heavily and locking, keys and chains clanking, and over all the uncompromising flagstaff looms like an embodied threat.

After my many dreary wanderings round London, the clambering in and out of omnibuses and other vehicles, and prison interviews, I found the old-world tranquillity of the Temple quite a relief.

Here began a new order of search. I had to find a barrister, and that without delay. But how, whom, and in what court or lane did the right man dwell? During one brief moment indeed my thoughts turned towards our family solicitor as a possible counsellor in this matter, but only to be promptly diverted into other channels. That worthy gentleman's feelings would certainly not have withstood so rude a shock. I could picture him, in my mind's eye, slowly removing his gold pince-nez and looking at me in blank but indulgent surprise, as at one who had suddenly taken leave of her senses. No, this would never do. Barristers by the score must surely reside in the labyrinths of the Temple, and I determined to seek one first hand.

And thus it was that, after some little hesitation, I finally ascended the stairs of a house in Fig Tree Court in the hope that J. B. Armstrong, Esq., selected at random, might answer my purpose.

The clerk who opened the door looked politely surprised at my appearance and inquired my business, into which I promptly plunged head-first. His eyebrows gradually ascended higher and higher into the regions of his hair, and his face grew stern and sad as I proceeded. "Allow me to inquire," he interrupted, "the name of the solicitor who is instructing the case."

"I have not got a solicitor," I replied, somewhat taken aback.

Then he re-opened the door. "I feel confident, madam, that Mr. Armstrong would not care to undertake such a case. Good morning."

I retired from this gentleman's presence neither

E

bent nor broken, though slightly disappointed.
"So it is usual to engage a solicitor first," I reflected, "and to communicate through him with the
barrister, is it? Well, a solicitor can't be afforded
here and we must do without him." The Anarchist
in me revolted at such red-tapeism. "Well, here's
for another plunge," I said to myself; "let us try
a B this time. C. Bardolph sounds promising."
And I ascended another staircase and knocked at
another inhospitable door.

Mr. Bardolph I saw in person, a very pompous
gentleman with manners the reverse of polite. He
could scarcely contain his outraged feelings when
it came to the question of the solicitor. "I can
have no connection with such a case," he said
firmly, and I again retired, feeling quite disreputable.

My next defeat occurred in the chambers of
Mr. Anthony C. Frazer. No sooner did my eyes
fall on that gentleman than I regretted my entry,
and the utter hopelessness of my mission was
borne in upon my mind, for I was beginning to
realise the difficulties of the situation and to scent
failure in the very air. Mr. Frazer requested me
to be seated and eyed me curiously, as though
I were some queer zoological specimen recently
escaped from captivity, and listened with an in-
credulous smile to my narrative. He did not even
wait for the missing solicitor. "This is scarcely

in my line, madam," he said, rising. "You have
certainly made some mistake." And he left his
clerk to accompany me to the door.

I descended the stairs from this gentleman's
chambers feeling distinctly crestfallen and tired,
and at my wits' ends as to where next to go, when,
turning the corner into another court, I became
aware of rapid footsteps in my pursuit, and next
moment I was overtaken by ·the youth who had
ushered me out from the scene of my last defeat.

"I think, miss," he began, "that I can direct you
to a—er—barrister who would just do for your
business. On no account say that I recommended
you to him, or you will get me into trouble. But
you try Mr. Curtis in Brick Court. He undertakes
the defence of burglars and swindlers and all sorts
of people, and you'll find him cheap and satisfactory."

I thanked the youth, and although this did not
strike me as altogether the most promising introduction, I thought it best to try my luck in this
new direction, and, having at length discovered the
house, I ascended the three rickety flights of stairs
which led to Mr. Curtis's apartment and entered.

This Curtis was a small, wizened old man, of
obsolete cut, but with remarkably up-to-date manners, and a pair of keen little eyes, penetrating as
Röntgen rays. His hair was weedy, and his clothes
snuffy and ill-fitting; but spite of this there was

something uncommonly brisk and wideawake about the little man, and a certain business-like directness in his manner which impressed me favourably.   I felt hopeful at once.

One of the first remarks he addressed to me— for we primarily discussed the financial aspect of his services—struck me by reason of its uncompromising common sense. "Five guineas down and another three next Tuesday, miss, and I make no inquiry where the money comes from," he said, "not so long as it is the current coin of the realm and paid punctually. Without this, however, I cannot undertake or proceed with the case."

On my immediately producing the required sum he requested me to be seated, and sitting down opposite me himself, he asked me for full particulars of the case. These I gave him to the best of my ability and he took notes.

The question of witnesses he tackled with the same uncompromising lack of veneer which had characterised his remarks on the money question. "Witnesses to character and so forth must be found," he said, "the more authentic and reputable the better, but at all costs they must be procured. Whom can you suggest ?"

I confessed that I could for the moment think of nobody.

"You will think of somebody," he replied persuasively, "you *must* remember somebody," and

there was that in his voice which did not brook
or encourage contradiction, "some one in a respectable position, of course," he continued, "a
man pursuing one of the liberal professions, or a
business man of means. Plenty of doctors and
professional men among your people, are there
not ? The evidence of such a man would carry
weight. The court's belief in a witness's veracity
is, generally speaking, proportionate to his means.
Doubtless you will be able to think of a desirable
man . . . who knows the prisoners," he added,
rapidly turning over his notes, and speaking in
such a manner as to convey to me the idea that
the exact extent of the witness's knowledge of the
prisoners was not of any very great consequence,
so long as he was prepared to swear to their
respectability, and that his banking account and
general appearance were satisfactory.

"I will look round and let you know the result
to-morrow," I answered.

"Good," replied Curtis, "two witnesses at least,
and men of position and education at all costs.
Good afternoon."

I had enough to do during the remainder of the
day in finding those witnesses, but found they were
at last, though not without a tremendous effort on
my part and some considerable degree of ingenuity.
When attired in some of my brother Raymond's
discarded clothes, and produced for Curtis's inspec-

tion the following day, they really made a respectable couple, and I felt proud of them—one a physician of superior accomplishments and aristocratic
appearance, the other a master-tailor, of prosperous
if not very *distingué* presence. I likewise discovered a cabman who had been present in Hyde
Park at an allegedly incriminating speech made
by Banter; and on jogging his memory with a
little whisky he distinctly recalled several points
valuable to the defence.

Up till the very day of the trial my time was kept
well occupied with such errands. Indeed, remarkable as the fact may appear, practically the whole
labour of preparing the defence devolved upon me.

It was neither an easy nor a very encouraging
task. The greater number of the English Anarchists mysteriously disappeared at this approach
of danger. Mindful of the truth of the axiom that
discretion is the better part of valour, A thought
it well to suddenly recollect his duties towards his
family; B discovered that he had a capacious
stomach, which required feeding; C, that the
Anarchist policy was in discord with his own true
principles. At such a moment, therefore, and surrounded, or rather unsurrounded by such men,
the task in front of me was not easy, and in the
actual state of public opinion it was not very
hopeful either.

Public feeling was against the Anarchists. So

long as violence and outrage had been reserved
entirely for the benefit of foreign climes, the
British public had regarded the Anarchists with
tolerance and equanimity. But the mysterious
death of Myers had alarmed and disquieted it, and
heavy sentences were generally invoked against the
prisoners.

That the whole conspiracy was a got-up affair
between Jacob Myers and the police was evident.
Neither Banter nor O'Flynn was a dangerous man ;
a little loud and exaggerated talk was the utmost
extent of their harmfulness. Neither of them was
any better capable of making a bomb than of
constructing a flying-machine, and they were less
capable of throwing it than of flying.

But political detectives would have a slow time
of it in this country unless they occasionally made
a vigorous effort on their own behalf, and an
unscrupulous and impecunious man like Myers
proved a valuable tool to help such gentlemen
along, and fools of the Banter type suitable
victims.

And thus it was that these two men now found
themselves in the dock with twelve serious-minded
tradesmen sitting in solemn conclave to consider
their crimes.

The trial itself was a ridiculous farce. Jacob
Myers, who would have been the one witness of
any importance, was not subpœnaed ; he had in

fact discreetly quitted the country under his wife's escort. The police, with imperturbable gravity, brought ginger-beer bottles into court which had been found in O'Flynn's apartment, and which, they averred, could be converted into very formidable weapons of offence. Many gaseous speeches made by the prisoners, or attributed to them, were solemnly brought up against them, and a shudder ran through the court at the mention of such phrases as "wholesale assassination" and "war to the death."

The evidence, however, sufficed to impress the jury with the extreme gravity of the case and to alarm the public, and the prisoners were found guilty.

I well recollect the last day of the trial, which I attended throughout in more or less remote regions of the Old Bailey, recruiting recalcitrant witnesses, sending food in to the defendants, &c. Two other cases were being tried at the same time, one of which was a particularly revolting murder, for which three persons were on trial. The prisoners' relatives were waiting below in a state of painful excitement. "Guilty or not guilty," was on all their lips, "release or penal servitude, life or death, which was it to be?" Friends were constantly running in and out of the court giving the women news of the progress of the trials. "It is looking black for the prisoners!" "There is more hope !" "There is no hope !" and finally "guilty" in all the cases was reported. The wife of a horrible German murderer who had strangled his employer's wife, while a female accomplice played the piano to divert her children's attention from her cries, swooned away at the news. O'Flynn's old mother went into hysterics and became quite uncontrollable in her grief when, a few minutes later the news, "Five years' penal servitude," was brought down.

CHAPTER V

TO THE RESCUE

THE first weeks of my experience in the Anarchist camp had flown by with astounding rapidity. The chapter of my experiences had opened with the expulsion of an alleged spy and *agent provocateur*, and had closed with a sentence of penal servitude passed on two of my new-found comrades. Between these two terminal events I seemed to have lived ages, and so I had, if, as I hold, experience counts for more than mere years. Holloway and Newgate, Slater's Mews and the Middle Temple, barristers and solicitors, judges and juries and detectives; appointments in queer places to meet queer people—all this had passed before me with the rapidity of a landscape viewed from the window of an express train; and now that the chapter had closed, I found that it was but the preface to the real business I had set my shoulder to.

The morning after the conclusion of the trial I met Armitage by appointment, and together we wended our way towards Slater's Mews. The doctor was preoccupied, and for some minutes we proceeded in silence; the problem of what to do with the *Bomb* was evidently weighing on his mind. At last he spoke: "It is our duty," he said, "to see that the movement be not unduly crippled by the loss of these two men. Poor fellows, they are doing their duty by the Cause, and we must not shirk ours. The *Bomb* must be kept going at all costs; we can ill afford to lose two workers just now, but the loss of the paper would be a yet more severe blow to our movement. How thankful I am that you are with us! It is always so. The governments think to crush us by imprisoning or murdering our comrades, and for one whom they take from us ten come to the fore. I am sure you must agree with me as to the paper."

"I quite agree with you in the main," I replied, "but I fear that the *Bomb* itself is past hope. It strikes me it had got into somewhat bad hands, and I fear it would be useless to try to set it on its feet again. It is hardly fair to a paper to give it a Jacob Myers for editor. Really it seems to me to have died a natural death. The entire staff has disappeared—Myers, the editor; Banter, the publisher; O'Flynn, the printer—who remains? where are the others? It seems to me they have all vanished and left no trace behind."

"Oh, that is hardly the case, I think," said the doctor in a tone of deprecation. "I went up to

the office last night and found Short sleeping on
the premises."

"Short? Is not he the man whom I first saw
wrapped in the red flag of glory?"

"Yes, that is the man; perhaps his appearance
is somewhat disadvantageous, but he is constant
to the Cause, anyhow."

"Well, I should not have thought him much of
a staff to lean on; still, appearances are often
deceptive. But, anyhow, do you not think it would
be advisable to start a new paper, rather than to
attempt to galvanise a corpse?"

"The idea would not be a bad one; in fact I
think you are right, quite right," returned Armitage.
"It is not wise to put new wine into old skins. Anyhow, here we are, I dare say other comrades have
mustered in the office who will have something to
say in the matter."

We had now reached our destination, and passing the curious scrutiny of several cabmen and
scavengers assembled at the entrance of the mews,
we prepared to ascend the break-neck ladder leading to the office. I had but put my foot on the
first step when I heard the loud yelping of a dog
followed by a string of oaths, and the office door
opened, emitting a tall brawny man in shirt-sleeves
with a very red face and close-cropped hair, who
appeared holding out at arm's length a pair of
tongs which gripped some repulsive-looking fronts

and collars. On seeing me, he exclaimed, "Take care," and proceeded to drop the objects on a heap of rubbish below. We were both somewhat surprised at this apparition, but realised without difficulty that the office was still in the possession of the police. They were, in fact, contrary to the doctor's expectation, the sole occupants of the place. The comrades had not seen fit so far to muster round the paper. To say there was none, however, is an injustice, for there on the sofa, still huddled in the red flag, lay Short, apparently little affected by what had taken place since I last saw him. He had been aroused from his slumbers by the yelping of his dog, whose tail had been trodden on by one of the detectives, and he had raised himself on his elbow, and was looking round, uttering curses volubly. He nodded slightly on seeing us enter, but did not change his position. There he lay, quite heroic in his immovable sloth ; of all the many fighters he alone remained staunch at his post ; and that because he was positively too lazy to move away from it.

Dr. Armitage on entering had gone up to one of the three detectives and spoken to him, and the man now turned to me.

"We are just having a final look round before leaving, miss," he remarked. "It is not at all pleasant work, I assure you, to be put in to search such a filthy place. Look there," he exclaimed,

pointing at the recumbent Short with his out-
stretched tongs. "I shall have to burn every rag
I have on when it is over, and I'd advise you to be
careful," and he resumed his occupation, which
consisted in raking out some old papers, while his
two companions, having contrived to resume an
official appearance, prepared to leave.

The police once gone Dr. Armitage and I found
ourselves in sole possession of the office and the
lethargic Short. It was no sinecure, to be sure.
Heaps of "pie," some due to the police and some to
Banter, who previous to his arrest had put his foot
through several "forms" which it was inadvisable
to let fall into the hands of the police, encumbered
the floor. Everything was intensely chaotic and
intensely dirty, from the type cases and the other
scanty belongings to the dormant compositor.
Armitage understood nothing of printing and I
very little, and there we stood in the midst of a
disorganised printing-office whence all had fled
save only the unsavoury youth on the couch. I
looked at Armitage and Armitage looked at me,
and such was the helpless dismay depicted in our
faces that we both broke into a laugh.

"Well," I said at last, "what shall we do? Suggest something. We cannot stay on here."

"The only thing I can think of," he rejoined after
a pause, "is that I should go around and look up
some of the comrades at their addresses whilst you

remain here and get Short to help you put up the type, &c., as best you can, so that we may remove it all elsewhere. Here certainly nothing can be done and we must start our new paper amidst new surroundings."

"So you are thinking of starting a new paper?"

We looked round, surprised at this interruption, for Short had apparently returned to his slumbers, but we now saw that he had emerged from the banner and was standing behind us, fully dressed (I discovered later on that he had discarded dressing and undressing as frivolous waste of time), a queer uncouth figure with his long touzled black hair and sallow, unhealthy face. He had a short clay pipe firmly set between his teeth, and his large lips were parted in a smile. He held his head slightly on one side, and his whole attitude was somewhat deprecatory and cringing.

"Well," said the doctor, "Isabel and I think that would be the best plan. You see the *Bomb* seems thoroughly disorganised, and we think it would be easier and better to start afresh. I was just saying that I would go round and hunt up some of the comrades and get their views on the subject."

"Oh," rejoined Short, "you can save yourself that trouble. One half of them will accuse you of being a police spy, the others will be ill or occupied —in short, will have some excuse for not seeing you. They are all frightened out of their lives. Since the arrest of Banter and O'Flynn I have not seen one of them near the place, though I have been here all the time."

This remark confirmed what we both half suspected; and as Short, who by right of possession seemed authorised to speak on behalf of the *Bomb*, seemed willingly to fall in with our idea of starting a new paper, taking it for granted—which I was not exactly prepared for—that he would install himself in the new premises as compositor, we decided to take practical steps towards the move. Short informed us that six weeks' rent was owing, and that the landlord threatened a distraint if his claims were not immediately satisfied; and in spite of the advice, "Don't pay rent to robber landlords," which stared us in the face, inscribed in bright red letters on the wall, I and Armitage between us sacrificed the requisite sum to the Cause.

Whilst we were discussing these matters the dog warned us by a prolonged bark that some one was approaching, and the newcomer soon appeared. He greeted Short, who introduced him to us as Comrade M'Dermott. He shot a scrutinising glance at us from his keen grey eyes and proceeded to shake hands with friendly warmth.

He was a very small man, certainly not more than five feet high, thin and wiry, with grey hair and moustache, but otherwise clean-shaven. His features were unusually expressive and mobile from his somewhat scornful mouth to his deep-set, observant eyes, and clearly denoted the absence of the stolid Saxon strain in his blood. His accent too, though not that of an educated man, was quite free from the hateful Cockney twang. His dress was spare as his figure, but though well worn there was something spruce and trim about his whole demeanour which indicated that he was not totally indifferent to the impression he created on others. He looked round the "office," took a comprehensive glance at Short, who was occupying the only available stool and smoking hard with a meditative air, and then walked over to me, and addressing me in an undertone, with the same ease as if he had known me all my life, he said, with a twinkle in his eye, jerking his head in the direction of Short, "There's a rotten product of a decaying society, eh?" This remark was so unexpected and yet so forcibly true, that I laughed assent.

"So you're the only ones up here," he continued. "I expected as much when I heard of the raid on the office. I was up in the North doing a little bit of peddling round the country, when I read the news, and I thought I'd come to London to see what was up. What do you think of doing with the paper anyway? It seems a pity the old *Bomb* should die. It would mean the loss of the only revolutionary organ in England."

F

"Oh, it must not die," I replied, " or at least if it cannot be kept up, another paper must take its place. Comrade Armitage agrees with me in thinking that that would be the best plan. You see this place looks altogether hopeless."

Armitage, who had been engaged in looking over some papers, now joined us and the conversation became general.

"Well, how did you get on up North?" inquired Short, who seemed to wake up to a sense of actuality. "How did you hit it off with young Jackson? Did you find him of much use?"

"Use!" retorted M'Dermott with an infinite depth of scorn in his voice. "A fat lot of use he was. If it was a matter of putting away the grub, I can tell you he worked for two, but as to anything else, he made me carry his pack as well as my own, on the pretext that he had sprained his ankle, and his only contribution to the firm was a frousy old scrubbing-brush which he sneaked from a poor woman whilst I was selling her a ha'p'orth of pins. He seemed to think he'd done something mighty grand—'expropriation' he called it; pah, those are your English revolutionists!" and he snorted violently.

Short gave vent to an unpleasing laugh. He always seemed to take pleasure at any proof of meanness or cowardice given by his fellows. Armitage looked pained. " Such things make us long for the

Revolution," he said. "This rotten society which breeds such people must be swept away. We must neglect no means to that end, and our press is one. So now let's set to work to move the plant and start a new paper, as we seem all agreed to that plan. Who'll go and look for a suitable workshop?"

Short volunteered, but M'Dermott scouted the idea, declaring that the mere sight of him would be enough to frighten any landlord, and this we all, including Short, felt inclined to agree with. At last we decided to fall in with M'Dermott's suggestion that he and I should sally forth together. "You see, my dear," he said with almost paternal benevolence, "you will be taken for my grand-daughter and we shall soften the heart of the most obdurate landlord."

The field of our researches was limited by a few vital considerations. The rent must not be high. For the present anyhow, the expenses of the paper would have to be defrayed by Armitage and myself. Short had proposed himself as printer and compositor, on the tacit understanding of free board and lodging, and the right to make use of the plant for his own purposes; I was willing to give my time to the material production of the paper, and to contribute to its maintenance to the best of my ability; and Armitage's time and means were being daily more and more ab-

sorbed by the propaganda, to the detriment of
his practice; but he was not of those who can
palter with their conscience. The individual initiative inculcated by Anarchist principles implied
individual sacrifices. Another consideration which
limited our choice was that the office must be
fairly central, and not too far from my home, as,
spite of my enthusiasm for Anarchy, I could not
wholly neglect household duties. We talked over
these points as we walked along, and M'Dermott
suggested Lisson Grove, where a recent epidemic
of smallpox had been raging, as likely to be a
fairly cheap neighbourhood, but after tramping
about and getting thoroughly weary, we had to
acknowledge that there was nothing for us in
that quarter. We were both hungry and tired,
and M'Dermott suggested a retreat to a neighbouring Lockhart's. Seated before a more than doubtful cup of tea, in a grimy room, where texts stared
at us from the walls, we discussed the situation,
and decided to inquire about a workshop which
we saw advertised, and which seemed promising.
Our destination led us out of the slummy wilder-
ness into which we had strayed, into cleaner and
more wholesome quarters, and at last we stopped
before some quite imposing-looking premises. "We
seem destined to consort with the cabbing trade," I
remarked; "the last office was over a mews, this
place seems to belong to a carriage-builder." There

was, however, no other connection between the unsavoury mews and the aristocratic carriage-yard, whose proprietor, resplendent in side-whiskers and a shiny chimney-pot hat, advanced to meet us, a condescending smile diffusing his smug countenance. I explained to him our object, and he showed us over the shop, which consisted in a large loft, well lighted and fairly suitable, at the back of the premises.

In answer to Mr. White's inquiries, I informed him that I needed it as a printing-office, for a small business I had, and he quite beamed on me, evidently considering me a deserving young person, and expressed the opinion that he had no doubt I should get on in that neighbourhood.

M'Dermott, who was greatly enjoying the fun of the situation, here broke in : "Yes, sir, my grand-daughter deserves success, sir ; she's a hard-working girl, is my poor Emily," and here he feigned to wipe away a tear, whilst casting a most mischievous side-glance at me.

"Dear, dear, very affecting, I'm sure," muttered the prosperous carriage-builder.

Everything was soon satisfactorily settled. I gave him my name and address, and that of my brother's Socialist friend as a reference, and we agreed that I should move in on the following Monday morning.

Great was the amusement at Slater's Mews at

the account of our adventures, given with a few enlargements by M'Dermott. He had an artist's soul, and would never consent to destroy the effect of a tale by slavish subservience to facts.

"Well, I fear he will find he has taken in wolves in sheep's clothing," Armitage remarked; "anyhow, I am thankful that matter is settled and that we can get to work without further delay. I met Kosinski, and he has promised to give us a hand with the move. I shall not be able to be here all the time as I have to attend an operation on Monday, but I will put in an hour or two's work in the morning. I suppose I can get in if I come here at five on Monday morning?" he said turning to Short who was "dissing pie," his inseparable clay pipe still firmly set between his yellow and decayed teeth.

"Oh, yes. I shan't be up, but you can get in," the latter surlily remarked. He was evidently no devotee of early hours.

On Monday a hard day's work awaited me. At Slater's Mews I found the poor doctor, who had already been there some two hours, packing up the literature, tying up forms, and occasionally turning to Short for instruction or advice.

The latter, seated on a packing-case, was regaling himself on a bloater and cheesecakes, having disposed of which he took up a flute and played some snatches of music-hall melodies. He seemed quite unconcerned at what took place around him, contenting himself with answering Armitage's questions. Soon after I arrived on the scene Kosinski appeared. It was the first time I had seen him since the memorable evening at Chiswick, and I felt a little nervous in his presence, overcome by a half-guilty fear lest he should think I was merely dallying, not working in true earnest. I was conscious of my own sincerity of purpose, yet feared his mental verdict on my actions, for I now realised that his uncompromising words and scathing denunciation of dilettanteism had had much to do with my recent conduct; more than all Armitage's enthusiastic propagandising, much as I liked, and, indeed, admired the latter. Kosinski shook hands with Armitage and Short. The latter had stepped forward and assumed an air of unwonted activity, having pulled off his coat and rolled up his shirt sleeves, and there he stood hammering up a form and whistling "It ain't all Lavender"—very appropriate verses, considering the surroundings. The Russian merely recognised my presence with a slight bow, not discourteous, but characterised by none of the doctor's encouraging benevolence; I, however, felt more honoured than snubbed, and worked away with a will.

"Well, I must be going," said Armitage; "it is nearly ten, and at half-past eleven I have an appointment at a patient's house. You will stay, won't you, Kosinski, and help our comrades to move the plant ?"

"I will do what I can," replied the Russian. "I do not understand printing, but I will wheel the barrow, and do anything I may be told."

"That's right. Well, good luck to you, comrades. I will try and get round about five. I suppose you will then be at the new place ?"

"Oh, yes," I replied, "you will be in time to help us get things ship-shape."

"Well, good-bye, Isabel; good-bye, comrades," and he was off.

For some time we all worked with a will. Kosinski was set to stowing away the literature in packing-cases. Short "locked up" forms and "dissed" pie, and I busied myself over various jobs. M'Dermott had come round, and he stood at my elbow discussing the propaganda and the situation generally. He was much rejoiced at the turn matters were taking on the Continent, and deplored the lukewarmness of English Anarchists. "You cannot have a revolution without revolutionists," was a favourite phrase of his, and he was at no trouble to conceal his opinion of most of the comrades. I was as yet too new to the movement and too enthusiastic to endorse all his expressions, but the little man was congenial to me ; his Irish wit made him good company, and there was an air of independent self-reliance about him that appealed to me.

"That Kosinski's a good fellow," he continued. "He knows what Revolution means. Not but what there is good material in England too, but it is *raw* material, ignorant and apathetic, hoodwinked and bamboozled by the political humbugs."

"Have you known Kosinski long?" I inquired, interrupting him, for I saw he was fairly started on a long tirade.

"Oh, some seven years," he replied. "He was over here in '87 at the time of the unemployed riots; he and I were at the bottom of a lot of that movement, and we should have had all London in revolt had it not been for the palaver and soft-soap of the official labour-leaders. After that he went to America, and has only been back in England some six months."

Our preparations were now well advanced, and M'Dermott and I set out to procure a barrow whereon to transport our belongings.

I had expected on my return to find everything in readiness. Short had spoken as if he would work wonders, and I had hoped that within an hour we should be off. What was my surprise, then, to find that during the half-hour of my absence a change had come o'er the scene. Instead of the noise of the mallet locking up

forms, the melodious notes of a flute greeted my
ear as I approached the office, and I must confess
that my heart sank, though I was not yet prepared
for the truth. On entering I found things just as
I had left them, not a whit more advanced, but
Short was again seated, and opposite him lounged
the weak-kneed youth whom I had noted on the
occasion of my first group-meeting, Simpkins by
name, as I had since found out ; between them
stood the small hand - press which Short had
promised to take to pieces for removal, on the
"bed" of which now stood three bottles of ginger-
beer, a parcel of repulsive and indigestible-looking
pastry, and a packet of tobacco. My look of
dismay and surprise was answered by Short, who
explained that his friend had come up, bringing
with him the wherewithal for this carouse ; which
statement Simpkins supplemented by the information that he had been occupied that week in
"planting" an aunt and possessing himself of his
share of the good lady's property.

"My married sister got in first, but father waited
his opportunity, and whilst they went out to 'ave
a 'alf-pint at the pub round the corner, he got in.
They thought themselves mighty clever, for they
had locked the door and taken the key, but father
got in by the scullery window which they had
forgotten to latch, and when they came back they
found themselves sold. The guv'nor's a sharp one,

'e is, but I was fly too; 'e always keeps me short, grumbles 'cause I won't let myself be exploited by the capitalists; but I did 'im this time. I 'ad a good old-fashioned nose round whilst the guv'nor left me in charge whilst 'e went for a drink, and I found ten bob the old girl 'ad 'idden away in a broken teapot, so I just pocketed 'em. We planted 'er the day before yesterday; she was insured for twelve quid, an' everything was done 'ansome. Yesterday I felt awful bad, but to-day I thought I'd come an' see 'ow the paiper was getting on."

"Well, you see we're moving," I said. "If you care to give us a hand you'll be welcome. Come, Short, the barrow's here; let's get the things down."

"Oh, I'm going to have a half-day off," was his cool reply; "I'm tired. Armitage woke me up at five this morning, and I couldn't get any sleep after he came, he made such a damned noise."

"But surely you're going to help us get this move over; to-morrow you can sleep all day if you like."

"You can do as you like; I'm not going to move," was his only reply, and he calmly filled his pipe and puffed luxuriously. Simpkins giggled feebly; he evidently was wavering as to his proper course, but Short's calm insolence won the day.

I confess that at the moment I was blind to the

humour of the situation. I fancy people with a keen sense of humour are rarely enthusiasts; certainly when I began to see the ludicrous side of much of what I had taken to be the hard earnest of life, my revolutionary ardour cooled. My indignation was ready to boil over; I could have wept or stamped with annoyance. "Oh, but you *must* help!" I exclaimed. "You promised. How are we ever to do anything if you go on like this?"

Short merely puffed at his pipe complacently.

For the first time since his arrival Kosinksi spoke. I had almost forgotten his presence; he was working quietly, getting things ready, and now he stepped forward.

"The comrade is right," he said; "he does not want to work; leave him alone; we can do very well without him. Let us get off at once. There is enough ready to make a first load, anyhow."

The calm indifference of Kosinksi seemed to take some of the starch out of Short, who looked more than foolish as he sat over his ginger-beer, trying to feign interest in the flagging conversation with Simpkins. I was relieved at the turn matters had taken, which threw the ridicule on the other side, and before long we were ready, little M'Dermott having made himself very useful, running actively up and down the ladder laden with parcels. We must have looked a queer procession as we set off. The long stooping figure of Kosinksi, wrapped in his inseparable dark-blue overcoat, his fair hair showing from under his billycock hat, pushing the barrow, heavily laden with type-cases and iron forms, packets of literature and reams of printing paper ; I in my shabby black dress and sailor hat, bearing the furled-up banner, and M'Dermott following on behind, carrying with gingerly care a locked-up form of type, the work of poor Armitage, which was in imminent danger of falling to pieces in the middle of the street. We found that quite a crowd of loafers of both sexes, the habitués of the "Myrtle Grove Tavern," had assembled outside to witness our departure, and, as I never missed an opportunity to spread the light, I distributed among them some hand-bills entitled " What is Anarchy ? " regardless of their decidedly hostile attitude. The London loafer has little wit or imagination, and their comments did not rise above the stale inquiry as to where we kept our bombs, and the equally original advice bestowed upon Kosinksi to get 'is 'air cut.

A half-hour's walk brought us to our destination, but our Odyssey was not so soon to end. The man who accompanied the carriage-builder when he showed us over the shop was waiting at the entrance to the yard, and, recognising me, he asked me to step into the office. He had a rather scared appearance, but I did not notice this particularly at the moment, and supposing that

Mr. White wanted to give me the keys I told my friends I should be back in a minute. The carriage-builder was awaiting me in the little office where he usually received his fashionable clients. He was still the self-same consequential figure, resplendent in broadcloth and fine linen, but the benevolent smile had vanished from his unctuous features, and he looked nervous and ill at ease.

"I am sorry to say, Miss Meredith," he began, "that I find I am unable to let you the shop. I much regret having caused you inconvenience, but it is quite impossible."

This was a staggerer for me. Everything had been settled. What could have happened?

"What on earth does this mean?" I exclaimed. "Why, Saturday evening you called at my house and told me you were satisfied with the references, and that I could move in to-day."

The poor man looked quite scared at my indignation.

"I am very sorry, I assure you, but I cannot let you the shop," was all he replied.

"But surely you will give me some explanation of this extraordinary behaviour. I am not to be trifled with in this way, and if you will not answer me I will get some of my friends to speak to you."

This last threat seemed quite to overcome him. He looked despairingly at me, and then determined to throw himself on my mercy.

"Well, you see, the fact is I did not quite understand the nature of your business—that is to say, I thought it was a printing business just like any other."

Light dawned upon me. The police had evidently been at work here. I was too new to the revolutionary movement to have foreseen all the difficulties which beset the path of the propagandist.

"And since Saturday night you have come to the conclusion that it is an *un*usual printing office?" I inquired somewhat derisively. I could still see in my mind's eye the benevolent smile and patronising condescension with which he had beamed on M'Dermott and me on the occasion of our first meeting.

"You are a sensible person, Miss Meredith," he said, with an almost appealing accent, "and you will, I am sure, agree with me that it would be impossible for me to have revolutionary papers printed on my premises. It would not be fair to my clients; it would interfere with my business success. Of course every one has a right to their opinions, but I had no idea that you were connected with any such party. In fact I had gone out of town, and intended staying away two or three days when yesterday afternoon I received this telegram," and he handed me the document. It was from Scotland Yard, and warned him to return at once as the police had something of importance to communicate.

"Of course I came back," continued the tremulous White. "At first I thought it must be all a mistake, but I was shown a copy of the *Bomb*, and told that that was what you intended printing. Now you must agree that this is not a suitable place for such an office."

"I cannot see," I replied with some warmth, "that it can make any difference to you what I print. I pay you your rent, and we are quits. Of course if you refuse to give me the keys of the shop I cannot force myself in, but I have reason to think that you will regret your extraordinary conduct."

"Is that a threat?" inquired White, growing visibly paler, and glancing nervously towards the door.

"No, it is only the expression of a personal opinion," I replied. At this moment the door opened, and M'Dermott appeared.

"Well, are you coming with the keys? We are getting tired of waiting," he inquired.

"This man," said I, pointing with scorn at the abject carriage-builder, "now refuses to let me the shop on the ground that he disapproves of revolutionary literature."

M'Dermott gave a low whistle, "Oh, that's how the wind blows, is it?" he remarked; "I thought I saw some 'narks' hanging round. So this is the turn your benevolent interest in my grand-daughter has taken? Well, come along, Isabel, we have no time to waste, and I am sure this good gentleman will not feel comfortable till we are off the premises. He is afraid we might waste some dynamite on him, I do believe."

At the word dynamite White seized a bell-pull and rang it violently, and we could not help laughing heartily, as we left the office, at his evident terror. Whilst crossing the yard we saw two well-known detectives lurking on the premises. White had evidently thought it necessary to take precautions against possible outrage.

We found Kosinski patiently waiting. He did not seem much surprised at our news, and in answer to my inquiry as to what on earth we were to do, he suggested that we should take the barrow back to Slater's Mews, and then resume our search for a shop. This advice was so obvious and tame that it almost surprised me coming from him, still there was nothing for it, and back we went, looking somewhat more bedraggled (it had now come on to rain) and decidedly crestfallen. We found Short as we had left him, but I was still too indignant at his conduct to deign to answer his inquiries. I was tired and worried, and could almost have wept with annoyance. Kosinski at last came to the rescue. When he had brought the last parcel up the stairs and deposited it on the floor he came up to me.

" If you like we might go and look at a work-shop I have heard of and which might suit. Some

G

German comrades rented it for some time ; I believe they used it as a club - room, but I dare say it would answer your purpose, and I believe it is still unoccupied."

Of course I readily assented ; it was indeed a relief to hear of some definite proposal, and together we set off. Little M'Dermott, who evidently did not much relish Short's company, armed himself with leaflets and set off on a propagandising expedition, and Kosinski and I wended our way in search of the office. At last we stopped in front of a little green-grocer's shop in a side street off the Hampstead Road. "The place I mean is behind here," explained Kosinski ; " the woman in the shop lets it ; we will go in and speak with her."

Kosinski stepped inside and addressed a voluminous lady who emerged from the back shop.

"Oh, good day, Mr. Cusins," she exclaimed, a broad smile overspreading her face ; "what can I do for you ? "

Kosinksi explained our errand, and the good lady preceded us up a narrow yard which led to the workshop in question. She turned out to be as loquacious as she was bulky, a fair specimen of the good-natured cockney gossip, evidently fond of the convivial glass, not over-choice in her language, the creature of her surroundings, which were not of the sweetest, but withal warm-hearted and sympathetic, with that inner hatred of the police common to all who belong to the coster class, and able to stand up for her rights, if necessary, both with her tongue and her fists. She showed us over a damp, ill-lighted basement shop, in a corner of which was a ladder leading to a large, light shop, which seemed well suited to our purpose, meanwhile expatiating on its excellencies. I was satisfied with it, and would have settled everything in a few minutes, but Mrs. Wattles was not to be done out of her jaw.

"I'm sure you'll like this place, my dear, and I'm glad to let it to you, for I've known your 'usband some time. I used to see 'im come when those others Germans was 'ere, and——"

"Kosinski is not my husband," I interrupted. "I'm not married."

"Oh, I see, my dear; just keeping company, that's all. Well, I don't blame yer; of course, 'e is a furriner; but I'm not one to say as furriners ain't no class. I was in love with an I-talian organ-grinder myself, when I was a girl, and I might 'ave married 'im for all I know, ef 'e 'adn't got run in for knifin' a slop what was always a aggravatin' 'im, poor chap. And I don't say but what I shouldn't be as well off as what I am now, for Wattles, 'e ain't much class."

I ventured some sympathetic interjection and tried to get away, but her eye was fixed on me and I could not escape.

"It was a long time before I forgot 'im, and when my girl was born I called 'er Ave Maria, which was a name I used to 'ear 'im say, and a very pretty one too, though Wattles does say it's a 'eathen-sounding name for the girl. I was just like you in those days, my dear," she said, surveying my slim figure with a critical eye. "No one thought I should make old bones, I was that thin and white, and nothin' seemed to do me no good; I took physic enough to kill a 'orse, and as for heggs an' such like I eat 'undreds. But, lor', they just went through me like jollop. It was an old neighbour of ours as cured me; she said, says she, 'What you want, Liza, is stimilant; stout 'ud soon set you right.' An' sure enough it did. I took 'er advice, an' I've never 'ad a day's illness since, though Wattles's been mighty troublesome at times, and would 'av driven me to my grave long ago if it 'adn't been for stout. You should take it, miss; you'd soon be as like me, and as 'arty too. Two glasses at dinner and two at supper is my allowance, and if I chance to miss it, why I jest seems to fall all of a 'eap like, an' I 'ears my in'ards a gnawin' and a gnawin' and a cryin' out for stout."

I felt quite overcome at this charming picture of my future self, if only I followed Mrs. Wattles's advice. I expressed my intention of thinking the matter over, and, after shaking hands, paying a deposit on the rent—which she informed me she should expend in drinking my health—and settling to move in on the morrow, I made good my escape.

Cheered and elated by our success, I returned with Kosinksi to the office of the *Bomb*. He was naturally very nervous and reticent with women, but the events of this long day had broken down some of the barriers between us, and I found it less difficult to talk to him as we trudged on our way.

"I hope you will help us with the new paper," I said. "I feel really very unfit for the responsibility of such a task, but Armitage thinks I shall manage all right, and I do not wish to be a mere amateur, and shirk the hard work entailed by our propaganda. You see, I remember your words that night at Chiswick. I hope you do not still think that I am merely playing."

He positively blushed at my words, and stammered out: "Oh no, I do not in the least doubt your sincerity. I am sure you do your best, only I have seen so much harm done by women that I am always on my guard when they propose to share in our work. But you are not a woman: you are a Comrade, and I shall take much interest in your paper."

We met Armitage coming up Red Lion Street. He greeted us with a look of relief. "Where on earth have you been?" he exclaimed; "I went to

the address you gave me, but when I inquired for
you the fellow looked as scared as if he had seen
a ghost, and said he knew nothing about you, that
I must have made a mistake; and when I insisted
and showed him the address you had written,
seemed to lose his head, and rang a bell and called
for help as if I were going to murder him. I
thought he must be mad or drunk, and so turned
on my heel and came away. In the yard I recognised some of our friends the detectives, and I felt
quite anxious about you. At Slater's Mews the
door is locked; there is no light, and nobody
answered when I knocked. I am quite relieved to
see you. I was beginning to fear you had all got
run in."

"Well, you see we are still alive and in fighting
form. As you say the *Bomb* has closed, I suppose
Short has gone off to the music-hall with Simpkins,
as he hinted at doing. Anyhow, come home with
me; you too, Kosinksi, if you don't mind; there is
a lot to say, and many things to settle, and we
can settle everything better there than here in the
street."

My proposal was agreed to, and we all three
repaired to Fitzroy Square, where over a cup of
tea we settled the last details of the move, including the name of our new paper, which was to be
known as the *Tocsin*.

CHAPTER VI

A FOREIGN INVASION

THUS was the question of the new paper and its quarters settled. The shop, as I had hoped, did well enough for our purposes. True, the district in which it lay was neither salubrious nor beautiful, and the constant and inevitable encounters with loquacious Mrs. Wattles and her satellites something of a trial; but we were absorbed in our work, absorbed in our enthusiasms, utterly engrossed in the thought of the coming revolution which by our efforts we were speeding on.

During the first months, besides writing and editing the *Tocsin*, I was very busily employed in learning how to set type, and print, and the various arts connected with printing—and as I grew more proficient at the work my share of it grew in proportion.

The original staff of the *Tocsin* consisted of Armitage, Kosinksi, and myself, with Short occupying the well-nigh honorary post of printer, aided by occasional assistance or hindrance from his hangers-on. But our staff gradually increased in number if not in efficiency ; old M'Dermott was a frequent and not unwelcome visitor, and as time went on he gradually settled down into an inmate of the office, helping where he could with the work, stirring up lagging enthusiasms, doing odd cobbling jobs whenever he had the chance, and varying the proceedings with occasional outbursts of Shakespearian recitation. These recitations were remarkable performances, and made up in vigour for what they perhaps lacked in elegance and *finesse*. Carter would at times put in an appearance, mostly with a view to leaning up against a type-rack or other suitable article of furniture, and there between one puff and another at his pipe would grumble at the constitution of the universe and the impertinent exactions of landlords. Another Englishman who in the earlier days frequented the *Tocsin* was a tall, thoughtful man named Wainwright, belonging to the working-classes, who by the force of his own intelligence and will had escaped from the brutishness of the lowest depths of society in which he had been born.

Thus with little real outside assistance we worked through the spring and early summer months. Besides bringing out our paper we printed various booklets and pamphlets, organised Anarchist meetings, and during some six weeks housed a French Anarchist paper and its staff, all of whom had fled precipitately from Paris in consequence of a trial.

The lively French staff caused a considerable revolution in Lysander Grove, which during several
weeks rang with Parisian argot and Parisian fun.
Many of these Frenchmen were a queer lot. They
seemed the very reincarnation of Murger's Bohe-
mians, and evidently took all the discomforts and
privations of their situation as a first-class joke.
Kosinksi detested them most cordially, though, spite
of himself, he was a tremendous favourite in their
ranks, and the unwilling victim of the most affectionate demonstrations on their part : and when,
with a shrug of his shoulders and uncompromising
gait, he turned his back on his admirers, they would
turn round to me, exclaiming fondly—

" *Comme il est drôle, le pauvre diable !* "

They could not understand his wrath, and were
obstinately charmed at his least charming traits.
When he was singularly disagreeable towards them,
they summed him up cheerfully in two words, *Quel
original !* They soon learned, however, not to take
liberties with Kosinski, for when one sprightly little
man of their number, who affected pretty things in
the way of cravats and garters, presumed to dance
him round the office, the Russian, for once almost
beside himself, seized his persecutor by the shoulders
and dropped him over the balustrade below, amid
the cheers of all present.

He appeared, however, to be their natural prey,
and his quaint habit of stumbling innocently into

all manner of blunders was a perpetual fount of
amusement to the humour-loving Gauls. His
timidity with women, too, was a perennial joy, and
innumerable adventures in which he figured as hero
were set afloat.

One little escapade of Kosinski's came somehow to the knowledge of the French Comrades,
and he suffered accordingly. Although careless
and shaggy enough in appearance in all conscience, Kosinski happened to be fastidiously clean
about his person. I doubt whether he was ever
without a certain small manicure set in his pocket,
and an old joke among his Russian friends was
that he had failed to put in an appearance on
some important occasion—the rescue of a Nihilist
from prison, I believe—because he had forgotten
his tooth-brush. This was of course a libel
and gross exaggeration, but his extreme personal
cleanliness was none the less a fact. Now when
he first reached London he had scarcely left
the station, besooted and begrimed after his long
journey, when his eye was arrested by the appearance of a horse-trough. "Most opportune!"
mused Kosinski, "how public-spirited and hygienic
this London County Council really is!" and
straightway divesting himself of his hat and collar
and similar encumbrances, and spreading out on
the rim of the trough his faithful manicure set
and a few primitive toilette requisites secreted

about his person, he commenced his ablutions, sublimely unconscious of the attention and surprise he was attracting. Before long, however, a riotously amused crowd collected round, and the Russian had finally to be removed under police escort, while attempting to explain to the indignant officer of the law that he had merely taken the horse-trough as a convenient form of public bath for encouraging cleanliness among the submerged tenth.

With the departure of the *Ça-Ira* the office resumed once more, during a brief interval, the even tenor of its ways. Kosinski who, in a spirit of self-preservation, had practically effaced himself during its sojourn, made himself once more apparent, bringing with him a peculiar Swede— a man argumentative to the verge of cantankerousness—who for hours and days together would argue on obscure questions of metaphysics. He had argued himself out of employment, out of his country, almost out of the society and the tolerance of his fellows. Life altogether was one long argument to this man, no act or word, however insignificant, could he be induced to pass over without discussing and dissecting, proving or disproving it. Free-love was his particular hobby, though this, too, he regarded from a metaphysical rather than a practical point of view. Like everything else in his life it was a matter

for reason and argument, not for emotion; and
he and Kosinski would frequently dispute the
question warmly.

One day, not long before Christmas, and after
I had been nearly a year in the movement, when
all London was lost in a heavy fog and the air
seemed solid as a brick wall, there landed at the
Tocsin a small batch of three Italians fresh from
their native country. It was the year of the
coercion laws in Italy, of the "domicilio coatto"
(forced domicile), and the Anarchists and Socialists
were fleeing in large numbers from the clutches of
the law.

None of these Southerners had ever been in
England before, and having heard grim tales of
the lack of sunshine and light in London, they
took this fog to be the normal condition of the
atmosphere. Stumbling into the lighted office
from the blind stifling darkness outside, the leader
of the party, a remarkably tall handsome man
well known to me by reputation and correspondence, gave vent to a tremendous sigh of relief and
exclaimed in his native tongue :

"Thank Heaven, friends, we have overcome the
greatest danger of all and we are here at last, and
still alive !"

They then advanced towards me and Avvocato
Guglielmo Gnecco held out his hand. "You are
Isabel Meredith?" he said in a sonorous voice,

and I gave an affirmative nod. "I am very glad
to meet you at last, Comrade," and we all shook
hands. "So this is London! I had heard grim
enough tales of your climate, but never had I
conceived anything like this. It is truly terrible!
But how do you live here? How do you get
through your work? . . . How do you find your
way about the streets? Why, we've been wandering about the streets ever since eleven o'clock this
morning, walking round and round ourselves,
stumbling over kerb-stones, appealing to policemen and passers-by, getting half run over by
carts and omnibuses and cabs. Giannoli here
sees badly enough at all times, but to-day he has
only escaped by the skin of his teeth from the
most horrid series of deaths. Is it not so, Giacomo?" Giannoli, who had been engaged in
enthusiastic greetings with Kosinski, who was evidently an old friend, looked up at this.

"Oh, I've had too much of London already,"
he exclaimed fervently. "We must leave here for
some other country to-night or to-morrow at the
latest. We should be better off in prison in Italy
than at liberty here. You see, Comrade," he said,
turning to me with a smile, "we Anarchists all
belong to one nationality, so I have no fear of
wounding your patriotic sentiments."

"But London is not always like this, I assure
you," I began.

"Oh, make no attempt to palliate it," Gnecco interrupted. "I have heard English people before now defending your climate. But I see now only too well that my compatriots were right in calling it impossible, and saying that you never saw the sun here," and all attempts to argue them out of this conviction proved futile.

The avvocato, as above mentioned, was an exceptionally good-looking man. Fully six feet two inches in height, erect and slim without being in the least weedy, he carried his head with an air of pride and self-confidence, and was altogether a very fine figure of a man. His features were regular and well cut, his abundant hair and complexion dark, and his eyes bright with the vivacity of the perennial youth of the enthusiast. The delicacy of his features, the easy grace of his walk, and the freedom and confidence of his manners, all suggested his semi-aristocratic origin and upbringing. He was evidently a man of romantic tastes and inclinations, governed by sentiment rather than by reason ; a lover of adventure, who had found in Anarchism an outlet for his activities. His eloquence had made him a considerable reputation all over Italy as an advocate, but the comparative monotony of the life of a prosperous barrister was distasteful to him, and he had willingly sacrificed his prospects in order to throw in his lot with the revolutionary party.

Giannoli, in his way, was an equally interesting figure. Between Gnecco and himself it was evident that there existed the warmest bonds of fraternal affection—a sentiment whose fount, as I discovered later, lay in a mutual attachment for a certain Milanese lady, who on her side fully reciprocated their joint affection. Both these Italians were warm exponents of the doctrine of free-love, and, unlike their more theoretic Northern confrères, they carried their theories into practice with considerable gusto. Many Anarchists of Teutonic and Scandinavian race evidently regarded free-love as an unpleasant duty rather than as a natural and agreeable condition of life — the chaff which had to be swallowed along with the wheat of the Anarchist doctrines. I remember the distress of one poor old Norwegian professor on the occasion of his deserting his wife for a younger and, to him, far less attractive woman— a young French studentess of medicine who practised her emancipated theories in a very wholesale fashion.

"I felt that as an Anarchist it would have been almost wrong to repel her advances," the distressed old gentleman confided to me. "Moreover, it was ten years that I had lived with Rosalie, uninterruptedly. . . . *Cela devenait tout-à-fait scandaleux, Mademoiselle.* . . . I no longer dared show myself among my comrades."

I felt quite sorry for the poor old fellow, a humble slave to duty, which he performed with evident disgust, but the most heroic determination.

Giannoli, when seen apart from Gnecco, was a tall man. But at the time of his arrival in London he was already falling a victim to ill-health ; there was a bent, tired look about his figure, and his features were drawn and thin. A glance at him sufficed to reveal a nervous, highly-strung temperament ; his movements were jerky, and altogether, about his entire person, there was a noticeable lack of repose. He was about thirty-five years of age, though he gave the impression of a rather older man. The fact that he was very short-sighted gave a peculiar look to his face, which was kindly enough in expression ; his features were pronounced, with a prominent nose and full, well-cut mouth hidden by a heavy moustache. There was a look of considerable strength about the man, and fanatical determination strangely blended with diffidence—a vigorous nature battling against the inroads of some mortal disease.

The third member of the trio was a shortish, thickset man of extraordinary vigour. He somehow put me in mind of a strongly-built, one-storey, stone blockhouse, and looked impregnable in every direction ; evidently a man of firm character, buoyed up by vigorous physique. He was a man rather of character than of intellect, of great

moral strength rather than of intellectual brilliancy
—a fighter and an idealist, not a theoriser. I knew
him very well by renown, for he was of European
fame in the Anarchist party, and the *bête noire* of
the international police. Enrico Bonafede was a
man born out of his time—long after it and long
before—whose tremendous energy was wasted in
the too strait limits of modern civilised society.
In a heroic age he would undoubtedly have made
a hero ; in nineteenth-century Europe his life was
wasted and his sacrifices useless. These men,
born out of their generation, are tragic figures ;
they have in them the power and the will to
scale the heights of Mount Olympus and to
stem the ocean, while they are forced to spend
their life climbing mole - hills and stumbling into
puddles.

Such, briefly, were the three men who suddenly
emerged from the fog into the office of the *Tocsin*,
and who formed the vanguard of our foreign invasion. All three were at once sympathetic to
me, and I viewed their advent with pleasure. We
celebrated it by an unusually lavish banquet of
fried fish and potatoes, for they were wretchedly
cold and hungry and exhausted after a long journey
and almost equally long fast, for of course they
all arrived in a perfectly penniless condition.

Seated round a blazing fire in M'Dermott's
eleutheromania stove (the old fellow had a passion

H

for sonorous words which he did not always apply quite appositely) the Italians related the adventures of their journey and discussed future projects. As the fog grew denser with the advance of evening, and it became evident that lodging - searching was quite out of the question for the time being, it was agreed that we should all spend the night in the office, where heaps of old papers and sacking made up into not altogether despicable couches. Moreover, publication date was approaching, and at such times we were in the habit of getting later and later in the office, the necessity for Short's assistance rendering it impossible to get the work done in an expeditious and business-like way.

We worked on far into the night, the Italians helping us as best they could with the printing, one or other occasionally breaking off for a brief respite of slumber. We talked much of the actual conditions in Italy, and of the situation of the Anarchist party there; of how to keep the revolutionary standard afloat and the Anarchist ideas circulating, despite coercion laws and the imprisonment and banishment of its most prominent advocates. Kosinksi joined enthusiastically in the discussion, and the hours passed rapidly and very agreeably. I succeeded at length in dissuading Giannoli and Gnecco from their original intention of precipitate flight, partly by repeatedly assuring them that the state of the atmosphere was not

normal and would mend, partly by bringing their
minds to bear on the knotty question of finance.

The three Italians settled in London ; Gnecco
and Bonafede locating themselves in the Italian
quarter amid most squalid surroundings ; while for
Giannoli I found a suitable lodging in the shape
of a garret in the Wattles's house which overlooked
the courtyard of the *Tocsin*. They were frequently in the office, much to the indignation of
Short, who could not see what good all "those ——
foreigners did loafing about." Short, in fact, viewed
with the utmost suspicion any new-comers at the
Tocsin.

"These foreigners are such a d——d lazy lot,"
he would say ; "I hate them !" and there was all
the righteous indignation in his tones of the hard-
worked proletariat whose feelings are harrowed
by the spectacle of unrighteous ease. Short had
a habit of making himself offensive to every one,
but for some mysterious reason no one ever took
him to task over it. It was impossible to take
Short seriously, or to treat him as you would any
other human being. When he was insolent people
shrugged their shoulders and laughed, when he
told lies they did not deign to investigate the
truth, and thus in a despised and unostentatious
way—for he was not ambitious of *réclame*—he was
able to do as much mischief and set as many false-
hoods afloat as a viciously-inclined person with

much time on his hands well can. His physical and mental inferiority was his stock-in-trade, and he relied on it as a safeguard against reprisals.

After a prolonged period of fog the real severity of the winter set in towards the end of January. One February morning, after all manner of mishaps and discomfort, and several falls along the slippery icy pavement, I arrived at the office of the *Tocsin*. The first thing that struck my eye on approaching was the unusual appearance of the Wattles's green-grocery shop. The shutters were closed, the doors still unopened. "What has happened?" I inquired of a crony standing outside the neighbouring pub. "Surely no one is dead?"

"Lor' bless yer, no, lydy," answered the old lady, quite unperturbed, "yesterday was the hanniversary of old Wattles's wedding-day, and they've been keepin' it up as usual. That's all."

I was about to pass on without further comment when my attention was again arrested by the sound of blows and scuffling inside the shop, mingled with loud oaths in the familiar voice of my land-lady, and hoarse protests and entreaties in a masculine voice.

"But surely," I urged, turning once more to my previous informant, "there is something wrong. What is all that noise?" as cries of "Murder! murder!" greeted my ear.

"Why, I only just told you, my dear," she

responded, still quite unmoved, "they've been cele-
bratin' their silver weddin' or somethin' of the sort.
It's the same every year. They both gets roarin'
drunk, and then Mrs. Wattles closes the shop next
mornin' so as to give 'im a jolly good 'idin'. You
see, these hanniversaries make 'er think of all she's
'ad to put up with since she married, and that
makes things a bit rough on poor old Jim."

Perceiving my sympathy to be wasted I proceeded,
and on entering the office of the *Tocsin* I found that
here, too, something unusual was going on.

A perfect Babel of voices from the room above
greeted my ear, while the printing-room was be-
decked with a most unsightly litter of tattered
garments of nondescript shape and purpose laid
out to dry. I was not surprised at this, however,
as I had long grown used to unannounced in-
vasions. Unexpected persons would arrive at the
office, of whom nobody perhaps knew anything;
they would stroll in, seat themselves round the
fire, enter into discussion, and, if hungry, occasionally partake of the *plat du jour*. The most
rudimentary notions of Anarchist etiquette for-
bade any of us from inquiring the name, address, or
intentions of such intruders. They were allowed
to stay on or to disappear as inexplicitly as they
came. They were known, if by any name at all,
as Jack or Jim, Giovanni or Jacques, and this was
allowed to suffice. Every Anarchist learns in time

to spot a detective at first sight, and we relied on this instinct as a safeguard against spies.

But on reaching the composing-room on this particular morning an extraordinary sight presented itself. Accustomed as I was to the unaccustomed, I was scarcely prepared for the wild confusion of the scene. What at first sight appeared to be a surging mass of unwashed and unkempt humanity filled it with their persons, their voices, and their gestures. No number of Englishmen, however considerable, could have created such a din. All present were speaking simultaneously at the top of their voices ; greetings and embraces mingled with tales of adventure and woe. The first object which I managed to distinguish was the figure of Giannoli struggling feebly in the embrace of a tall brawny, one-eyed man with thick curling black hair, who appeared to be in a state of demi-déshabille. By degrees a few other familiar figures became one by one discernible to me as I stood mute and unobserved at the head of the stairs. Bonafede and Gnecco were there ; they, too, surrounded by the invading mob, exchanging greetings and experiences. Old M'Dermott, standing up against his stove, was striking a most impressive attitude, for the old fellow had to live up to the reputation he had established among foreigners of being the greatest orator in the English revolutionary party. Two cloddish - looking *contadini*

stood gazing at him, rapt in awe. Kosinksi stood
a little apart from the rest, not a little bewildered
by the enthusiastic reception which had been
accorded him by old friends. In one corner, too,
I recognised my old friend Short, fully dressed,
as usual, in his frowsy clothes, as though eternally
awaiting the call-to-arms, the long-delayed bugles
of the social revolution; there he lay, much as
when I first set eyes on him, wrapped up in old
banners and rugs, blinking his eyes and muttering
curses at the hubbub which had thus rudely interrupted his slumbers.

The others were quite new to me. They were
evidently all of them Italians—some ten or twelve
in number—though at the first glance, scattered as
they were pell-mell among the printing plant of the
overcrowded work-room, they gave an impression
of much greater number. They appeared mostly
to belong to the working-classes. Their clothes, or
what remained of them, were woefully tattered—
and they were few and rudimentary indeed, for
most of what had been spared by the hazards of
travel were drying down below. Their hair was
uncut, and beards of several days' growth orna-
mented their cheeks. Their hats were of incredible
size and shape and all the colours of the rainbow
seemed to be reproduced in them. Littered around
on divers objects of furniture, they suggested to me
a strange growth of fungi.

My advent, as soon as it was perceived amid the confusion and noise of the scene, created something of a sensation, for by now my name had become well known in the International Anarchist party. "Isabel Meredith" was exclaimed in all manner of new and strange intonations, and a host of hands were extended towards me from all directions.

At last Gnecco managed to make his voice heard above the din of his compatriots. "All these comrades," he explained in Italian, "have escaped like ourselves from the savage reaction which actually holds Italy in its sway. They arrived this morning after a fearful journey which lack of money compelled them to make mostly on foot."

Before he could get any further an outburst of song interrupted his words as the whole band broke into an Anarchist war-whoop. This over, my attention was arrested by the groans of a dark young man of extraordinarily alert physiognomy who had shed his boots and was gazing dolefully at his wounded feet. "What would I not give," he exclaimed, "to be back in prison in Lugano! Oh for the rest and comfort of those good old times!" He was utterly worn out, poor fellow, nipped up with the cold, and seemed on the verge of tears.

"Well," exclaimed M'Dermott at last, "propaganda implies propagandists, and propagandists entail bellies! All these fellows seem pretty well starving. What would they say to a little grub?"

On my interpreting the old fellow's suggestion he and it were received with universal acclaim. Bonafede produced from the innermost depths of his pockets a huge quantity of macaroni which was put on to boil, and several bottles of wine; one of the new arrivals, a sober-looking young fellow with a remarkably long nose, contributed an enormous lobster which he had acquired *en route*, while Kosinski volunteered to fetch bread and other provender. A Homeric repast ensued, for all these Anarchists had cultivated the digestions of camels; they prepared for inevitable fasts by laying in tremendous stores when chance and good fortune permitted. While they were eating a noticeable silence fell on the scene, and I had leisure to observe the immigrants more in detail.

Beppe, the tall, one-eyed man, already referred to, seemed to be the life and spirit of the band. He was a rollicking good-natured fellow, an unpolished *homme du peuple*, but not inadmirable in his qualities of courage and cheerfulness—the kind of man who would have cracked a joke on his death-bed and sung lustily *en route* to the gallows. He possessed, too, a heroic appetite, and as he made away with enormous heaps of macaroni his spirits rose higher and higher and his voice rose with them.

The long-nosed youth was something of an enigma. From the scraps of conversation which, during the repast, fell principally on the subject

of food, or the lack of food, during the tramp, I
gathered that they had relied principally on his
skill and daring in the matter of foraging to keep
themselves from actually dying of hunger on their
journey. Yet there was about him such a prudent
and circumspect air that he might well have
hesitated to pick up a pin that "wasn't his'n." He
was evidently of an acquisitive turn, however, for
over his shoulder was slung a bag which appeared
to contain a collection of the most heterogeneous
and unserviceable rubbish conceivable. "*Eh!* . . .
possono servire!" . . . was all he would volunteer
on the subject when I once chaffed him on the
subject of his findings. "They may serve yet! . . ."

Somehow this youth struck me at once as a man
who had made a mistake. At home as he appeared
to be among his comrades, there was yet something
about him which suggested that he was out of his
proper sphere in the midst of the Anarchists, that
he was *desorienté*. He was cut out for an industrious
working-man, one that would rise and thrive in his
business by hard work and thrift; he was destined
by nature to rear a large family and to shine in the
ranks of excellent family men. He was moulded
for the threshold, poor boy, neither for the revolutionary camp nor for the scaffold, and it was
thwarted domestic instinct which led him to steal.
There was good nature in his face and weakness;
it was the face of a youth easily led, easily influenced

for good or bad. As a revolutioniser of his species he was predestined to failure, for years would certainly show him the error of his ways. Old age seemed to be his proper state, and youth in him was altogether a blunder and a mistake. I found myself vainly speculating what on earth could have led him among the Anarchists.

The others comprised a silent young artisan who was evidently desperately in earnest with his ideas, a red-haired, red-bearded Tuscan of clever and astute aspect, a singularly alert and excitable-looking young man of asymmetrical features, who looked half fanatic, half criminal, and others of the labouring and peasant class. One other of their number arrested my attention, a stupid, sleepy young man, who seemed quite unaffected by the many vicissitudes of his journey. His features were undefined and his complexion undefinable, very greasy and suggestive of an unwholesome fungus. He was better dressed than his companions, and from this fact, combined with his intonation, I gathered that he belonged to the leisured classes. There was something highly repellent about his smooth yellow face, his greasiness and limp, fat figure. M'Dermott christened him the " Buttered muffin."

Dinner over, the one-eyed baker, Beppe, proceeded to give us their news, and to recount the vicissitudes of their travels. Gnecco and Giannoli were anxious for news of comrades left behind in

Italy. So-and-so was in prison, another had remained behind in Switzerland, a third had turned his coat, and was enjoying ill-gotten ease and home, others were either dead or lost to sight.

The present party, who were mostly Northern Italians, had left Italy shortly after Giannoli and Gnecco, and had since spent several weeks in Italian Switzerland, whence at last they had been expelled in consequence of the circulation of an Anarchist manifesto. Beppe gave a glowing account of their stay in Lugano, and consequent flight to London. "You know," he said, "that I reached Lugano with two hundred francs in my pocket in company with all these comrades who hadn't got five francs among them. It is not every one who could have housed them all, but I did. I could not hire a Palazzo or a barrack for them, but we managed very comfortably in one large room. There were fourteen of us besides la Antonietta. There was only one bed, but what a size! We managed well enough by sleeping in two relays. However, even in two relays it took some organisation to get us all in. It was a fine double bed, you know, evidently intended for three or four . . . even for five it was suitable enough, but when it came to seven! . . . there was not much room for exercise, I can tell you. . . . But with four at the top and three at the bottom, we managed, and Antonietta slept on a rug in a cupboard. We did our best to make her comfortable by sacrificing half our clothes to keep her warm, but we might have saved ourselves the trouble, for she deserted us for the first bourgeois who came along. She was not a true comrade, but I will tell you all about her later on.

"We had some trouble with the landlord, a thick-headed bourgeois who got some stupid idea into his head about overcrowding. I have no patience with these bourgeois prejudices. One day he came round to complain about our numbers, and at not receiving his rent. But we were prepared for him. We assembled in full force, and sang the *Marseillaise* and the *Inno dei Lavoratori*, and danced the *Carmagnole*. I took out my eye and looked very threatening—one glance at us was enough for the old fellow. He made the sign of the cross and fled before we had time to tear him to pieces.

" Well, my two hundred francs was a very large sum, and not paying the rent was economical, but it dwindled, and I had to look round again for ways and means to feed us all. The money came to an end at last and then the real struggle began. Old Castellani, the landlord, kept a large stock of sacks of potatoes in a cellar, and every day he used to go in and take a few out for his own use, and then lock the cellar up again, mean old brute ! But once again I was one too many for him. I

collected large quantities of stones in the day-time,
and then at night with a skeleton key I had acquired
—it came out of Meneghino's bag which we always
jeered at — I let myself in and from the farthest
sacks I abstracted potatoes and refilled them with
stones. I calculated that at the slow rate he used
them he would not notice his loss till March. What
a scene there will be then, *Misericordia !* During
the last fortnight of our stay we lived almost entirely on my potatoes. I don't know how the devil
they would all have got on without me. It is true
that a waitress at the Panetteria Viennese fell in
love with Meneghino, and used to pass him on stale
bread ; but then you all know his appetite ! He ate
it nearly all himself on the way home. One day I
sent Bonatelli out to reconnoitre. He returned
with *one mushroom !*" It would be quite impossible
to convey an idea of the intense contempt contained in these last words. It was a most eloquent
denunciation of impotence and irresolution.

"All the same we had a grand time in Lugano.
And the week I and Migliassi spent in prison was
a great treat. Why, they treated us like popes, I
can tell you—as much food as you like, and the
best quality at that ; no work, a comfortable cell,
and a bed all to yourself ! And the bread ! I never
tasted anything like it in my life : they sent to
Como for it all. Lugano bread was not good
enough. Ah, Swiss prisons are a grand institution,

and I hope to spend a happy old age in such a place yet.

"Then came Bonafede's manifesto, and that scoundrel Costanzi betrayed us all to the police. Then the real trouble began. We had not ten francs among the lot of us, and we twelve had orders to clear out of the country within forty-eight hours! Once again they were all at a loss but for me!" and here he tapped his forehead in token of deference to his superior wits. "I had noticed the fat letters Morì received from home the first day of every month, and how jolly quiet he kept about them. I also noticed that he used to disappear for a day or two after their receipt, and return very sleepy and replete, with but scant appetite for dry bread and potatoes."

At this point Morì, the greasy Neapolitan youth, blinked his eyes and laughed foolishly. He seemed neither ashamed of himself nor indignant at his companions, merely sluggishly amused.

"Well," continued Meneghino, "that letter was just due, and I intercepted it. It contained one hundred and eighty francs; would you believe me? and that went some way to get us over here. Altogether we managed to collect sufficient money to carry us to the Belgian frontier, and for our passage across from Ostend. But that tramp across Belgium, *dio boia !*"

Here a clamour of voices interrupted Beppe,

as each one of the travellers chimed in with a separate account of the horrors of that ghastly tramp across country in mid-winter.

For many years Europe had not experienced such an inclement season. Everywhere the cold counted innumerable victims. Along the country highways and byways people dropped down frozen to death, and the paths were strewn with the carcasses of dead birds and other animals who had succumbed to the inclemency of the elements. All the great rivers were frozen over, and traffic had to be suspended along them. Unwonted numbers of starving sea-gulls and other sea-birds flocked to London in search of human charity, for the very fishes could not withstand the cold, and the inhospitable ocean afforded food no longer to its winged hosts. All Europe was under snow ; the railways were blocked in many places, and ordinary work had to be suspended in the great cities ; business was at a stand-still.

Neither the temperaments nor the clothes of these Italians had been equal to the exigencies of their march in the cruel Northern winter. As they tramped, a dismal, silent band across Belgium, the snow was several feet deep under foot, and on all sides it stretched hopelessly to the horizon, falling mercilessly the while. Their light clothing was ill adapted to the rigours of the season ; boots gave out, food was scanty or non-existent, and they had to rely entirely on the fickle chances of fortune to keep body and soul together. By night, when chance allowed, they had crept unobserved into barns and stables, and, lying close up against the dormant cattle, they had striven to restore animation to their frozen limbs by means of the beasts' warm breath. Once an old farm-woman had found them, and, taking pity on their woebegone condition, had regaled the whole party on hot milk and bread; and this was now looked back on as a gala day, for not every day had afforded such fare. At times in the course of their weary tramp the Anarchists had made an effort to keep up their flagging spirits by means of song, revolutionary and erotic, but such attempts had usually fallen flat, and the little band of exiles had relapsed into gloomy silence as they tramped on noiselessly through the snow. One of their number had quite broken down on the road and they had been compelled to leave him behind. "Lucky fellow, that Morelli," exclaimed Meneghino, "enjoying good broth in a hospital while we were still trudging on through that infernal snow!"

"And Antonietta?" inquired Giannoli, when the relation of these adventures had terminated. "You have not yet told us her end, nor how she incurred your displeasure."

"Oh, Antonietta!" exclaimed Beppe. "I was forgetting. You who believed her to be such a

I

sincere comrade will scarcely credit her baseness. She ran away with a horrible bourgeois; she was lured away from the Cause by a bicycle! Yes, Antonietta weighed a bicycle in the scales against the Social Revolution, and found the Social Revolution wanting! So much for the idealism of women! Never speak to me of them again. The last we saw of her she was cycling away in a pair of breeches with a disgusting banker. She laughed and waved her hand to us mockingly, and before we had time to utter a word she was gone. I never shall believe in a woman again!"

His indignation choked him at this point, and only the expression of his mouth and eye told of the depth of scorn and disgust which he felt for the young lady who had thus unblushingly cycled away from the Social Revolution.

CHAPTER VII

THE OFFICE OF THE *TOCSIN*

To the ordinary citizen whose walk in life lies along the beaten track there is a suggestion of Bohemianism about the office of any literary or propagandist organ; but I doubt whether the most imaginative among them in their wildest moments have ever conceived any region so far removed from the conventions of civilised society, so arbitrary in its hours and customs, so cosmopolitan and so utterly irrational as the office of the *Tocsin*.

In other chapters I attempt to describe the most noticeable among the genuine Anarchists who belonged to it, but I wish here to convey some faint idea of the strange medley of outside cranks and *déclassés* whose resort it in time became. There appeared to be a magnetic attraction about the place to tramps, *désœuvrés* cranks, argumentative people with time on their hands, and even downright lunatics. Foreigners of all tongues assembled in the office—Russians, Italians, French, Spaniards, Dutch, Swedes, and before very long they practically

swamped the English element. The Anarchist and
revolutionary party has always been more serious
on the Continent than in England, and what
genuine Anarchists there are here are mostly
foreigners.

Trades and industries of the most heterogeneous
kinds were carried on at the *Tocsin* by unemployed persons who could find no other refuge
for their tools nor outlet for their energies. In
one corner old M'Dermott settled down with his
lasts and leather, and there industriously hammered
away at his boots, alternating his work with occasional outbursts of Shakespearian recitation. In
winter the old fellow was positively snowed up in
the office, where he crouched shivering over the
fire until the advent of spring revived him. On the
first warm sunny day he suddenly flung down his
tools, and rushing out into the courtyard amazed
and terrified Mrs. Wattles and her colleagues by
shouting at the top of his voice, " Let me shout,
let me shout, Richard's himself again ! " " 'E gave
me such a turn, Miss, with 'is carryin's on that I
got the spasims again, an' I don't know what ever
I shall do if I can't find the price of a 'alf-quartern
o' gin." And I took the hint, for Mrs. Wattles's
alliance was no despicable possession among the
savages of Lysander Grove.

A shed was erected in the corner of the composing-room, which served by night as a dormitory

for numbers of otherwise roofless waifs, and here during the daytime a young Belgian and his wife set up a small factory of monkeys up sticks, which when completed they proceeded to sell in the streets.   In another corner two Italians settled down to manufacture a remarkable new kind of artificial flower with which they traded when opportunity permitted.   Small plaster - casts of Queen Victoria and Marat were also manufactured here.   When the influx of starving Italians necessitated it, a kind of soup-kitchen was inaugurated over which Beppe presided, and very busy he was kept too, manufacturing *minestras* and *polenta*, a welcome innovation to me, I may mention, after a long régime of small and nauseous tarts, bread and jam, and cheese.   In short, the headquarters of the *Tocsin*, besides being a printing and publishing office, rapidly became a factory, a debating club, a school, a hospital, a mad-house, a soup-kitchen and a sort of Rowton House, all in one.

When I look back on the scene now, and recall all the noise and hubbub, the singing, the discussions and disputes, the readings, the hammerings on this side, the bangings on that, the feeding, and M'Dermott's Shakespearian recitations, I find it very difficult to realise the amount of hard work which I and the other few serious and earnest comrades got through.

The chief impediment to the progress of the

work, however, was Short, the compositor. On close acquaintance with this creature, I found that he did not belie my first impression of him as the laziest and most slovenly of men; and I soon realised the two dominant characteristics which had made of him a Socialist—envy and sloth. So deeply was he imbued with envy that he was quite unable to rest so long as anyone else was better off than himself; and although he did not care one jot for "humanity" of which he prated so freely, and was incapable of regenerating a flea, he found in a certain section of the Socialist and Anarchist party that degree of dissatisfaction and covetousness which appealed to his degraded soul. Besides which the movement afforded him grand opportunities for living in sloth and sponging on other people.

Short was not without his humorous side, however, when only you were in the right mood to appreciate it. His envy of the superiority which he noted in others was only equalled by his intense contempt for himself.

I can still picture the poor brute lying with his dog in a corner of the office amid a heap of rubbish, unwashed, unkempt (he never divested himself of his clothes), and verminous in the extreme. There he would blow discordant notes on a mouth-organ, or smoke his rank old pipe, eat jam tarts, and scowl his wrath and envy on the world. If he could get hold of some unoccupied person to whom he could retail all the latest bits of Anarchist scandal, or from whom he could ferret out some little private secrets, he was contented enough, or, leaning out of the office window he would deliver a short autobiographical sketch to the interested denizens of the surrounding courts. A small bill, posted outside the office door, announced that Short was prepared to undertake extraneous jobs of printing on his own account; and this was responsible for many of the queer customers who found their way to the office of the *Tocsin*.

One of the queerest of all the queer oddities who haunted it was a small man of hunted aspect, known to every one as the "Bleeding Lamb." He had acquired this peculiar name from the title of a booklet which he had written under the direct inspiration of the Holy Ghost, a sort of interpretation of the Apocalypse, wherein was foretold a rapid termination of the universe. The printing of the "Bleeding Lamb" was undertaken by Short, whose dilatoriness in executing his work doubtless prolonged by a few years the existence of the terrestrial globe.

There was all the fervour of a prophet in the eye of the "Bleeding Lamb," but inspiration ceased here, and even what there was of inspired and prophetic in his eye was overcast by a certain diffident and deprecating look. He was the victim, poor man, of a twofold persecution in which heaven and earth joined hands to torment him—the arch-angel Michael and the Metropolitan police being the arch offenders.

One of the first things that struck you about the Bleeding Lamb was the helpless look of his feet. They were for ever shuffling and stumbling, getting in the way, and tripping up himself and others. His hands too had a flabby and inefficient expression, and his knees were set at a wrong angle. His stature was insignificant, his colouring vague; longish hair and beard of a colourless grey matched the grey of his prophetic and persecuted eye.

He would enter the office furtively, and cast a rapid glance round as though he almost expected to find the archangel Michael or an inspector of the Metropolitan police lurking in a corner, and it would take him some few seconds before he could muster up sufficient courage to inquire, as was his invariable custom, whether anyone had been round to ask after him. On being assured that no one had called for that purpose he appeared relieved, and gradually, as he became more and more reas-sured, he would warm to his subject of the coming cataclysm, and launch out into prophecy. "Ah," he exclaimed to me one day after a long discourse on the universal destruction at hand, "won't Queen Victoria just shiver in her shoes when she receives the revised edition of the 'Bleeding Lamb.' Little does she dream at this moment of what is in store for her." I recollect also that Nelson was in some way connected with his prophecies and his perplexities, but in what particular connection is not quite clear to my mind. The sympathy which he apparently felt for the Anarchists was, I suppose, due to the fact that they too were engaged—on a somewhat smaller scale it is true—on a policy of destruction, and also to their avowed antagonism to the law and the police, whether metropolitan or otherwise.

The Bleeding Lamb had a formidable rival in the field of prophecy in the person of another strange frequenter of our office—a demure-looking gentleman named Atkinson who professed to be the reincarnation of Christ, and who preached the millennium. He was a less depressed-looking person than the Bleeding Lamb—whom he treated with undisguised contempt—and affected a tall hat and Wellington boots. The Lamb, on his side, denounced the Messiah as a fraud, and went so far as to suggest that he had only taken to prophecy when the alteration in the fashion of ladies' pockets compelled him to abandon his original profession. "That Lamb is not quite right in the upper storey," whispered Atkinson to me one day; "he may even become dangerous, poor creature!" Shortly afterwards I was taken aside by the gentleman in question who warned me to keep my purse in safety as "that Messiah is no better than a common thief."

The approach of either of these prophets was invariably the signal for a stampede on Short's part, who, never having completed his work, dreaded encountering the mournful scrutiny and reproachful bleating of the Lamb no less than the sad, stern rebukes and potential Wellington boots of the Messiah. Into no single item of the day's programme did he put so much zest as into the grand dive he would make into any available hiding-place, and he would lie for hours flat on his stomach under M'Dermott's bed sooner than "face the music."

One day the perspiring Lamb entered the office red in the face and considerably out of breath, rapidly followed by a lugubrious individual, talking volubly in an argumentative monotone. This person seemed to be very indignant about something.

"Marcus Aurelius was a just ruler and a philosopher," he was saying, "and he saw the necessity for suppressing the Christian factions. He was among the severest persecutors of the early Christians.—What does that argue, you fool?"

"Nothing against my contention with regard to the seven-headed beast in the Apocalypse," replied the Bleeding Lamb with a defiant snort.

"The seven-headed beast has nothing to do with the case," retorted his interlocutor, putting all the warmth into his monotonous drawl of which he appeared capable. "The seven-headed beast can't alter history, and my case is conclusively proved in the course of this little work, to the production of which I have devoted the best years of my life. The seven-headed beast indeed! Pshaw for your seven-headed beast, you dunder-headed dreamer!"

Whilst I gazed on dumbfounded at this little scene, making futile efforts to grasp the vexed point under discussion, the strange new-comer, whom the Lamb addressed as Gresham, deposited on the floor a huge and shapeless brown-paper parcel, under whose weight he was staggering, and sitting down by its side he carefully untied the string, and dragged triumphantly forth tome after tome of carefully-written MSS., which he proceeded to read out without further preamble.

"'Atheism *v.* Christianity,'" he drawled, commencing at the title, "'being a short treatise on the Persecutions of the Early Christians, the object of which is to prove that they were persecuted by the just emperors and protected by the unjust; that, consequently, they were wrong; that Christianity is wrong, and the Deity a palpable fraud; by Tobias Jonathan Gresham,'—and let the seven-headed beast in the Apocalypse put that in his pipe and smoke it!" casting a defiant glance at the Bleeding Lamb.

As this concluding remark was made in the same monotone as the foregoing sentence, I was at some

loss to determine whether or not it formed part of
the title of that momentous work.

The Bleeding Lamb here cast me a knowing
glance, which said as plainly as words that his
unfortunate acquaintance was mad, but that it was
as well to humour him, and so he magnanimously
sat down on a stool facing his rival, while the latter
proceeded to read out his book, which was destined soon to mount up the long list of Short's
sins of typographical omissions. This was but
the herald of a long series of readings from the
"short treatise," which were carried on at intervals
for some weeks.   Minute after minute and hour
after hour Gresham drawled on from one tedious
reiteration to another, never raising his voice nor
altering its key, till a sense of dizziness overcame
his audience, and his voice became as the singing
in one's ears which accompanies high fever or
heralds a faint.   Indeed I have never suffered from
fever or faintness since that date without my sen-
sations recalling Gresham's dreary, argumentative
drawl;   then gradually his voice would grow
fainter and somewhat spasmodic, until at length
it gave way to snores, as the weary Lamb and the
atheist Lion, like the kid and the leopard of Isaiah,
sank down together in a confused heap on the
floor, and there slept out a miniature fulfilment of
the word of the prophet.

Then there was a Polish count who found his

way to the *Tocsin*—a most deplorable aristocratic
débris, who might have stepped straight out of
the pages of Dostoievsky. I never set eyes on a
more depressed-looking mortal than Count Voblinsky. He looked as though he bore on his
bent shoulders the weight of all the ill-spent lives
in Christendom. He was a damp, unwholesome-
looking man, whose appearance suggested long
confinement in a cellar. He was pale and hollow-
eyed, and almost mouldy ; altogether a most cada-
verous-looking person. He was always attired,
even at eleven A.M., in an old dress suit, green and
threadbare with age, and a furry tall hat, into
which garments he seemed to have grown and
taken root. But despite the decay of his person
and his attire, there was a certain degree of
aristocratic refinement about Voblinsky's features,
last ghastly traces of his ancient nobility. He
vaguely recalled to my mind a long-ago Continental trip of my childhood, and an unfortunate
elephant in the Marseilles Jardin des Plantes who,
from long inactivity in the corner of his cage, had
become overgrown with moss. There was the
same incongruous touch of erstwhile nobility, the
same decay, the same earthy smell. By what
shady and circuitous paths had the unfortunate
count reached this unhappy pass ? Perhaps his
wife was responsible ; for if ever woman was
calculated not to lead her mate on to higher and

better things it was the Countess Voblinska. The countess was worse than slovenly : she was down-right dirty. Her tumbled, frowsy hair, with patches of golden dye in it, was surmounted by an appalling hat of incongruous dimensions and shape, trimmed with what appeared to be archæological relics, thick in dust. To approach it brought on a per-fect paroxysm of sneezing. Her clothes, which were very greasy and never brushed, hung together by strings, tatters, and safety-pins. Her hands and face were begrimed with several coats of dirt, and a top coat of *poudre de riz*. No ordinary imagina-tion dared speculate on what lay hidden beneath those tattered rags she wore. She gesticulated much, and discoursed on the subject of some lecture she was to give, in the intervals of volley-ing forth abuse and swearing in Parisian argot at her long-suffering husband, who received it all with most ludicrous courtesy. Often a strong smell of gin mingled with the eloquent flow of the countess's language.

On the whole, however, the Anarchists and their queer associates might be regarded as a fairly tem-perate set. One of the most potent causes of drink is the monotony of the existences led by most people, the hopeless dreariness of their con-fined, narrow lives, the total lack of interest and excitement. This is not the case in revolutionary circles, where not only are there plenty of ideas afloat to occupy men's minds and distract them from the narrow circle of their dreary domestic lives, but where also the modern craving for excitement, factitious or otherwise, finds plenty of nourishment.

The office of the *Tocsin*, however, did not lack the occasional presence of the habitual drunkard. There was one queer fellow who frequently put in a dissipated appearance for the purpose of complaining of the ill-usage to which his wife's tongue subjected him. He looked forward to the Social Revolution as the only escape from this thraldom, and certainly no man ever made more strenuous, albeit ill-directed efforts, on its behalf.

Then there was a bibulous Welshman who at times would startle the unwashed denizens of the neighbouring slums by appearing in a tall hat and irreproachable shirt front. He was a doctor by profession, who succeeded in maintaining a certain reputation in polite circles, but an alcoholic soaker by inclination, one of those men who somehow contrive to keep ahead of ruin by sleeping out periods of financial distress in friends' houses.

Our proof-reader was a benevolent old gentleman of obsolete customs, who in an age of open-air cures still wore a mouth and nose respirator. He was such an eminently respectable person that I never could quite understand why he associated himself with anything so disreputable as the *Tocsin*. I always half suspected that he came there principally on my account, chivalrously determined that I should not be surrounded *solely* by scum. But besides this motive he had some pretensions to being a man of advanced views, and was a purchaser of "advanced" literature. The introduction of this into the precincts of his home was a great trial to his better half, who had no kind of sympathy with such leanings. New-fangled ideas of any description were tabooed by her, and all preachers and holders of such she unconditionally consigned to hell-fires. Her husband she regarded as a brand to be snatched from the burning, and she and a few select female relatives worked hard to snatch him. But although new-fangled ideas on social organisation and political economy were bad enough, one thing alone was beyond all human endurance to the mind of Mrs. Crawley, and that one thing was free-love.

One day Mr. Crawley brought home "The Woman Who Did," and neglected to conceal it. It was found by his wife lying on the dining-room sofa.

"My fingers itched to seize and burn the impudent huzzy, lying there as unconcerned as though she had been the 'Private Meditations and Prayers of the Rev. Bagge,'" Mrs. Crawley confided to her Aunt Elizabeth, "but it was a six-shilling book, and I knew how Crawley valued it, and for the life of me I did not dare touch it."

It was a sore trial indeed to Mrs. Crawley to live under the same roof with such a person, but she dared not so far outrage the feelings of one whom she had sworn to love, honour, and obey, as to execute the offending lady. She long meditated some revenge, some outlet for her outraged feelings ; it was long in coming, but come it did at last. The " Man Who Didn't " followed in the footsteps of his irregular mate, and in a fourpenny-halfpenny edition. This was more than the worthy matron could stand, and either he or she herself must leave the house. She summoned Aunt Elizabeth, a lady of irreproachable moral standard, the whites of whose eyes had a habit of turning up spasmodically, and the corners of whose mouth down, and to her she unburdened her feelings.

" My dear Eliza," she said, " I have too long tolerated 'The Woman Who Did,' but when it comes to the 'Man Who Didn't,' that—er—well, that *disgusting* 'Man Who Didn't'—and how am I to know that he didn't, the brazen creature !—it is time I asserted my authority. I cannot and I will not stand him."

The offending and irresolute gentleman was then seized upon with a pair of tongs, carried in solemn procession to the remotest room in the house, and burnt. The sanctity of matrimony had reasserted its rights.

A young bank clerk who accompanied Crawley to the office was a type of what I might call the

K

conscientiously unprincipled man.   It being wrong
to steal, he made a point of annexing small objects.
Cleanliness is next to godliness, and he devoted himself heroically to dirt ; it was not at all his natural
tendency, and the more disagreeable he found it
the more strenuous was he in its pursuit.   Being by
nature punctual, he made it an absolute point of
honour never to keep an appointment ; and, as a
lover of domestic peace, he was for ever working
his way into scrapes and rows.   He was a comical
object, with his limp yellow hair brushed ferociously
on end, and his mild yellow eyes scowling defiance
at mankind.

When the Cuban revolution broke out a wave of
sympathy for the oppressed islanders passed over
the whole civilised world, and nowhere did this
find a warmer echo than in the Anarchist party and
the *Tocsin* group.   Many Anarchists were in favour
of going out to the assistance of the insurgents.
Opinion was divided on the question.   Some said :
" It is our duty to remain in Europe to carry on the
work of Anarchist propaganda here.   The Cuban
revolution is a race struggle, and no concern of
ours."   Others said : "We Anarchists are inter-
nationalists, and in whatsoever part of the world
there is revolt against oppression, and wherever
the revolutionary forces are at work, there is our
opportunity to step in and direct those forces into
the proper course, towards Anarchism."   These

Anarchists saw in the uprising of this small and comparatively insignificant race against the Spanish throne the possible dawn of a wider, vaster struggle, in which the whole world would join hands to lay low thrones, altars, and judgment seats.

A small band of Italian comrades, led by an adventurous Sicilian, got up a subscription for the purpose, and left the office of the *Tocsin*, amid great revolutionary enthusiasm, to journey to the assistance of the insurgent island. Only one of their number ever returned alive to Europe to tell of the horrors and hardships of the fierce struggle there endured, of the cruelty of the Spaniards, and the uselessness of the fight from the Anarchist point of view.

The Cuban fever was very catching, and after the departure of this first band there was a regular epidemic of departure at the *Tocsin*. Carter and Simpkins turned up at the office one afternoon very much in earnest about it all and persuaded that a little British grit was what was needed in Cuba, "to keep things humming." Simpkins recalled his old army days and the valour he had several times displayed when under the influence of liquor. He waved an old belt appertaining to those times, and would, I believe, have sung something about the Union Jack and the beer of old England, had not his friend recalled him to a better sense of his duty as an Anarchist and Internationalist. It appeared that Carter had come into a small sum of money consequent on the death of an uncle, with which he was bent on paying their passage out to Cuba. "What is an Anarchist to do in this wretched country?" he asked. "I am tired of lying in bed waiting for the revolution. It's too slow coming." "Yah!" muttered Short under his breath to me, "the springs are out of order, and he finds it hard. That's about how much he cares for the revolution."

After Carter and Simpkins had taken their leave of the staff of the *Tocsin* I watched a very moving scene from the window, when they bade good Mrs. Wattles farewell. The good lady was very deeply affected, and with tears in her eyes she begged them to think again before betaking themselves to "them furrin' parts" where she had heard "the drink was something awful and not fit for a Christian stomach." She was only half reassured when told that rum came from somewhere in that direction.

But Carter and Simpkins never reached Cuba. Some few minutes' walk from the office of the *Tocsin*, at the corner of Lysander Grove, stood an inviting house of call, the "Merry Mariners," where the valiant warriors dropped in on their way, to refresh themselves, perhaps in anticipation of the dreary prospect which Mrs. Wattles's words had opened before them. When several hours later Short returned from his accustomed evening stroll round the neighbourhood, he described with great relish the pitiable termination of their voyage. He had found Carter just sober enough to cart his incapacitated disciple home on a wheelbarrow, after which he painfully betook himself to his bed, there to bemoan the tardiness of the revolution, and the broken condition of the spring mattress.

"And won't his guv'nor just give Simpkins a ragging when he gets home. He'll give him Cuba," gloated the unsympathetic printer.

Another relief expedition from the *Tocsin* met with scarcely more brilliant success. Beppe and Meneghino set out under the guidance of old M'Dermott, on tramp to Cardiff, whence they hoped to work their way out to the insurgent island. They, too, set out full of brave hopes and generous enthusiasm, but with too confident a trust in the beneficence of Providence as caterer to their material needs on the journey. Before a fortnight had elapsed, they also were back at the office, Beppe bearing the poor old Irishman on his shoulders in a quite crippled and exhausted condition. He had to be put to bed, and remained there several weeks, before he was in a fit state to get about again. They all complained bitterly of the inhospitality of the country-

folk to whom they had appealed for help, and
of the uncourteous reception they had met with
in the Cardiff docks. Poor Meneghino reached
London barefooted, his faithful canvas bag hanging disconsolately over his shoulder—and all with
woefully vacant stomachs. They formed a comic-
ally dismal group as they collapsed into the office
in an exhausted heap.

Amid these many strange and dubious, ludicrous
or pathetic characters, some few heroic figures
appeared. From time to time there came into
our midst Vera Marcel, the Red Virgin of the bar-
ricades, the heroine of the Commune of Paris—a
woman of blood and smoke and of infinite mercies
towards men and beasts. I can see her still, almost
beautiful in her rugged ugliness, her eyes full of
the fire of faith and insane fanaticism, her hair
dishevelled, her clothes uncared for. I can hear
the wonderful ring of her tragic voice as she
pleaded the misery of the poor and suffering, of
the oppressed, the outcast, the criminal, the rejected, and as it rose higher and higher to invoke
fire and sword and bloodshed in expiation. Then
I seem to hear its magic and inspired ring as her
wonderful faith conjured up visions of the future
when the whole of humanity shall live in peace
and brotherhood, and the knife, which in time
of revolution had shed the blood of the oppres-

sors, shall " cut nothing deadlier than bread." A
strange gaunt figure she was, a woman who had
never hesitated at shedding blood in the good
Cause, nor feared to face death for it; but with
her friends, and especially with children and dumb
animals, she was as gentle as the gentlest of her
sex ; and no words can describe the extreme
sweetness of her voice.

As publication time approached, all-night sittings
became necessary, when all this heterogeneous
assembly met together, and amidst Anarchist song
and Anarchist enthusiasm forwarded or hindered,
each in his degree, the publication of the *Tocsin*.
I can see in my mind's eye the much-littered, overcrowded office in all the confusion of those nights,
with its dark corners hidden in shadow, where slept
tired fighters weary of the fray, and its brightly-
lighted patches, under the lamps, where the work
of the night was being carried on. Some dozen
voices, more or less musical, are chanting Anarchist war-songs, and the *Inno di Caserio* and the
Marseillaise ring out through the open windows
to the dormant or drunken denizens of Lysander
Grove. The Reincarnation is patiently turning
the wheel of the printing machine, and rolling
out fresh *Tocsins*, thinking, no doubt, of that
tocsin which, at no distant date, shall ring out
from a loftier sphere to rouse the deluded inhabitants of this globe to a different millennium from

that dreamed of by Anarchists. But, whatever his thoughts, he grinds away with much Christian endurance and fortitude. Wainwright, who is tired after a long turn at the wheel, subsequent to a hard day's work in the brick-yard, is relating to a few interested listeners the strange story of his life, or discussing points of Anarchist principle and propaganda.

Then, somehow, the Bleeding Lamb would find his way in, and looking over at his reincarnated rival at the wheel with undisguised contempt, he whispers: "I know what sort of a wheel his unhallowed hoof ought to be turning!"

Armitage and Kosinski at such times would be busy folding the papers, both absorbed in their work, happy to think that they were thus advancing the great Cause. And Short, shivering discontentedly at the cold, or swearing amid much perspiration at the heat, would smoke his pipe and eat his unattractive pastry, whilst crawling into his rugs and banners, until Beppe, in an outburst of indignation, drags him out by the scruff of the neck and compels him to lock up the forms.

One night there was a grand banquet, for Beppe had turned in, bearing under his long cloak a prime conditioned tom-cat, whose disconcerted mews were rapidly ended by a dexterous twist of the neck, and whose plump person was before long stewing in wine and vinegar in the *Tocsin* stockpot, after his liver had been previously fried for the private consumption of the ever-hungry Beppe.

When this succulent repast had been disposed of towards 3 A.M. (all the *Tocsin* workers had admirable digestions) a brief respite from work ensued, during which Beppe sang pieces of Italian opera, accompanied by Gnecco on his mandolin, and M'Dermott treated us to brief recitations from Shakespeare. Much stamping and gesticulation accompanied, I remember, the soliloquy of Hamlet, and our flesh crept at the witches' incantations from "Macbeth." The old cobbler delighted in Shakespeare and dictionaries, between the perusal of which he spent most of his time. "Like Autolycus in the 'Winter's Tale,'" he said to me one day, "I am a 'snapper-up of unconsidered trifles,' and during the riots of 18— I snapped up a sufficient number of these to enable me to set myself up with a small library, and I did no work during eighteen months, devoting my entire time to Shakespeare and Johnson's Dictionary."

Sometimes a phrenologist who had strayed into our midst would follow on with a brief phrenological séance, and nothing afforded the comrades more satisfaction than to be informed that their bumps showed undoubted criminal propensities.

Then again the heavy roll of the machine would

drown all lesser noises with its monotonous grinding, as the most resolute and earnest among us
returned undaunted to the fray, whilst others, less
energetic, curled up on the floor in varying uncomfortable attitudes about the office—inside the
dormitory shed and out, propped against posts
and type-racks, or stretched on stacks of paper—
and slumbered in blissful ignorance of the future
fortunes of the *Tocsin*.

CHAPTER VIII

THE DYNAMITARD'S ESCAPE

MAY-DAY was at hand, and we had been working all night at the office of the *Tocsin* in order to have the paper ready in time to distribute to the provincial groups. Since Friday morning I had hardly left the office at all—merely going home for dinner and returning at once to the fray—and by four o'clock Sunday morning we had rolled off the last of the five thousand copies of the *Tocsin*, which, along with two thousand leaflets drawn up by myself and Armitage, were ready for distribution. The 1st of May fell on the following Wednesday, and we had for once the satisfaction of knowing that we had taken Time by the forelock.

Short had retired to his shake-down in the dormitory about midnight, and the loud creaking of his boots against the boards was the only sign he gave of life. Kosinski, Armitage, and Giannoli, after making up and addressing the last parcel, had left for their respective abodes ; Beppe and Meneghino, having turned the wheel the whole evening, had fallen to sleep exhausted, stretched

on a bench in the machine-room; and I, after
having partaken of a cup of tea and some hot
buttered toast which old M'Dermott had provided
for me, sat nodding and dozing on one side of the
fire. The old cobbler had fallen fast asleep on the
other side while poring over a dictionary, noting
down sonorous and impressive-sounding words
with which to embellish the oration he intended
to deliver on May-day in Hyde Park.

About half-past five, just as the first cold rays
of the chilly spring dawn cast a ghastly blue light
on the dormant figures around me, deadening the
yellow flame of the lamp which was burning itself
out, I was roused from my torpor by a light rap
at the outside door. In the office all was quiet,
but for the heavy and rhythmic snores of the
weary comrades, and wondering who could claim
admittance at such an unearthly hour, I rose with
a shiver and opened the door. To my surprise I
found myself face to face with Bonafede.

Since that bitter January day when Bonafede
and his companions had emerged from the London
fog and made their unexpected entrance on the
scene of the *Tocsin*, I had not seen very much of
him, though we had never quite lost sight of one
another, and I frequently heard his news through
mutual friends. As I have already stated, Gnecco
and Bonafede had retired to lodgings in the Italian
quarter in the unsavoury neighbourhood of Saffron

Hill. They had a little money, but only enough to last for two or three weeks. Gnecco had a few valuables in the shape of a gold watch and chain, a pearl breast-pin, and a fur-lined coat, and he soon had recourse to my friendly help to dispose of these articles to the best advantage with a pawnbroker, and on the proceeds, eked out by some small help which he received from his family, he managed to rub along, and he and his mandolin were soon familiar features at the office. But with Bonafede the case was different. He was a man of too active and independent a character to be long idle. He was by profession an engineer, and in Italy, before his career had been interrupted by his political activity, he had held an important post on the Italian railways. But for many years his life had been a stirring one, and he had learned to turn his hand to whatever offered, and had in turn worked as a dock labourer, a sailor before the mast, a gilder employed in church decorations, a house-decorator in a lunatic asylum and a cutter-out of military trousers at Marseilles, a warehouse porter and a navvy. Whatever job turned up he accepted; if it was work at which he had no experience he would look up some comrade in that line and get from him a few hints, and this, supplemented by reading up particulars in some trade encyclopædia at a public library, enabled him to accomplish his task satisfactorily.

He had hardly been in London a fortnight when he looked about him for work, and, nothing better offering, he engaged himself as washer-up at one of Veglio's many restaurants. After six weeks he was rescued from the uncongenial drudgery of scullion by a comrade, a fellow-Calabrian, who earned a good living as decorator of West-end cafés, and who took on Bonafede to assist him in frescoing a ceiling at the Trocadero, not, however, before the latter had laid the foundations of a *lega di resistenza* between the Italians employed in restaurant kitchens. At the end of a month the ceiling was painted, and Bonafede parted company with his compatriot, pocketing £10, plus his keep whilst the job lasted. One of his first steps was to visit me at the office of the *Tocsin* and arrange for the printing of an Italian pamphlet and of a booklet of revolutionary songs, the production of Gnecco, which were to be smuggled into Italy for distribution. The cost of paper and carriage of these works ran into the better part of £3. With the remaining cash in his pocket, Bonafede went to look up old friends and comrades in the French and Italian quarters. A's wife was expecting her confinement, B needed an outfit in order to enter on a job as waiter which he had secured at a club ; C had been out of work for three months and had five small mites to feed and clothe, and so forth. At the end of this expedition rather less than 15s. remained in his pocket, and once more he sought employment. This time he got taken on by a contractor who asphalted the London streets, a work done entirely by Italians. Here he remained for nearly two months, during which time he organised the men into a union and induced them to strike for better conditions. The men won their point, and returned to work on the condition that the agitator who had got up the strike should be dismissed, and Bonafede left of his own accord, unwilling to cause loss to the men by prolonging the struggle. After a few weeks' enforced idleness, during which he was lost sight of by the comrades, he reappeared one evening at a group meeting held at our office, and informed us that he was taken on as electrician at the Monico.

Ten days had now passed since I last saw him, and my expression was eloquent of my amazement at his unexpected appearance.

"You are surprised at my coming at such an unusual hour, Comrade," he began with his strong Calabrian accent; "but you will understand when I tell you that ever since yesterday evening I have been awaiting an opportunity to get round here without being followed by my guardian angels of Scotland Yard. Gnecco told me that you were passing the night in the office, and so I seized on a favourable moment and came." He stopped, glanced round the room, walked up to the bench on which the two Italians were sleeping the sleep of the just, and having satisfied himself that no one could overhear us he explained the motive of his visit to me.

"You doubtless know that Jean Matthieu, suspected of complicity in the P. . . . bomb explosions, has been hiding in London for some time past." I nodded assent : he had even been pointed out to me one evening by Giannoli at a meeting in the East End.

"Well, since yesterday we have the certainty that the police are on his track, that they are aware of his whereabouts. It has become absolutely necessary for him to leave London without further delay—within the next twenty-four hours. Everything is arranged. The police will be watching the Continental trains, so he will go for the present to Leicester, and stay with a comrade who has a French wife, and who will pass him off as his wife's uncle. From there we hope, within a week or so to get him off to America ; but all this requires money : the least that we can give him is twenty pounds. I had five by me, left with me to make use of for the Cause, a few French comrades have handed me over another seven. But we are still in need of eight pounds to make up the necessary sum. Could you let us have it ?"

The last days of the month always found me at the end of my resources. I had but two pounds in my purse. "What a pity," I exclaimed, "that you could not let me know yesterday! To-day is Sunday; it will be impossible for me to get at any money. Raymond is certain only to have a pound or two on him, if he has as much; the Bank is closed. I have some jewellery by me on which I could easily raise ten or twelve pounds, but the pawn-shops are not open on Sundays. What am I to do? Can you not wait until to-morrow?"

Bonafede explained that every minute was of consequence: Matthieu must leave at once or he would inevitably be arrested. We both remained silent, hesitating, for a few minutes. At last he spoke: "Madame Combrisson has the money by her, I am sure, but she will never give it. You say, however, you have some jewellery that you would be willing to pledge: perhaps with that as security she would advance us the money. Any-how we can but try."

It was arranged that I should go home for my valuables and repair to the house of the Com-brissons, where, Bonafede informed me, Matthieu was at that moment concealed.

"But do you think he is safe there?" I inquired.

"Oh yes, perfectly. Jules is a good comrade, and both he and his wife have every reason to

L

wish to remain on good terms with the Anarchists.
They know on which side their bread is buttered.
I shall go now and you will find me at the
Combrissons'."

I knew the French couple well by reputation,
though I had never yet crossed their threshold.
Combrisson had come over to England some
twelve years ago ; he had been mixed up in the
Anarchist propaganda, and had seen fit to expa-
triate himself ; it was rumoured that he had been
actively mixed up with a gang of coiners, amongst
whom were several Anarchists who thought it
good warfare to make the hated bourgeois pay
for the propaganda by falsifying the currency.
They had not been long in London when they
took a large house in Grafton Street, letting
out rooms to comrades. They also kept on the
ground floor a small *depôt* of foreign revolutionary
literature, and received for a consideration the
correspondence of the refugees. Combrisson, who
worked as a carpenter and joiner, had the reputation of being a good comrade, and always set
down to his wife's account all actions not strictly
in accordance with the principles of solidarity,
such as turning out comrades who did not pay
their rent, refusing small loans and subscriptions,
and such like.

By eight o'clock I was in Grafton Street. As
I turned down the corner which leads from the

Tottenham Court Road, I became aware that I
was being followed. A young man with a sandy
moustache, a celestial nose, and fishy blue eyes,
got up to look like a counter-jumper on a holi-
day, whom I had long since learned to know as
Detective Limpet, was walking a few steps behind
me on the other side of the road. I stopped at
Number 9, my destination, and I saw Limpet
likewise stop outside a public-house which stood
opposite, and exchange a few words with a hulking
brute leaning against the wall, characterised by
a heavy jaw, lowering brows, and a strong Irish
brogue, in whom I recognised Detective O'Brien.
They both turned their eyes on me as I stood
on the door-step pulling the bell handle, and I
saw a stupid grin overspread the countenance of
the Limpet.

The door was opened by a little maid-of-all-work
who seemed doubtful as to whether she should let
me in or no, till a head adorned with curl-papers
appeared above the kitchen steps, calling out in a
shrill voice, "Jane, you fool, show the young lady in."

Next minute I was in the front kitchen, where
Madame Combrisson, her husband, and Bonafede
awaited me.

The house was a good-sized, solidly-built one,
originally intended for a gentleman's residence,
but fallen now on evil days. An odour of fried
onions and sawdust pervaded the establishment,

for Madame Combrisson boarded three or four
of her lodgers, regaling them principally on "*soupe
à l'ognon*," and Combrisson carried on in the back
kitchen his carpentry business at which he kept
these same lodgers employed, paying them in
kind with food and house-room, and doling out
a few shillings now and again as pocket-money.
In this way he succeeded in combining philan-
thropy and business, and though, after a few
months, his employees invariably left as soon as
they had learned a little of the English language
and English prices, still there were always new-
comers willing, nay anxious, to replace them.

After a few preliminary words of introduction,
I produced the jewellery for Madame Combrisson's
inspection. She was a small wiry woman, with
hard, covetous grey eyes, grizzled hair screwed
up in a tight knot on the top of her head, a nose
like the beak of a bird of prey, and thin blue
lips. Her eyes lit up as her hands turned over
the little diamond brooch and finely-chased gold
bracelet which I submitted to her inspection.

"Of course I am not a judge," she said, "but
I should think we could easily raise a little money
on these. I wish I had it myself, I would willingly
give it for the Cause, but, *que voulez vous, mademoiselle?* we are but poor folk ; however, I know
some one near here who might perhaps be able
to oblige us ; I will go and see."

Bonafede winked at me and I could see that he considered the matter settled. He and Combrisson left the kitchen and I remained alone with madame, who proceeded to take her fringe out of the curl-papers, and to exchange her petticoat and red flannel jacket for a somewhat rusty black dress. Whilst performing her toilette she eyed me carefully. I noticed that since she had inspected the jewellery she had involuntarily assumed a more respectful tone in addressing me. "I hear from the comrades that you are very active in the Cause, mademoiselle; have you been long in the movement?"

I replied that it was getting on for two years.

"And your family, are they Anarchists also?"

I explained that my parents were dead and that I was the only one of my family who worked in the movement. She seemed surprised at this information, "But you must be rich," she said : "that jewellery you have brought is very beautiful; you are young, you could enjoy yourself, mix with those of your own class; why do you work in a printing-office instead?"

"But I am an Anarchist. We must all do what we can to help the Cause, I do my best; not more, however, than other comrades."

She seemed by now to have summed me up, though I was evidently still somewhat of a mystery to her, and she merely said :—

"Oh, of course we are all Anarchists; we all do our best for the Cause."

As she was leaving, Bonafede came down and said that Matthieu would like to see me if I saw fit, and together we mounted to the back attic where the dynamitard was concealed.

Nobody could have guessed on sight that the puny little man before me could be the dreaded Anarchist for whom the police of Europe had been searching high and low during the past seven months. Matthieu was a tailor by trade, and his physique bore traces of the sedentary work and of the long hours passed in close unhealthy rooms. He was slightly hunchbacked, his chest narrow and hollow, his legs bowed; his pale blue eyes with their swollen red lids had the strained expression of one accustomed to make use of the last rays of daylight before lighting the lamp. His massive jaw and firm round chin, and high narrow forehead were the only features which revealed in him the man of action and the fanatic. Yet this was the man who, by a series of explosions culminating in the blowing up of a police station, had spread terror in the ranks of the French bourgeoisie.

We shook hands, and I told them how I had been followed by Detective Limpet and how he and O'Brien were stationed opposite the house.

"Yes," said Bonafede, "it is certain that they

suspect Matthieu's presence here; we must try to get rid of them in some way for a short while; set them off on some false scent, so as to enable our comrade to leave the house."

"If you would only let me do as I wish," broke in Matthieu, "I would soon be out of this. I have a good revolver and I am not afraid to use it. I would make a rush for it, and ten to one I should get off scot-free; and anyhow better be taken fighting than caught like a rat in a hole."

We both tried to dissuade him, arguing that there was always time to take such a step, and that with a little patience and ingenuity it was almost certain that a means would be found for his safe escape.

In a few minutes Madame Combrisson entered the room. She handed me over £10 and a receipt for the pledges, adding that her friend would not be induced to lend more. I handed the sum over to Bonafede. He had now £22 in hand, so that the financial side of the difficulty was solved. Madame Combrisson, however, had news. A neighbour had informed her that Chief Inspector Deveril had been seen in the street, and that, after giving instructions to his two subordinates not to move from their post of observation, he had left, it was supposed, in order to procure a search-warrant. This news filled us with alarm.

Almost any minute now the police might claim
entrance to the house, and then Matthieu would
inevitably be caught.   What was to be done?
I was told off to look out of a front window
from behind a curtain and report on the situation, but only to return with the news that Limpet
and O'Brien were both leaning airily on their
sticks studying the heavens with imperturbable
calm.   Matthieu was growing restless.   He walked
up and down the small room like a caged beast,
nervously clutching at the revolver which he kept
in his trouser pocket.   Madame Combrisson kept
bemoaning her fate, saying that it would be the
ruin of her house if the police entered.   Bonafede
alone remained calm and collected.   At last he
exclaimed, looking at his watch, "It is now past
eleven, in another half-hour the public-houses will
open, let us hope that our friends below may
turn in to refresh themselves.   In that minute
Matthieu must escape; we must have everything
ready; he had better change his clothes and disguise himself as much as possible.   We will leave
together; we are both armed, and if the worst
comes to the worst we will sell our lives dearly."

"Oh, my poor house, my poor house!" moaned
madame, "this business will be the death of us all."

Bonafede turned on her savagely.   "This is no
time for recriminations," he exclaimed.   "Sharpen
your wits and see if you cannot find some means

of getting rid of those spies. You are clever enough when it is a question of serving your own interests."

Madame Combrisson seemed electrified by these words.

" I will try, Comrade, only give me time to think." Next minute, she exclaimed, " How would it do to send down two of the comrades to pick a quarrel in the street ? They could start a fight, a crowd will assemble, the detectives will go to see what is up, and you and Matthieu can avail yourselves of the confusion to escape."

" Good ! " replied Bonafede, " go and see about it at once. I will help Matthieu to get ready, and you, Isabel, be on the look-out, and let us know when the right moment has come."

I stationed myself behind the curtain at the front parlour window. In a few minutes I saw a young German who lodged in the house rush up the area steps into the street, followed by Combrisson. They were both shouting and gesticulating loudly, and Combrisson seemed to be demanding money which the other refused. A few passers-by stopped to listen to the two foreigners, who danced around, growing ever more noisy ; but Limpet and O'Brien stood firm. They looked at the combatants, but seemed to consider the matter as a joke, and only crossed over to our side of the way when they saw a crowd begin to

assemble. The quarrel between Combrisson and
his lodger began to flag when they saw that their
object had failed, and the German soon walked
off in the direction of Tottenham Court Road. I
watched the detectives cross over to their former
post of observation, and was just going to inform the
comrades of the negative result of this manœuvre
when I saw Inspector Deveril coming down the
street. For a second I stood paralysed with ap-
prehension : all was up with my friends ! Next
moment I had climbed the four flights, and given
the dreaded news.

Matthieu rushed to the attic window. It gave
on to a wide gutter which ran along several roofs.
"This is my only means of escape. I will get
into one of these other houses by the skylight, and
escape at the front door whilst they are searching
here."

"And if any one tries to stop you ? " I exclaimed.

"So much the worse for them," he replied,
clutching his revolver.

He was already outside the window when
Bonafede spoke, advising him to wait a minute
whilst we saw what was going on. As soon as
the police knocked, he could carry out his plan.
To be noticed by them on the roof would be fatal
to its success.

At that moment Combrisson rushed in. "I
cannot tell what has happened. Deveril spoke to

those two spies and has walked off. The public-house has opened, Limpet has gone inside, and only O'Brien remains on guard."

We all three went downstairs to watch proceedings, leaving Matthieu by the window, ready at a moment's notice to put his desperate project into execution.

Sure enough, all was quiet in the street below; passers-by were hurrying home to their Sunday dinners, the smell of which pervaded the street and house, and O'Brien stood at the door of the opposite pub, leaning gracefully on his stick and gazing at the windows of our house. We stood watching for about a quarter of an hour, fully expecting to see the police appear; the room had gradually filled with the lodgers, all on the *qui vive*, and jabbering fluently in foreign tongues. As nobody came and all seemed quiet, Bonafede and I returned upstairs to reassure Matthieu.

In a few minutes we heard a ring at the door.

" It is they ! " we exclaimed, and Matthieu leapt to the window, whilst Bonafede rushed to the door, which burst open, giving admittance to a strange-looking figure. The new-comer had the slight build and nervous carriage of a Frenchman, but was got up in the most aggressively British attire. Clean-shaven, with a short bulldog pipe in the corner of his mouth, a billycock hat set rather jauntily on his head, a short, drab-coloured overcoat of horsy cut, black and white check trousers, red-skin riding gloves, square-toed walking shoes, a light cane, and a rose in his buttonhole; you would have taken him at first sight for a sporting tipster. Matthieu, who had stopped short at this sudden apparition, and Bonafede, both stood staring in amazement. The new-comer looked at them with a wicked twinkle in his eye, and burst out into a hearty laugh.

"Why, it is you, Sylvestre," the Italian at last said, whilst Matthieu jumped down into the room. "But what on earth have you done to yourself? I should never have recognised you?"

"Ah! so I look in character, then? If you did not recognise me no wonder that I was able to take in those gaping clodhoppers, fresh from their turnip-fields, in the street below. I have news for you. Just listen," but here he broke off, for, looking round the room, he had caught sight of me (I had stood speechless in a corner whilst this scene was enacted). "First though, my dear fellow, I must beg you to introduce me to the lady. The emotions of the moment seem to have made you and Matthieu forget all manners."

Bonafede turned smilingly towards me, and introduced us: "Armand Sylvestre, a French comrade; Isabel Meredith, editor of the *Tocsin*."

The Frenchman made me an elegant and pro-found bow in strange contrast with his sporting appearance, removing his hat, which he had till then kept on.

"But what has happened to you, Sylvestre?" exclaimed Matthieu. "Your hair has turned purple."

"Oh, for Heaven's sake don't look at my hair. A most awful fate has befallen it. Yesterday I heard from Cotteaux that you intended leaving soon, so I settled to come down here this morning, and thought it would be as well to disguise myself; one never knows, one can sometimes get such a lot of fun out of those heavy-witted, pudding-eating police. So I asked Marie to go into a West End hairdresser's and procure some black hair-dye, as I know my gold locks are well known to our friends below. She asked for some, explaining that it was for theatricals, and last night I tried it. With what result you see!—and mind I only made up my mind to come out after washing it some dozen times. Now, with a hat on, it's not very noticeable, but if you could have seen it last night; it had turned the real imperial shade of purple! It was a sight for the gods!"

We all laughed heartily at his adventure, the humour of which was heightened by the mock pathos and tragedy with which he narrated it. But Matthieu, who was straining his ears to catch the slightest sound downstairs, asked him to proceed with his news.

"*Oh, mais vous savez, mademoiselle, votre pays*

est tout-à-fait épatant," he began, turning to me.
"As I came down the street I noticed Deveril
speaking with those two satellites of his outside
the 'Cat and Mouse.' I at once guessed something
was up here, and thought I would try and pump
them, so I walked into the bar and asked in my
best English accent for a whisky and soda, throwing down a half-sovereign to pay for it, and began
talking about racing bets with the barman. As
I expected, after a few minutes, Limpet entered,
asking for a glass of bitter ; he soon got interested
in our talk. I was giving tips with the air of a
Newmarket jockey, and as he had finished his
drink I offered to treat him. He hesitated, saying
that he was in a hurry, and I then pumped the
whole tale out of him, how he and his comrade
were watching this house, where they had reason
to know that a dangerous French Anarchist was
concealed, and so forth and so on.

"'But,' I said, 'if this is so, why do you not get
a warrant to search the house?' And he then
explained to me that the inspector had wished so
to do, but that the magistrate, spite of his entreaties, had refused to sign the warrant because
it was Sunday ! ! Yes, this is an extraordinary
country. Society must be saved, but before everything the Sabbath must not be broken. *C'est
delicieux !* Having gained this information, I
politely wished him good day, and walked over

to this house. You should have seen the faces of
those two men.   I expect their mouths are open
still."

We all stared at each other at this information.
This, then, was the secret of the situation. The
English Sunday had saved our comrade ! Bonafede
went downstairs to summon the Combrissons and
relieve their minds. We had now nearly twenty-
four hours before us ; it was certain that till nine
o'clock on Monday morning the search-warrant
would not be signed. In this interval Matthieu
must leave the house, but how ?

Sylvestre, who evidently looked upon the whole
question as a good joke—*une bonne blague*—suggested that the dynamitard should dress up in his
sporting attire ; he urged that the detectives had
seen him enter and could not be surprised at his
leaving, and that this would be the best solution
of the difficulty. The idea seemed feasible, and
it was tried on.   Matthieu got into the check
trousers and horsy overcoat, but the effect was
too ludicrous, and he was the first to laugh at
the figure he cut in the looking-glass. Something
else must be found. Madame Combrisson came
to the rescue. She reminded us of a Jewish
comrade, also a tailor by trade, who was not unlike Matthieu, being slightly hunchbacked. Her
idea was to get him round, dress him in the
fugitive's clothes, let Bonafede call a cab in an

ostentatious style, into which the false Matthieu
was to jump and drive off; the detectives would
probably follow on their bicycles, and then was
our opportunity. Only, how to get this man on
to the scene without his advent being noticed by
them ? For if he were seen to enter, the game
was up; his exit would not cause surprise. We
were still face to face with the same difficulty, and
Matthieu once more began to pace the room like a
wild beast in a cage.

Sylvestre broke the silence. "The only way out
of the difficulty is to disguise our man. Dress him
up as a woman ; he will then enter without causing
observation."

In a few minutes all was settled. I was to leave
with the hand-bag in which I had brought in the
jewellery to be pawned ; but this time it was to
contain a dress belonging to Madame Combrisson.
With this I was to proceed to the lodging of the
Jewish comrade, Yoski, taking care to lose on the
way any detective who might be following me.
Yoski was to dress himself in the woman's clothes,
and return with me to Grafton Street, care being
taken that the detectives should notice his entry.
He was then to exchange his female attire for
Matthieu's clothes and drive off in a cab, as previously arranged, and then Matthieu, in his turn
donning the skirt and blouse, was to leave the
house on my arm, whilst the police would be rush-

ing after a red-herring. Sylvestre turned a somersault to express his joy, and, slapping Matthieu on the shoulder, said, "Why, before long, *mon vieux*, you will again be treading the flags of Paris, and, let us hope, frightening the bourgeois out of their wits."

By two o'clock I was on my way. When I left the house Deveril was talking with O'Brien over the way; Limpet had disappeared for the time being. The inspector at once noticed my presence, and, calling to a corner-boy lounging at the public-house door, he spoke to him, pointing me out, and this "copper's nark" followed doggedly in my steps. Yoski lived in a turning off the Mile-End Road, but anxious to give no inkling as to my destination, I turned in the opposite direction, and after a lengthy *détour* stopped at my own door. I stayed indoors nearly an hour, hoping that my attendant's patience would give out, but he showed no signs of moving, time was precious, and I decided to set out once more. This time I walked down the Euston Road to the beginning of Marylebone Road, where I jumped on to a 'bus going towards Maida Vale. The youth did likewise, and at the beginning of the Kilburn High Street I descended, making my way up that dreary road. I began to despair of ridding myself of my pursuer. I was miles out of my way, the hours were passing, and he still dogged my steps. I trudged along,

M

weary and worried, weighed down with the responsibility of my position. Suddenly my eyes caught
sight of a solitary hansom coming slowly towards
me, I hurried forward, the youth was some paces
behind me on the other side of the road, and before
he had time to realise what I was up to I had
boarded that hansom and shouted to the cabman,
"Five shillings, if you set me down at Baker Street
Station in ten minutes," and away we went. I
looked out of the spy window in the back of the
cab and saw my "nark" standing staring in the
middle of the road. At Baker Street I took a ticket
for the Edgeware Road and there I jumped into a
train for Aldgate Station. When I once more found
myself in the streets I looked carefully around me
and to my relief was able to assure myself that no
one was following me. Taking a circuitous route,
for greater precaution, I at last reached my destination.

I seemed to be in a foreign country. Dark-eyed
comely women and pretty children, dressed in gay
colours, were walking up and down. The shop-signs
and advertisements were mostly written in Hebrew
characters, loud conversation in a foreign language
accompanied by vivacious gesticulation, caught the
ear. The narrow, dirty street was swarming with
inhabitants, the front doors were mostly open, and
many people had placed chairs on the doorsteps
and pavement and were sitting out, though it would

be an euphemism to speak of enjoying the fresh air in such a neighbourhood. The house at which I stopped was a six-roomed "cottage," but whilst I stood on the doorstep, waiting to gain admittance, at least fourteen persons passed in and out. At last a wizened old woman, scrutinising me suspiciously, answered my inquiries.

"Yoski! yes, he live on the tird floor back, vis his vife and schwester. Yes, you will find him in."

Yoski was a small, unhealthy-looking man, not much unlike Matthieu, though darker in colouring, and of a weaker type of face. He was a serious, silent, earnest man, a model of solidarity, regularly setting aside his weekly contribution to the Cause out of his meagre earning on which he had to maintain a wife and four children and a young sister. They all lived in the one room, but one felt that this did not cause them any suffering; they were evidently used to it. The three grown-ups were all at work when I entered, and the children clustered round like inquisitive little animals. I explained briefly my identity and the object of my visit, talking English, which was not understood by his female relatives. He nodded gravely, and said: "But I cannot change here; it would cause too much curiosity. I will tell my wife that I must go with you for some work, and I will go into the room of a friend of mine who is out and dress there." He did as he said and we left the room together.

On the landing I handed him the bag. "Is every-thing here ? " he inquired, "hat and all ? "

The hat ! Who had thought of it ? And yet without that it was impossible to go out.

"Cannot you get at your wife's or your sister's ?" I inquired.

"Impossible," he replied, " they would never give me a moment's peace till they knew why I wanted it. You might, however, try with Rebecca Wies-mann ; she is a comrade and lives two streets farther down. Do not, however, tell her all this matter ; make up some story and see if you can manage."

Much doubting my success, I went round to Rebecca's. I had seen her sometimes at meetings, but I felt that she would be surprised at my appear-ance, and still more at my errand. Still there was nothing for it, the shops were all shut, and so I went round to her. This girl lived alone, having separated from her parents, who were strictly ortho-dox and intolerant Jews. She was indeed taken aback at seeing me, but did not like to refuse my request. I told her that I was expected at a com-rade's house, that I had been followed by detectives and wished to lose sight of them, and she, with the foreign Jews' dread of policemen as omnipotent be-ings, swallowed the tale and provided me with a showy best hat quite unlike my own. This I donned and left with my own in a paper under my arm, in spite of her pressing offer to keep it for me.

In a few minutes I was knocking at the door Yoski had pointed out to me. I found him ready, carefully shaved of his moustache, and quite transformed in appearance. The hat and veil completed the disguise. By six o'clock we were in Grafton Street. I was relieved to find that Deveril had left, and that only Limpet and O'Brien were on guard. They took a good stare at us as we passed them by.

Combrisson himself opened to us. "Oh, here you are at last. We began to fear you would never come. It has been as much as we could do to prevent Matthieu from spoiling everything by making a rush for it. Come in, there is not a moment to lose. Deveril may be back any minute, and he's not so easily gulled as those two mugs."

We found Matthieu in a state of great nervous excitement. The long, anxious hours of waiting had told on him. A nervous twitch convulsed his mouth. He jumped spasmodically to his feet as we entered the room. "At last," exclaimed Bonafede, with a sigh of relief on seeing us. "Now, Matthieu," he said, laying a hand encouragingly on the man's shoulder, "there is no time to be lost. Isabel will go downstairs whilst you two exchange clothes. As soon as you are ready I will fetch the cabs. Be courageous, and, above all, calm, and in half-an-hour all will be over."

I went downstairs with Madame Combrisson, and we paced nervously up and down the front parlour. Every other minute one of us went to look out of the window. It was nearly dark. The street lamps were lighting up, and still the two detectives watched on the other side of the road.

"Where is Sylvestre?" I at last inquired, to break the tense silence.

"Who knows? He left about half-an-hour ago, saying he would soon be back. He is off on some madcap expedition, you may be sure. He is a dreadful *farceur*."

At that moment no fewer than three barrel-organs came up the street, stopped nearly opposite the house, and started playing "The man who broke the bank at Monte Carlo," and other similar classics. I was at the window and saw Sylvestre go gravely up to the detectives, bow, say a few words, and cross over to our door. Madame rushed out to open to him.

"So here you are, Mademoiselle. All is well, I hope?" he inquired.

I nodded assent.

"Oh, what a game it will be to see their faces to-morrow when Deveril comes round with his warrant! Meanwhile, I was sure those poor devils were boring themselves to death, so I went down to the Italian quarter and brought back these musicians. I have just told them that I hope the music will help them to pass a pleasant half-hour."

Just then Bonafede came down, followed by the false Matthieu. The lower part of his face was concealed in a muffler, and the illusion was really very deceptive.

"I am going now for the cab," said the Italian. As soon as I return Yoski must hurry out, jump in rapidly, and drive off. I shall be waiting for you, Isabel, and Matthieu with a cab just by Shoolbred's; time to leave the house five minutes after the departure of Yoski. Here is Matthieu; you, Madame Combrisson, see if his dress is right; now I am going."

"Wait a minute," exclaimed Sylvestre, "give me a bottle of whisky and two glasses, I will go over and offer some to the 'tecs; it will look as if I am trying to distract their attention from Bonafede and the cab, and will lend truth to the scene."

All passed off to perfection. As the hansom drew up, Sylvestre, with a polite bow, offered a drink to Limpet and O'Brien. The latter caught sight of the cab, just as the false Matthieu hurriedly jumped in, and, pushing the Frenchman roughly aside, he leapt on his bicycle and rushed off in pursuit just as the cab disappeared round the street corner. Bonafede had quietly slipped off down the Tottenham Court Road. Limpet was pacing up and down distractedly, uncertain whether to stick to his post or join his comrade in pursuit. In five minutes' time I quietly walked out, arm in arm with Matthieu, turning round on the doorstep to shake hands with Madame Combrisson. We walked boldly past Limpet, and were soon at Shoolbred's, where I left the dynamitard with Bonafede, and, taking a roundabout walk, returned within half-an-hour to Grafton Street. In an hour's time Bonafede joined us. "All is well!" he exclaimed; "within a couple of hours our comrade will be safe in Leicester. It has been an anxious day, but it has ended better than I had dared hope for."

"And now let us get some dinner," broke in Sylvestre, "I am just fainting with hunger. Here is a sovereign, Madame; see if you can get us something fit to eat, though I fear that, with this hateful English Sunday, everything will be shut."

"Do not abuse the English Sunday," rejoined Bonafede, "to its sanctity we owe our friend's escape."

We were soon enjoying a supper which Madame Combrisson got in from the neighbouring Italian restaurant. We were all in high spirits, and laughed and chatted freely. Limpet, and O'Brien who had returned after satisfying himself as to the true identity of the false Matthieu, who had driven straight home, kept pacing up and down in front of the area railings, evidently half suspecting that we had played them a trick.

All that night we sat round the kitchen fire, chatting and dozing alternately.   At midnight Deveril came, accompanied by two other officers, who relieved Limpet and O'Brien.   The next morning, as the clock hands pointed to 9.15, a loud rat-tat resounded through the house.   Deveril, with our two friends of the previous day, accompanied by three uniformed policemen, were on the door-step.   Combrisson opened to them with his most engaging smile.   He politely read the warrant which the inspector handed him, and bowed him in, saying that he was happy that he should per-suade himself that Matthieu was not, and never had been, on the premises.   Deveril seemed rather taken aback by this reception, but was too sure of his case to feel much doubt.

Never shall I forget that man's face when, after a three hours' hunt in every hole and corner of the building he had to come down persuaded that his victim had escaped him.

He was perfectly green with rage.   Turning to Bonafede who, with us others, was sitting in the front parlour, he said, " Well, Signore, you have been one too much for me on this occasion, but remember, he laughs best who laughs last.   We shall doubtless meet again soon."

Bonafede merely shrugged his shoulders and turned aside, whilst the crestfallen Limpet, who had evidently received a severe wigging from his superior for allowing his quarry to escape, turned on me a look of intense hatred and hissed out,

"Remember, miss, you may not always be in London ; you will yet pay me for this !" and with this melodramatic threat he and his comrades departed amidst the jeers of the assembled lodgers.

In the street they were met by deafening shouts of "Vive Deveril ! Hurrah for the detective force !" Sylvestre, who had slipped out a few minutes before the arrival of the police, had assembled in the road all the Italian comrades of the *Tocsin* group, several Frenchmen of his own acquaintance, and four or five organ-grinders, and amidst the ironic cheers of their enemies, the dejected guardians of law and order made their shamefaced exit from the scene.

CHAPTER IX

SOME ANARCHIST PERSONALITIES

THERE has been of late years a remarkable, and, on the whole, a very futile tendency among certain men of science to dissect and classify abnormal people and abnormal ideas, to discover that geniuses are mad, and that all manner of well-intentioned fanatics are born criminals.

But there were elements in the Anarchist party which defied the science of the psychological analyst, so strangely and intricately were the most heterogeneous qualities blended in certain of their number—fanaticism, heroism, criminality, and not unfrequently a spicing of genius.

The primary difference between the ordinary normal man and the fanatic—as between the normal man and the madman or the genius—is the totally different standpoint whence each views life. This it is which renders it impossible for the normal man really to understand or judge fanatics. He cannot grasp their motive, their point of view, and is therefore morally incapable of judging them.

Among the Anarchists, who may be said to re-present the intellectual rather than the material side of the Socialist movement—there were many fanatics. This fanaticism showed itself in different ways—sometimes in the most admirable self-abnegation, in the sacrifice of wealth, position, and happiness ; frequently in abnormal actions of other kinds, and most noticeably in deeds of violence.

Very diverse in nature were the motives which prompted the committal of these acts of violence —these assassinations and dynamite explosions— in different men. With some it was an act of personal revolt, the outcome of personal sufferings and wrongs endured by the rebel himself, by his family or his class. In others violence was rather the offspring of ideas, the logical result of speculation upon the social evil and the causes thereof. These Anarchists referred to their actions as Propaganda by Deed.

Émile Henry, the dynamitard of the Café Terminus, belonged to the number of what I may call the theoretical dynamitard. His terrible acts were the outcome of long and earnest thought ; they were born of his mental analysis of the social canker. He committed them not in moments of passion, but with all the *sang froid* of a man governed by reason. His defence when on trial was a masterpiece of logical deduction and eloquent reasoning.

To the average man it is no doubt very difficult to conceive that when he threw his bomb among the crowd in the Café Terminus, maiming and killing indiscriminately, Émile Henry was performing his duty according to his own lights just as much as a soldier when he obeys orders and fires on the enemy, a city man when he embarks on the day's business, or a parson when he preaches a sermon against prevailing vices. It was his sermon—however vigorously preached—against the prevailing vices and injustices of Society, and against the indifference which all classes displayed towards these. He took upon himself to strike a blow against this indifference on behalf of all the weaker and more unfortunate members of society. Being a man of intellect and some culture, he could not, like his more ignorant *confrères*, imagine that one man or one small group of men, was responsible for these. Earnest thought and reflection told him that if any section of society suffered, then society at large was guilty: all the thoughtless, all the indifferent members of society were equally responsible for its abuses. Now this may be true enough theoretically, but no one but a fanatic or a madman would carry the reasoning farther to the point of saying: "Society at large is guilty; society at large must suffer. Society is fairly well represented by the mixed crowd in a café. I

will attack this crowd indiscriminately, and kill as
many of their number as I can. I will unreluct-
antly end my days on the scaffold in order to
accomplish this very obvious duty; " and proceed
from words to deeds.

There is something terribly, if pervertedly logical
in this reasoning, and although nothing could be
farther from the attitude of the ordinary delinquent,
it is no doubt more dangerous to the peace and
continuance of society; and such was the attitude
and the reasoning which rendered the Anarchists so
formidable, and which led up to many of their
most terrible outrages. Émile Henry was in his
own way a well-meaning youth; kindly in private
life, frugal in his habits; studious, industrious, and
free from vice, he lived with his old mother and
mixed little with his fellows, and no one who knew
him could have suspected that this quiet, studious
boy would have developed into the terrible assassin
whose act sent a thrill of horror through the
world.

To Anarchists of this order, abstract ideas and
opinions replaced all the ordinary forces of life.
Their every action was prompted by some theory,
and they fashioned their lives to fit their peculiar
views of what it ought to be. Émile Henry
belonged to this number no less than Kosinski,
Bonafede, and certain so-called Christian Anarchists.
For in some fanatics the Anarchist ideas, instead of

leading to violence, led to the absolute negation and rejection of it.

Among the many frequenters of our office and of the weekly discussion meetings held there, was a Christian Anarchist, one of those holding what was known as the "non-resistance to evil" creed. He, too, was a man who fitted his life to his ideas, who lived in ideas, whose whole being centred round his ideas. He was a religious fanatic whose course had deviated into strange paths.

Norbery was a pale, anxious-looking Lancashire man, with weak, restless eyes and a resolute mouth, who did not lack a certain dignity of bearing.

Both the organisationists and the individualists united in abusing and despising the Christian Norbery, but no amount of insults or invective ruffled his temper or aroused his wrath. "When you preach force or use force," he said to his opponents, "you imitate the very methods used by Governments. You will never attain universal peace and brotherhood by such means. As Anarchists we have no right to use other than passive resistance, for by using coercion we are defeating our own ends and justifying the actions of our persecutors."

The more indignant his Anarchist opponents became in the course of debate, the calmer and more complacent grew Norbery. "Abuse me," he would say, "insult me, use violence towards

me, if you will; I shall turn the other cheek."
Once a hot-headed Italian Anarchist lost patience
with him and threw him downstairs. He lay
where he fell with a sprained ankle, repeating
good words from the Sermon on the Mount, until
his adversary, overcome with shame and remorse,
picked him up and bandaged his injured limb.
Once during certain strike riots in the North of
England, Norbery journeyed to the scene of
trouble to preach passive measures and the
Anarchist principles to the rioters. He was
dragged from his platform by the police and badly
hustled and knocked about. But Norbery was
determined on having his say; he procured a
chain and padlock, chained himself to a lamp-
post, threw away the key, and resumed the interrupted course of his harangue. A large crowd
gathered round the persistent orator, attracted
partly by his eloquence and partly by the novelty
of his situation. The police hurried to the scene
and tried to drag him down; his coat and shirt,
torn to shreds, remained in their hands, while the
semi-naked Anarchist preached away to the constantly increasing crowd. The officers of the law
foamed with rage, and threatened and pommelled
the enchained and defenceless Norbery. Norbery
grew more eloquent and more argumentative
under this treatment. Nearly an hour passed
before a file could be procured and the chain

severed, and by that time Norbery had ample opportunity to finish his discourse, and was conveyed to the police station in a fainting and exhausted condition.

Armitage and I engaged in endless discussions with Norbery on the question of violence, maintaining on our side that violence could only be overcome by violence, and that, however peaceful our ultimate aims might be, force must inevitably be used towards their attainment. We argued and adduced reasons in support of our views, and Norbery argued and adduced counter-reasons in support of his views, but neither the one nor the other of us was ever in the least affected by his opponent's eloquence, and at the end of the discussion we were all, if anything, more staunchly persuaded of the sense and justice of our own case than at the start. So much for the profitableness of debate between confirmed partisans.

Émile Henry was representative of the theoretical dynamitard ; Matthieu, like Ravachol, of the dynamitard by passion. A——, who belonged rather to the Ravachol type, and ended by killing one of the crowned heads of Europe, was during a few weeks a frequenter of the *Tocsin*. He had turned Anarchist in revolt against the society which had cramped his life, starved him in childhood, overworked his body, underfed his mind, where he had found neither place nor welcome.

N

Born into the lowest depths of society, dragged up amid criminals and drunkards, he had spent his early years between the streets and the jail-house, at times working his undeveloped muscles, at other times begging or picking pockets.

"It is all very well," he said to me one day, "for those on the top rungs of the ladder to talk of the unrelenting laws of nature and the survival of the fittest. For my part I have felt very forcibly one great law of nature, the law of self-preservation : the right to live when you have once been born, the right to food and to the pleasures of life, and I determined to survive at all costs. When my stomach is empty and my boots let in water, the mere sight of a replete and well-clothed man makes me feel like murder. It may be true that it is natural for the strongest and the best men to rise above their fellows, but even this is not the case in our society of to-day. The weakest and the worst have somehow got to the top, and giants are bolstering up the impotence of dwarfs. These dwarfs are crushing the life-blood out of us. We must pull them down, exterminate them ; we must turn the whole world upside down before we can create a new and better order of things."

His action was not a theoretical protest translated into deeds ; it was an act of vengeance, of personal and class revenge.

Giannoli was a type apart. His desires and

actions were responsible for his views. They coloured and distorted his opinions and destroyed all sense of proportion. An incident in his private life would stand up giant-like in the way of all the doctrines in the world, dwarfing opinions and creeds. He was a physically active man and his ideas grew out of his life, whereas men like Kosinski might be said to abandon the material life in the pursuit of an ideal.

Giacomo Giannoli was a man of some education, and no ordinary degree of natural refinement and culture, one whom you would pronounce at first sight to be a gentleman. He was the son of a fairly well-to-do builder in a provincial town of Lombardy, and had received a good general education in boyhood. Early left an orphan by his father's death, he had inherited his business, and for some years he carried it on prosperously, living with his mother and sisters. But before he was two-and-twenty his naturally erratic disposition asserted itself, and he chafed under the restraints and monotony of life in a small provincial town. He sold up his business at a great loss, well-nigh ruining his family, had it not been for his mother's small private means ; and with his share of the proceeds of the sale he travelled about for some years, leading a roving life, and devoting most of his time and cash to the Anarchist propaganda, constantly getting into troubles and bothers, at times in hiding, at others in prison, always in difficulties, growing harder and harder up as the months went by, and his moderate means slipped through his untenacious fingers.

Two convergent factors had led up to this sudden change in his life. Firstly, an incident of a private nature which revolutionised his notions of individual morality, and secondly, the discovery of the Anarchist doctrines which gave form to his new views. The incident which was primarily responsible for his new views of life, he recounted to me not long after his arrival in London.

"It was a woman," he said, "who completely altered my views of life, and made me see how perverted and unnatural are our ideas of sex and love and morals, and, in short, of everything. She was an ignorant peasant girl who lived in a neighbouring village, but a woman of rare mind and character. I shall never forget her, nor what I owe her. I was a young fellow of some twenty-one years at the time, and I loved this girl with all the passion and faith of a youth of those years. Teresina loved me in return, and for some two years we lived on happily till one day it was brought to my knowledge that she was unfaithful to me. I was beside myself with grief and mortification and jealous fury. For some hours I just raged up and down my room like one demented, crying like a child one minute, cursing and meditating revenge the next. I felt that I must have blood at all costs to appease my passion—Teresina's or her lover's, or somebody's. I was to meet Teresina that evening as usual towards nine o'clock, and I thought the intervening hours would never go by. One hope suddenly suggested itself to me, and I clung desperately to it. 'Perhaps it is false!' I said to myself. 'I will ask Teresina. It is all a lie,' and then 'Proofs, proofs, I must have proofs!' I cried, and once more my thoughts turned back to murder. Thus I went through the long hours, and at last evening came—a beautiful warm May evening, and long before the appointed hour I was at our rendezvous in a deserted *podere* on the mountain-side, overgrown with flags and other spring flowers, among which the fireflies were flitting noiselessly. I had no eyes for the beauty of the scene, however. I paced up and down waiting for my sweetheart, cursing the treachery of women and the blindness of men. Suddenly she appeared, dark against the clear evening sky, graceful, gay, and unconscious as ever. Without a word of welcome I rushed at her, seized her by the arm, and hurled forth all my accusations and all my reproaches.

"'Tell me it is not true,' I cried at last, 'tell me it is not true, or I will kill you where you stand!'

"I expected the usual routine of tears and pro-

testations of innocence, all the lies and subterfuges
with which women are wont to defend themselves
against the unreasoning savagery of their mates.
I was disappointed.   Teresina stood perfectly silent
till I had finished speaking ; then without flinching,
without one instant's hesitation, she answered, ' It
is true.   Every word of it is true.'

" If the moon and the stars had all dropped
simultaneously out of heaven at my feet I should
not have been more astonished.   The calmness of
her answer, the steady earnestness of her gaze as
she looked back fearlessly into my eyes, her utter
lack of subterfuge, took away my breath.   I dropped
her arm and stood staring at her, bereft of speech
and understanding.   At last I blurted out stupidly
that I did not understand her, that I must be going
mad, and entreated her to explain.

" ' I said it was true ; that I love Giordano, and
have accepted his love,' she answered.   Still I did
not fully grasp her meaning.

" ' But, Teresina, I thought that you loved me ;
have you lied to me then ? ' I exclaimed.

" ' No, I have not lied,' she answered me.   ' I have
never lied to you,' and she took my hand in her
strong little hand, and led me like one blind or
intoxicated to the projecting root of a tree close
by, and there sat down by my side.

" ' Listen,' she said, still holding my hand in hers,
' I ought to have told you what I have to say before

now. I only hesitated because I knew it would cause you acute suffering at first . . . until you could understand. Believe me, I do love you as much as ever I did, and I could not bear even the thought of living without you. I love Giordano too, in a different way it is true, but still I love him. He has not got your mind or your heart, or your wonderful knowledge' (she was a very ignorant girl, so far as learning was concerned, and my small knowledge of books appeared to her little short of miraculous, poor child!), 'but then he has some qualities you do not possess. Well, I love him for these, and I enjoy being with him in a quite different way from what I experience with you.'

"I was silent, and she continued after a short pause :—

"'Nothing is more brutish or more selfish than jealousy, my friend. If I thought another woman could give you a moment's happiness, I should say: "Take it, enjoy it!" We do not grudge our friends every moment of enjoyment not enjoyed in our company. We wish them other friendships and other joys. What is there in the love between man and woman which should make us so selfish and so unreasonable? For my part, I must have freedom at all costs, absolutely at all costs. It is dearer to me than anything else in life, and I had sooner sacrifice even love and happiness; indeed, I cannot love or be happy without it. For God's sake grant me this liberty as I grant it to you ! Take my love as I can give it to you, but do not ask me to be your slave on its account ! Be sure you have my heart, and little of it remains to be squandered in other directions. What does the rest matter ? I do not grudge you your loves, your pleasures, your caprices ! Do not grudge me mine. Life is necessarily full of sorrows ; do not let us embitter it unnecessarily.'

" She ceased speaking. She had risen to her feet and stood in front of me as she spoke, then as she finished she sank down on her knees by my side.

" ' Do you understand ? ' she asked me. ' Can you love me on these terms ? liberty—absolute liberty for us both ? '

" I answered ' Yes,' nor did I ever regret the answer.

" I think that was the most momentous day in my life, for it wrought the greatest change in me. My eyes were opened by the peasant girl's words, and from that evening forward I regarded life quite differently. For the first time I realised the necessity to the individual to enjoy absolute personal freedom in love as in all else in life. All my previous ideas and prejudices appeared to me monstrous and iniquitous. I saw the falseness of all our ideas of morality, the absurdity of placing conventions before nature and the detestable character of our dealings with women and of our attitude in such matters.

And with this suddenly awakened vision I looked anew on life, and it seemed to me that till then I had never lived. All that which I had before taken for granted I now began to question. I found that instead of thinking out life's problems for myself I had allowed myself to grow into other peoples' ideas, that I had tacitly taken for right what they had pronounced right, and for wrong what they had stigmatised as wrong. My spiritual world now turned, as it were, a complete somersault, and I was re-born a new man—an Anarchist.

"I and Teresina and Giordano lived very happily for some months, much to the scandal of the narrow-minded, bigoted village folk, until I was compelled to absent myself from the country owing to some little disturbances in the neighbourhood in which I had got implicated.

"Teresina followed me into exile, and with little intermission remained with me during all those early years of wanderings and adventure. She cared little about Anarchist doctrines, though herself a born rebel and an innate Anarchist. She did more for me than all the doctrines in the world. Poor child! When at last I got through all my money, and life from day to day grew harder and more precarious, food scantier, clothes raggeder, and surroundings more dangerous, she still remained faithful to me in her own way, but the life was too hard for her. We had spent the summer

in Paris, and there I had got seriously implicated
in a little Anarchist venture and found it necessary
to flee the country with all haste. Teresina followed me into Belgium in the bitter winter weather.
She died of consumption in a Brussels hospital
shortly after our arrival."

Such, in his own words, were the influences and
the circumstances which revolutionised Giannoli's
entire life and his outlook on things. He became
one of the leaders of the most advanced section of
the "Individualist Anarchists," who maintain that
not only is government of man by man wrong and
objectionable, but that no ties or obligations of any
sort bind men together. The ethics of "humanity"
and "brotherhood" are unknown to these Anarchists.
They recognise no laws, social or moral, no obligations or duties towards their fellows, no organisation
or association of any sort. They claim absolute
freedom for the individual, freedom to live, die,
love, enjoy, think, work, or take—this freedom in
each individual only curtailed by others claiming
equal rights. And I am bound to admit that the
question whether such individual freedom would
not tend to individual licence and domination by
the stronger and cleverer or more unscrupulous
man in the future, met with little consideration.

That it led to such licence in the present among
themselves was an indubitable fact. All the individualist Anarchists agreed that, being at war

with existing society, which interfered with, co-
erced, and used violence towards them, they were
at liberty to use all means against society in re-
taliation—force and even fraud if expedient. But
the less intelligent and more ignorant men who
came in contact with these principles considered
themselves not only at liberty to use all means
against society, the enemy; but honour or scruples
of any sort among themselves were tabooed. A
naturally honourable man like Giannoli was, of
course, free from the danger of falling victim to
such perverted sophistry. But the manner in
which these doctrines succeeded in perverting the
minds of fairly intelligent and well-meaning men
is illustrated by the following incident.

One evening, some months after the advent of
Giannoli and his friends, there arrived at the office
of the *Tocsin* a small party of three men and one
woman—all of them Spaniards. They requested
me to help them to procure lodgings for the night,
and, as they knew nothing of the English language,
to assist them the following morning in procuring
tickets, etc., with a view to their immediate re-
departure for the States. Giannoli, who knew the
men, having spent some years in Spain, explained
to me that the leader of the party, a handsome,
well-spoken young man, was an engineer belonging
to a good Barcelona family. The second one, a
good-natured giant, was his brother and an en-

gineer like himself. The third male member of
the party was a lanky, scrofulous journalist, a man
of many words and few wits. The lady, a pretty
brunette, was their "compagna." She had escaped
from her family and eloped with Fernandez, the
engineer, but was apparently shared on communistic
principles.

I settled the party for the night in a small hotel
and procured their tickets for the morrow's journey,
after which they proceeded to hand over to Giannoli,
with many cautions and precautions, a mysterious
linen bag which, it was whispered, contained some
twelve thousand lire in bank-notes (about five
hundred pounds sterling). Then, having been
assured by Giannoli that I was to be trusted, they
told me their story.

The two brothers, the engineers, had till quite
recently been employed by a large electrical engin-
eering firm in Barcelona, of which an elder brother,
some years their senior, was the manager. For
some time the two younger men had been engaged,
unknown to their family, in Anarchist propaganda,
and had fallen in with the section of the *in-
dividualisti*. Fernandez was in love with Adolfa,
the daughter of a well-to-do merchant, and had
secretly talked her over to his own ideas. The
girl's parents objected to the match on account
of the extreme youth of the couple—the girl was
not quite eighteen and the young man still con-

siderably under age. Therefore they settled to
elope, and Fernandez's brother and Vanni, their
journalist friend, expressed a desire to form an
addition to the elopement. This Fernandez had at
first objected to, but the girl, who had made rapid
strides into the Giannolian free-love theories, insisted. Lack of money formed the only obstacle
to this scheme, but an unforeseen circumstance
enabled them to remove it.

The eldest brother, who had charge of the finances
of the establishment, and whose business it was to
pay the men their wages, wished to absent himself
from the works for a few days, and, without the
knowledge of his employers, he broke rules to the
extent of handing over to his brother Fernandez,
as to one beyond suspicion, the men's wages—the
five hundred pounds now contained in the
mysterious linen bag.

"Now," argued Fernandez to himself, "I, as
an Anarchist, do not recognise private property,
nor any set moral laws. The company's money
is the result of plunder; they can afford to lose
it and have no right to it; I stand desperately
in need of it—and it is in my hands. . . . My
brother? . . . oh, my brother, he is after all
nothing but a bourgeois, and I, as an Anarchist,
admit of no family ties."

Thus when, two days later, the unfortunate
manager returned, he found his brothers gone,

the money nowhere to be found, and disgrace and ruin ahead. Driven to despair, and not knowing in what direction to turn for the necessary sum, the wretched man ended his perplexities with a bullet. This was the first news which greeted the runaways on their arrival in the States.

Now the younger brothers who had perpetrated this cruel thing were not hardened criminals. From what little I saw of them, they appeared to be kindly, courteous, and, by nature, fairly honourable men. What they lacked was moral strength. Under ordinarily good influences they would have acted in an ordinarily proper way. They had not the force of character necessary for handling the Anarchist individualist doctrines, which, excellently as they may work with men of character, are fatal to weaker men. The man who recognises no law outside himself must be capable of governing himself.

The office of the *Tocsin* was the constant scene of debate and dispute between the two rival camps in the Anarchist party—the organisationists and the individualists. Bonafede and Gnecco belonged to the former, while most of the active staff of the *Tocsin*—myself among others—adhered to the latter section. A curious feature of the matter —and I fancy it is not exclusively characteristic of the Anarchist party—was the amount of invective

and hatred, which both factions ought properly
to have expended on the common enemy, but
which instead they spent most of their time in
levelling at one another. A casual witness of
these internal strifes might have imagined that
the two parties were at the antipodes in their
ideas and objects, rather than comrades and parti-
cipators in a common belief. Their dissensions
were alone forgotten in a common hatred of
government and existing society. And even in
their efforts to upraise the social revolution—the
great upheaval to which all Anarchists aspired—
I doubt whether there lurked not some secret
hope that the detested rival faction might be de-
molished in the fray. Bonafede and Giannoli
were warm friends personally, and held one another in great esteem. Yet I can clearly recollect
Giannoli one evening, with tears in his eyes, assuring me that his first duty when the Revolution
broke out would be to bisembowel his dear
friend.

"He is my friend," Giannoli said to me, "and
I love him as such, and as a man I admire him.
But his doctrines are noxious; in time of Revolution they would prove fatal to our Cause; they
would be the undoing of all the work for which
we have suffered and fought. Organise a Revolution, indeed! You might as well attempt to organise a tempest and to marshal the elements into

order ! I know Bonafede to be above personal ambition, but, take my word for it, most of these organisationists hope to organise themselves into comfortable places when their time comes ! It is our duty to destroy them."

CHAPTER X

A FLIGHT

No man, having once thrown himself into an idea, was ever more sincerely convinced of the truth of his beliefs or more strenuous in his efforts to propagandise them than Giannoli. To destroy utterly the fabric of existing society by all possible means, by acts of violence and terrorism, by expropriation, by undermining the prevailing ideas of morality, by breaking up the organisations of those Anarchists and Socialists who believed in association, by denouncing such persons and such attempts, by preaching revolution wherever and whenever an opportunity occurred or could be improvised, to these objects he had blindly devoted the best years of his life. His was a gospel of destruction and negation, and he was occupied rather in the undoing of what he had come to regard as bad than with any constructive doctrines.

All existing and established things were alike under his ban : art no less than morals and religion. He nourished a peculiar hatred for all those links which bind the present to the past, for

ancient customs and superstitions, for all tradition.
Had it been in his power he would have destroyed
history itself. "We shall never be free," he used
to say, "so long as one prejudice, one single in-
grained belief, remains with us. We are the slaves
of heredity, and of all manner of notions of duties,
of the licit and the illicit."

One day I took him to the National Gallery.
I was quite unprepared for the effect of this step.
He walked about nervously for some time, looking
from one picture to another with evident displeasure. At last he stopped in front of Leonardo's
"Madonna delle Roccie," and remained gazing at
it for some minutes in silence, while a heavy frown
gathered round his brows. "I hate art," he exclaimed at last. "I consider it one of the most
noxious influences in the world. It is enervating
and deteriorating. Art has always been the slave of
religion and superstition, from the ancient Egyptians
and Assyrians to our own times. You see something beautiful, perhaps, in these pictures, in these
saints and Madonnas and Immaculate Conceptions? Well, when I look at them, all the darkest
pages of history seem to open before me, and
generations upon generations of superstitious slaves,
toiling on and suffering with the ever-present terror
of hell-fires and chastisement, pass before my
mental vision. I should love to burn them all,
to raze all these galleries and museums to the

ground, and libraries with them. For what are libraries but storehouses of human superstition and error? We must free ourselves from the past, free ourselves utterly from its toils, if the future is to be ours. And we shall never free ourselves from the past until we have forgotten it. Let us leave here. I cannot stand it any longer! I do not know which is most repugnant to me, the asceticism of these early Christians or the senseless fantasies of the Greeks," and without further ado he fled.

Fired by this gospel of destruction, he spent his life wandering about Europe, never resting for a month together, wrenching himself free from all those ties which might curtail the freedom of his actions. Although not fashioned by nature for enduring hardships, he alternately suffered cold, hunger, heat, fatigue, privations, and dirt. In Paris one week, making a brief sojourn in Spain the next, fleeing thence under warrant of arrest to find himself some days later in hiding in Italy; at times in prison, always in danger and uncertainty; starving one day, in fairly flourishing conditions the next, never certain what fortune the morrow might bring: thus the years went by, until, escaping from *domicilio coatto*, or worse, in Italy, he had at length made his way to London and the office of the *Tocsin*, quite broken down in health after the long winter tramp. As I knew him, among his few personal friends, Giannoli was loyal and honourable in the extreme, independent and proud. Like many other Anarchists he entertained an almost maniacal prejudice against plots and conspiracies of any kind, maintaining that such organisations were merely police traps and death-gins. "Propaganda by deed"—outrage, in short—they maintained should, and could, be the outcome only of entirely individual activity. Never, indeed, did police or press make a greater blunder than when they attributed deeds of violence to associations and large conspiracies, and sought for or denounced accomplices. Every one of those outrages and assassinations which startled Europe was the act of a single man, unaided by, and frequently unknown to other Anarchists.

This horror of plots and associations was, when I first met him, one of the most noticeable traits about Giannoli. He was beginning to lose his earlier assurance, worn out by the roving life he had led, and was growing suspicious in the extreme. "Such-a-one is a police emissary," or "So-and-so is not to be trusted" were words constantly on his lips.

To me he took a great liking, and he always showed implicit faith in me both as an Anarchist and an individual. "You are a true Anarchist," he said to me one day, "and I would trust you with anything, *even*," and he emphasised the word so as to give greater weight to the compliment, "*even* with *explosives*."

His suspiciousness, however, grew by leaps and bounds during his sojourn in London. Every day he threw out hints against some new person or some fresh imaginary conspiracy. There was a plot brewing, he informed me, among various false comrades to ruin him. He was the victim of a conspiracy to deprive him of his liberty and perhaps even of his life. Not a day passed but some covert threat was made against him; men whom he had believed his comrades, and to whom he—fool that he was!—had confided the deadliest secrets in the past, had given him to understand the power they held over him, and had made it clear that they would avail themselves of it should it serve their purpose. "What fools we Anarchists are," he exclaimed to me one day, "ever to feel any confidence in any one! We are no longer free men when we have done this. We are slaves."

I watched the progress of this monomania with painful interest, for among all the Anarchists there was no individual for whom I entertained a more genuine regard than for Giannoli. One of the worst aspects of the matter, moreover, was that I was really unable to judge how far Giannoli's suspicions were true and how far imaginary. As to his sincerity there was no possibility of doubt, and this lent to all he said an air of verisimilitude which

was most convincing. I did not know the majority
of the other Italians well enough to feel positive as
to their honesty, and many of them were uncertain
and somewhat suspicious characters. Morì, for instance—the youthful Neapolitan already referred to,
the enigmatic "buttered muffin"—was quite incomprehensible. He was a youth of no particular intelligence, and certainly of no ideality or genuine
political or anti-political convictions, and I was
quite at a loss to conjecture why he had followed
the Anarchists into exile—his only apparent reason
being a disinclination to study and a desire to
escape from school. When Giannoli informed me
that he was a police-spy I really did not know
whether to believe him or not.

And as the weeks passed on, Giannoli's condition
grew worse and worse, and I could see that a crisis
must inevitably follow. Nor was I mistaken in this
conviction.

Late one afternoon, towards the end of September,
I was busy in the printing-room "making up" the
pages of the forthcoming number of the *Tocsin*,
when, looking up from my work on which I was
very intent, I saw Giannoli walk in hurriedly with
his usual restless step, and look about the place in a
nervous short-sighted way, evidently in search of
somebody. He was just about to leave again, not
having noticed me, when I called to him. "Oh,
Isabel," he replied, evidently much relieved, "are

you here then!" and he came up to me. "I did
not see you!" and then, casting a glance round the
room, he inquired, "Are we quite alone?"

"There are others upstairs," I answered. "If
you wish to speak to me alone I will come to your
room a little later, when I have finished this
work."

"Oh, thank you, thank you," he exclaimed; "I
must speak to you; I shall wait for you till you
come;" and he hurried away, once more looking
furtively round the office as though fearing he were
watched.

From his manner it was evident to me that he was
terribly perturbed about something and that his
fears and suspicions were reaching a climax.
"Whatever can be the matter?" I asked myself
as I hammered away at my form. "Has anything
serious really happened?"

Towards seven o'clock I left the printing-office
and the work to the tender mercies of Short, who
was just writhing out of a peaceful sleep of some
hours' duration on the "bed" of the machine, and
made my way towards Giannoli's room, which
though quite close was by no means easy of access.
Turning to my right, half-way down the court-yard,
I passed into Mrs. Wattles's house, at the summit of
which my friend was located; and here at once my
progress was arrested by that lady herself, only half
sober and in a mood evidently requiring sympathy.

"Oh, my dear," she exclaimed, "are you going up to see that pore young man? I don't know what's gone wrong with 'im of late, but for all the world 'e looks as if 'e were sickening for something. To look at 'im's enough. It just sets my inn'ards all of a 'eave and a rumble, and I 'ave to take a little drop o' something warm to settle 'em again."

"Damnation!" I muttered inwardly at finding myself trapped at such a moment; but there was nothing for it; I had to wait and hear out the long and weary recital of the sickness and agony of her deceased son, to whom she had suddenly discovered a resemblance in Giannoli. At the end of a long discourse, full of those "sickening details" in which women of her class delight, she summed up her case with a brief but telling epitome of his career, to the effect that he never smoked, nor drank, nor swore, but that he "only gave one sniff and died;" and I, determined to escape from the inevitable sequel, when Wattles senior's vices would be declaimed in contrast to the son's virtues, beat a hasty retreat. A few scraps of this anti-climax, mingled with hiccups and sobs, wafted after me as I wended my way up the uneven wooden stairs. At the top of these a perilous-looking ladder gave access to a trap-door, through which I dexterously made my way into Giannoli's room.

The interior was familiar to me—a squalid little

den, some ten feet square, whose dirty, brown-paper-patched window looked out over the chimneys and yards of the "Little Hell" district. In one corner of the room was a mysterious cupboard, through which a neighbouring chimney contrived to let in a constant supply of filthy black smoke. The bare unwashed boards were rotting away, and at one spot the leg of the bed had gone through the floor, to the considerable alarm of its dormant occupant. The wall-paper, which had once been a gorgeous combination of pink and cobalt and silver, was tattered and discoloured, and so greasy that one might imagine that generations of squalid lodgers had made their meals off it. The furniture consisted of a small table, now covered with a perpetual litter of papers; a ramshackle wash-hand stand, on which a broken vegetable dish served as a receptacle for soap and such objects; a bed, which bred remarkable crops of fleas, and to which clung an old patchwork quilt, but which was otherwise poor in adornment; a chair, and an old travelling-box. As I have already mentioned, a trap-door in the floor gave access to this apartment. There was no other door.

When I entered Giannoli was sitting at his table with his face buried in his hands, so deeply absorbed in his own reflections that for some seconds he did not notice my advent. When at last I made my presence known to him he gave a violent start, and, holding out both his hands, he wrung mine for some moments in silence. Then he motioned me to the box; I seated myself; once more he became silent; then, suddenly raising his head, he looked me full in the face.

"Do you know why I wished to speak to you?" he asked; "can you guess? Oh, it is no light matter, Isabel, which has led me to trouble you, no pleasant matter either. I am on the brink of ruin, threatened and betrayed by my most trusted friends. I must leave here at once, go right away from London and England. My life is not safe here for another day." He spoke in Italian, and as he grew more excited his voice rose higher and higher, though every now and again he was minded to control it, as though fearing he might be over-heard. "Yes," he continued, "those men whom I have most trusted, whom I have treated as my own brothers, with whom I have often shared my last shilling and the very clothes off my back, have turned against me. They are in league to destroy me. They are plotting against my liberty and my life!" For some minutes he raved on in this style, every now and again breaking off into curses, while I listened half horrified, half in-credulous.

"For goodness' sake," I exclaimed at last, "do try and be calmer, Giannoli, and tell me what has happened and what you wish me to do."

"You are right," he answered, making an effort to control himself; "I must explain the matter or you cannot understand. . . . I will talk to you frankly, for you at any rate are above suspicion. You may perhaps be aware that I have been connected with many serious Anarchist ventures in the past. The explosions at St. ——, the affair in V—— three years ago, the sacking of the bank in Barcelona. All of these were, of course, very dangerous matters, in which I risked my life; but it all tended towards the destruction of society, and I readily took the risk. As far as possible I avoided taking other comrades into my confidence —partly out of regard for my own safety, partly with a view to theirs. To one or two well-trusted men, however, I confided my projects, so that in case of my arrest all proper measures might be taken." (Gnecco was one of these "trusted comrades," B—— and Morì were others.) "I was mistaken in my estimate of these men, mistaken in my confidence in them. From their lips my secret has been wormed or bought by others, until now it has become a byword, and every indiscreet fool and paid spy in our midst knows the tale of my past better than I do myself. I no longer dare attend our meetings, for all around me I hear whisperings and insinuations, and my name being passed from one mouth to another along with references to my past actions. The torture is becoming unendurable. Some of these cowards even descend to taunting me with their knowledge; and when I, in any way, cross their purposes in our discussions, they threaten me covertly with exposure. That disgusting young fool, Morì, only to-day, being jealous of me in some trivial matter, tried to intimidate me by hinting at the V—— affair. I felt that I could have struck him down where he stood; and then a sense of my own impotence overtook me, and I stood there, silent and confused, trying to laugh the matter off, as though I had not grasped his meaning. But I can stand this state of things no longer: it is driving me mad. When I am alone now I suddenly start with the feeling that some one is coming on me unawares. This afternoon, wishing to be alone and to think matters over, I took a walk about the Park, but the very trees seemed to be whispering about me, and before long I perceived that I was followed, that my movements were being dogged step by step. When I am alone in my room they do not even leave me in peace. They obtain entrance here by means of that Wattles woman, who is evidently in their pay. B—— cannot forgive me for not having appropriated to our private use the money expropriated in Barcelona for the propaganda; and this indeed is one of their principal grievances against me. Would you believe it, Isabel, last night he actually got into this house and woke me from sleep by shouting the name of the bank through that hole? When I rushed down to find him, determined to teach him a sound lesson, he was gone. But what use is there in my enlarging on this subject? You cannot fail to see the danger I am in, and the absolute imperative necessity for flight. Another day's procrastination may be my undoing. Who knows what signal they are awaiting to denounce me, and how many others may be implicated in my ruin? I must get away from here; I must flee in absolute secrecy, and none of them must be allowed to suspect where I am gone. You and Kosinski alone I can trust. You alone must be in the secret of my flight. Will you help me, Isabel?" and at this point Giannoli seized my hand, and then, overcome and unnerved by excitement, he allowed his head to sink on to the table and sobbed convulsively.

My head was fairly swimming by this time. How far was all this true? how far the imaginings of an over-wrought, over-excited brain? However, the immediate urgencies of the situation gave me no time to carefully weigh the matter. I must either act or refuse to act, thereby leaving my friend alone to his despair and possible ruin. I decided on the former course.

"I think that you exaggerate, Giannoli," I answered him. "You are ill and over-wrought, and require rest and change. Get away from here by all means if there is any danger in remaining, but do not take too gloomy a view of the situation. I am at your disposal and willing to help you in every way in my power. Tell me where you think of going, and what I can do. But in the meantime, had we not better get supper somewhere, and discuss the situation over a little reassuring food ?"

This unheroic but practical suggestion met with poor Giannoli's approbation, and he confessed to not having broken his fast all day. He also seemed relieved at the prospect of leaving the vicinity of the office where he was convinced that spies surrounded him, and having thanked and re-thanked me over and over again for my proffered assistance, he led the way down the ladder, and together we gained the street. I was horribly shocked at the haggard strained look of the unfortunate Italian which the clearer light down here revealed. He had aged ten years since his arrival. We made our way towards a small restaurant in Soho frequented principally by the lower order of *cocotte*, and here over a savoury but inexpensive meal we discussed our plans.

"I can scarcely dare believe that this hell is coming to an end!" exclaimed Giannoli. "The assurance of your sympathy is already lightening my burden. I am beginning once more to take hope and courage ! Oh, to have at last left that

awful den where night and day I have felt myself
watched by unseen treacherous eyes, and my every
breath noted by my enemies! I shall never put
foot there again. You and Kosinski must get my
things away from there to-night, and to-morrow I
leave London by the first continental train."

"Where do you purpose going?" I inquired.

"To South America, as soon as the arrival of
funds will allow it, but, this not being practicable
for the moment, I propose going first to Lisbon.
There I will hide for a few weeks until I restart
for Buenos Ayres, and I trust that this will have the
advantage of putting my 'friends' off the track.
Even for this little voyage I do not at the present
moment possess the necessary funds, but in this
you can no doubt assist me, for in a few days I
expect some thirty pounds from my relations in
Italy. If you will return to my room to-night
you might rescue my guitar and what few little
objects of value I possess and pawn them, and burn
all papers and documents of any kind."

"You have left everything till rather late!" I
could not help exclaiming, not a little taken aback
at the amount to be done, and at the rapidly
advancing hour.

Supper over, I left Giannoli in Oxford Street, and
made tracks for his lodging, which by great good
luck I reached without any obstruction. I locked
myself in, rescued a few papers of importance,

burnt the rest, put his scanty personal belongings
together in a box which it had been agreed I was
subsequently to send Kosinski to fetch, and having
secured his guitar, a silver-handled umbrella, and
two or three other articles of small value, I proceeded with these to a neighbouring pawnbroker.
I may mention here that since my connection with
the Anarchist movement, and its consequent de-
mands on my pocket, I had become quite familiar
with the ins and outs, and more especially the ins,
of these most invaluable relatives.

I reached the side door of Mr. Isaac Jacob's
establishment on the stroke of eleven, but as Providence and would-be drunkards had mercifully or-
dained that pawnbrokers should remain open later
than usual on Saturday, I was still able to effect
an entrance.   I laid my goods down on the counter,
and politely requested the temporary loan of £3.
"Three pounds for this damned lot of old rubbish,"
exclaimed the indignant Jew.   "Do you take this
for a public charity?   It's not worth fifteen shillings
to me, the whole lot!" and he turned the things
over with his greasy hands, as though they were
objectionable offal.   We finally compromised for
thirty-two shillings, with which sum in my pocket
I triumphantly sallied forth.

My next move was to disinter Kosinski, whom I
felt pretty certain of finding at a certain coffee-stall
where, at that advanced hour, he was in the habit

of making his one and only diurnal, or rather nocturnal repast. This coffee-stall was situated at the corner of Tottenham Court Road and a side street, and there, sure enough, stood Kosinski, munching sardines on toast, and buns, and drinking coffee, surrounded by a motley group of cabmen and loose women. These had evidently grown used to his regular attendance and treated him with marked respect and friendliness, many of the unfortunate women having often had to thank him for a meal and the price of a night's lodging when luck had failed them in other directions.

Kosinski was somewhat taken aback at my sudden appearance. " You, Isabel ! " he exclaimed in some confusion, "what can have brought you here ? But may I offer you a little supper ? These buns are excellent ! "

Tired and worried as I was, I could not help smiling at the awkward manner in which he made this offer. " No, thank you," I answered, " I am not hungry. I have come to fetch you in connection with a rather important matter. Can you come with me when you have finished your supper ? "

" Yes, certainly," answered Kosinski, " if there is anything I can do. Just let me finish these few mouthfuls and I will follow you. In the meantime will you explain what is the matter ? "

Without further ado I explained to him the

P

whole Giannoli affair as I understood it. It was
a relief to me to do so, and I was anxious to hear
his opinion. He was silent for some minutes after
I had finished speaking, and munched reflectively
the last relics of his supper.

"I am afraid," he said at last, "that Giannoli is
not quite well—not quite well, mentally, I mean,"
he added after a slight pause. "At the same time,
it is quite possible that there is some truth in what
he suspects. Spies have always been abundant
in our party and Giannoli is a very likely victim.
He has been imprudent in the past, too believing
and too foolhardy. I do not know very much
about the men whom he primarily suspects, but
Gnecco certainly I believe to be above suspicion.
In any case it will be safer for him to leave. . . . I
am ready now. . . . What can I do? Where are
you going?"

"Home, and to bed," I answered. "I have
been on my feet all day and I am very tired.
Moreover, there is nothing that I can do till
to-morrow."

I then explained to him what he was to do,
where we were to meet on the following morning,
and where he could find Giannoli that night. He
acquiesced and we parted.

Early the following morning I found Giannoli
and Kosinski, as prearranged, awaiting my arrival
under the bridge of Waterloo Station. Both

looked very washed out, with the fagged and
pasty look of people who have been up all night.
They were strolling up and down, carrying Giannoli's box between them, and making a fine but
very obvious show of indifference towards a
policeman who eyed them suspiciously. "Here,
move on, you fellows," he was saying gruffly as
I came up with them, and on perceiving me they
seemed glad enough to be able to do so.

"That stupid policeman wanted to arrest us as
rogues and vagabonds," Kosinski explained to me
as we made our way towards a neighbouring
coffee-shop for breakfast. "A pretty fix that
would have been just now! We had scarcely
settled down for a quiet sleep on the box when
the meddlesome fool came up and asked our
names and addresses, what we had there, what we
were doing at that hour, and threatened to take
us in charge unless we moved on. When I explained that we were simply waiting for our train
he laughed, and said that was a likely tale! If
you had not come along and thus confirmed our
assertion that we expected a friend, I really believe
he would have arrested us."

"Well, is everything arranged?" I inquired as
we settled down to our breakfast. "How did you
get on last night?"

"Oh, we have had nothing but mishaps and
adventures all night," returned Kosinski. "What

a night! Thank goodness it is over at last. After
you left, towards one o'clock, I went off to Giannoli's room to fetch his box. I confess that I
felt a little nervous about this, for I dreaded an
encounter with that horrible Mrs. Wattles. She
talks and talks and talks to me whenever she sees
me, and insists upon asking the most indelicate
questions. She is a perfect savage. But no matter; let me get on. As I crawled upstairs, I heard
her in her room abusing her poor husband in the
most disgusting terms. I held my breath and
crept up. I found the trunk right enough in the
corner, though it was none too easy to find, as
there was no light in the room, and I was afraid
of lighting even a match for fear of attracting
attention. But on the way down a terrible acci-
dent occurred. My foot caught in a scrap of oil-
cloth at the top of the stairs, just outside Mrs.
Wattles's room, and I fell. Crash down the stairs
went the box, and I rattled after it. The noise,
of course, brought Mrs. Wattles screaming and
swearing to the door. Then, bruised and bewildered as I was, I seized on the box and fled. Down
the remaining stairs, out through the door, and
into the street, I ran as for dear life. Oh I have
never run like that before, Isabel! I remember
years ago, when escaping from prison in Russia,
my life depended on the efficiency of my legs.
But I did not run with such fervour as I ran last

night from that woman. I still feel unspeakably grateful when I think that I escaped without being recognised. She raced down after me, but being half-drunk she fell in the passage, and it was that which saved me. . . . I found Giannoli in Trafalgar Square."

The remainder of the night they had spent peacefully enough, wandering about the streets, occasionally being " moved on " by a policeman, until the sceptical officer already referred to had evinced an intention of arresting them both as rogues and vagabonds. I could not help smiling at the peremptory manner in which poor Giannoli's adventures had almost been brought to a conclusion.

I gave Giannoli the proceeds of the previous night's pawnings, and I and Kosinski turned out on the table what money we had about us. It was just sufficient to cover the expenses of the first stage of Giannoli's journey.

We proceeded — a quaint procession — to the station. Kosinski led the way with head bent forward and even resolute tread, apparently untired and unaffected by his night's vicissitudes, with the much battered box on his shoulders. Behind him followed Giannoli and myself, the former nervous and unstrung, constantly turning from right to left with the idea that we were being followed. In the station, half deserted this Sunday morning, we had

another long wait.　We talked of many things together, and I had never found Kosinski so friendly
and communicative before.　There existed between
Giannoli and himself the keen sympathy and understanding of two men equally devoted to an idea,
equally willing to sacrifice everything to it.　The
Russian was more of a philosopher than the Italian,
more engrossed in abstractions, more oblivious of
his own personality, and this it was that had saved
him from the possibility of Giannoli's terrible
malady.　At the same time he was by no means
inclined to make light of Giannoli's fears, and together they talked them over, Kosinski promising
to investigate them after his friend's departure,
and to see if it was possible to discover who was
really at fault.

"No man can ever hold such threats over me,"
said Kosinski, "for I have never taken any one
into my confidence.　I have always acted alone.
Some day it may fall to my lot to pay with my
life for some action on behalf of our ideas.　When
that moment comes I shall be ready for the
sacrifice."

"I too," exclaimed Giannoli with fervour—"I
too would not hesitate to make the sacrifice if I
felt the right moment had arrived.　If to-morrow
—if at this very moment—I saw the means of
advancing the Anarchist cause by the sacrifice of
my life, I would give it without regret or hesitation.

But to lose it for no purpose, before I have finished my work, to fall a victim to the envy and treachery of my own comrades, and to involve others in my own ruin, I cannot bear. When my time comes to die I wish to feel that my death is at any rate of some use. There are moments when an Anarchist can help his ideas on better by dying than by living. But for me the moment is not yet quite ripe."

He then relapsed into silence, and the two friends sat together, engrossed in their own reflections, without saying a word.

After a time Giannoli turned to me : " I will write to you as soon as I reach Lisbon, Isabel, and let you know how I am getting on. There at least I am little known, and I will stay with an old friend whose sincerity is above suspicion— Avvocato Martini. You and Kosinski are the only two persons whom I regret in leaving London. You have done more for me than I can ever thank you for. You have saved my life, and although I do not value life for itself, it may be of value to our Cause, and I hope yet to give it for some good purpose. Give what explanation you think fit of my disappearance. Above all, let no one suspect where I am gone."

The train left at ten o'clock. Giannoli was deeply affected at parting from us, and as the train was about to leave he seized our hands and embraced us. "Something tells me," he exclaimed, "that I shall never see either of you again. Write to me sometimes and bear me in mind. Do not believe any lies you may be told about me. I have only our principles at heart. Good-bye," and the train steamed out of the station.

I remained alone with Kosinski. The hour was still quite early, and there was much to be talked over together. "Let us go to some picture gallery," I suggested, "so as to talk things over and to settle what we are to give out concerning Giannoli's disappearance."

"No, please, don't," answered the Russian in genuine alarm; "you know how I hate art, Isabel. It goads me to madness. We must think of some other place."

We strolled out of the station together and wended our way across the bridge and along the Strand, up by St. Martin's Church, and eventually found ourselves close to old St. Giles's Churchyard. "Let us sit down here," I said, indicating a seat; "I am tired of walking."

"It is little better than a picture gallery," murmured Kosinski, "but it will do if you are tired," and we sat down. Kosinski advised me to feign absolute ignorance of Giannoli's whereabouts and to set afloat the idea of his having committed suicide. He asked me to let him know as soon as I received news from the fugitive, and he, in the meantime, would investigate the matter of the "conspiracy." As we parted he said to me:

"I am very glad, Isabel, that I have had to deal with you in this matter. You may sometimes have thought me unduly harsh in my estimate of your sex. I am not without reason in this. Women are rarely of much use in a movement like ours. They so rarely seem able to forget *themselves*, to detach themselves from the narrow interests of their own lives. They are still the slaves of their past, of their passions, and of all manner of prejudices. But you are different. . . . There have even been moments when I felt that I had other things to say to you, things which it is better to leave unsaid. I must not be guilty of the weakness which I condemn in women. An Anarchist's life, you see, is scarcely his own. He has no time to indulge in personal sentiment. Good-bye," and before I had time to answer he was gone.

I returned home and spent the remainder of the day locked in my room, absorbed in many conflicting thoughts. I was grieved beyond words at Giannoli's trouble, at the possibility of foul play, at the almost more grievous possibility of mental disorder in him. Then again and again Kosinski's last words recurred to me, and I could not help reflecting that, slight as they were, he had probably never said so much to any other woman. I was compelled to admit to myself that the Russian, for all his strange ideas and brusque manners, had grown to be a great deal to me. But I felt that he was a hopeless case—the kind of man to whom personal happiness was unknown, and who would succeed in rendering unhappy any one rash enough to care for him. "How easy happiness might be," I reflected, "with our ideas, with our freedom from prejudice. And yet it is these very ideas which will ruin his life, which——" Half unconsciously I found that my thoughts had been drifting from abstract ideas and abstract enthusiasms to persons, and with this divorce from abstractions began a feeling of weariness, of nausea. I thought of Kosinski's words again, of his contempt for personal sentiment in an Anarchist, of what he had said about women; and I struggled hard within myself to turn my thoughts into other channels. It was useless, and at last, weary of the effort, I retired to bed and took refuge in slumber.

During the following weeks I worked on fairly regularly at the *Tocsin* and saw Kosinski not unfrequently, on which occasions he most carefully avoided any recurrence of personalities, however vague these might be. Giannoli's disappearance created considerable commotion, and every one was at a loss to imagine what could have become of him. My relations with those Italians whom he had suspected were naturally very strained and uncomfortable, for I did not know what to think of them, how far to trust or mistrust them. Kosinski, as promised, investigated the matter as carefully as he could, but the exact truth was difficult to ascertain. Gnecco we neither of us for one instant suspected, but we felt some degree of uncertainty about the others. Whether or no there had been some amount of unclean work going on, it was anyway quite certain that a great part of Giannoli's suspicions were the outcome of his overwrought and exhausted mental condition.

About a fortnight after his departure I received at last a letter from Giannoli. This consisted of a few words, written evidently in much hurry and perturbation of spirit. He thanked me for the money from his relatives, which I had forwarded, which would, he said, enable him to leave at once for Argentina. "It has arrived in the very nick of time," he wrote, "for here I am no longer safe. Avvocato Martini, of whom I spoke to you in such high terms, is not to be trusted. He intercepts my letters, and has, I believe, communicated with my enemies in London. Thank Heaven! I am now able to get away. In South America I shall once more settle down to the propaganda work, and I shall be out of the power of these informers. My old friend, Giovanni Barelli, awaits me there. We shall live together and life will once more become endurable. I am anxious to hear from Kosinski. What is the result of his inquiries? My best love to him and to you, dear friend, and again a thousand thanks to you both. I will write at greater length from America."

I showed the letter to Kosinski. He read it through with a serious expression. "I fear," he said, "that it is a case of hallucination, and that there is but very slight foundation of truth to his suspicions. I have looked into the matter and can see no adequate grounds for suspecting the men whom he regarded as his enemies over here. Giannoli exaggerates and distorts everything. I must write to him and try to reassure him about this. I will tell him that he is mistaken. We cannot afford to lose such a comrade."

"Beware," I returned half in jest—"beware, lest you too fall under his ban."

"Oh, there is no fear of that," answered Kosinski with assurance. "He knows me too well. I am the oldest friend he has. I can and must tell him the truth."

Kosinski wrote, and the weeks passed on. A month after Giannoli's arrival in Buenos Ayres I received another letter from him. Once again he declared that he was not safe, that he must take flight. Barelli, of whom he had always spoken with the most brotherly affection, had turned against him. He and other false comrades had entered into a plot to murder him, and at the time of writing he had fled from their ken and was in hiding in some remote and populous district, awaiting the arrival of money which would enable him to return to Europe. Then, later on, there arrived another letter from Lisbon, disconnected in matter, shaky in writing, full of the wildest and most improbable statements.

"I feel like a hunted animal," he wrote; "I have been driven about from pillar to post, from one end of the civilised world to another. I am growing very weary of all this, and am trying to devise how to terminate a situation which is growing intolerable. Here I am again in hiding, and dare not venture from my lair till the dead of night. What money I had is almost at an end. My clothes are falling off my back. I have not changed my linen for weeks, having forgotten my old valise in my hurried departure from Buenos Ayres. My health is failing, and I feel utterly helpless and wretched. You would be horrified if you could see me now. I am ill, and at night I can get no sleep. Every moment I expect them to break in, murder me, and seize my papers. Those devils from Buenos Ayres are already on my track. I have not heard from Kosinski. His letter has no doubt been intercepted. As soon as possible I shall proceed to Gibraltar. I am thinking out a plan to end all this. *Do you understand?*"

Some weeks later I received from Gibraltar a letter in which Giannoli informed me that yet once more he was compelled to abscond himself, further plottings against him rendering this necessary.   He had been seriously ill, he wrote, and his strength was quite giving out.   He was, at the time of writing, on the eve of departure for Barcelona, where he was determined "to end it all."   He had at last received Kosinski's letter, and would write at greater length from Barcelona.   He warned me to beware of false friends.

These last sentences troubled me very much. What could it all mean ?   What was impending ? And Kosinski; did he doubt *him* too ?

But this state of uncertainty as to his meaning was destined to be but of short duration.   Barely a week had elapsed since my receipt of the above letter when, as I stood alone in the composing-room one morning, I was surprised to see the figure of an unknown man appear above the balustrade leading from below.   He was evidently a foreigner and a Southerner, and walking straight up to me he asked in Italian, but with a distinct Spanish accent, "Are you Isabel Meredith ?"

On my answering in the affirmative, he handed me a sealed note on which was written my name in Giannoli's familiar hand.

"This is for you," he said, "I bring it direct from Barcelona.   It is strictly private.   Good morning," and as mysteriously as he had appeared he was gone.

Even before opening it, the shaky writing on the envelope told me only too eloquently that matters were no better with Giannoli at the time he penned it. Moreover, I felt certain, from the extraordinary nature of its delivery, that it must contain news of exceptional moment. A dull, sick feeling of dread overcame me as I stood irresolute, holding the unopened letter in my hand. I was tempted to put it aside and postpone the knowledge of any unpleasant news it might contain. I knew this, however, to be a weakness, and so with an effort I tore it open. It read as follows :—

"DEAREST FRIEND,—This is a letter which it would be unsafe to consign to the post. Therefore I send it to you by hand, by means of an old friend who can be trusted. He is not a comrade, and has no knowledge of its contents. A few days back I wrote to you from Gibraltar, telling you of the serious break-down in my health, and of the circumstances which had compelled me once again to leave Lisbon. Now, at last, I feel in a measure more composed, for my resolution is taken, and I mean to end my life—not without benefit to our Cause, I hope. You are the only person with whom I am com-

municating. Even Kosinski has been bought
over by my enemies. A letter from him was
forwarded to me in Lisbon, in which he sided
with the spies who have been trying to ruin me,
and which contained covert threats which I
understood only too well. Thus another illusion
is shattered ! The burden of all these disillusions,
all these disgusts and disappointments, is too
heavy to bear any longer. I must get away from
it all before my health and intellect are completely
shattered. I have always thought suicide a cowardly
death for an Anarchist. Before taking leave of life
it is his duty to strike a final blow at Society and
I, at least, mean to strike it. Here the moment
is in every way ripe. Ever since the explosion
in Madrid, eight months ago, the Anarchists have
been the victims of the most savage persecutions.
I have seen one man with his nails torn off, and
another raving mad with thirst, after having been
kept without water, and fed on salt cod during
sixty hours. Others have been tortured in prison
in other ways—some tortures so vile and filthy
that I would not tell you of them. I write this
in order to show you that the moment is ripe
here for some vigorous act of reprisal. It is
impossible to strike a blow at all those who are
responsible, for the whole of Society is to blame :
but those most guilty must suffer for it. I am
prepared to strike my final blow before I take

my leave, and you will learn from the papers in a few days' time the exact nature of the act I contemplate.

"And now I must beg you to pardon me for all the trouble and disturbance I have occasioned you, dear friend; I can never thank you enough. You, and you alone, have been true to me. For your own sake, I entreat you also to beware of false friends—especially avoid Kosinski. — Yours ever, GIACOMO GIANNOLI."

CHAPTER XI

A CRISIS

THE flight of Giannoli, and all the worry and turmoil occasioned thereby, told on my health. I did not admit as much to myself, and I still kept on at the paper as usual through the very thick of it all. For one thing, this was necessary in order not to arouse the curiosity of many of the comrades, and moreover there is no doubt that whatever line of life we may adopt we gradually become the creatures of our habits, however much we may scoff at such a notion. Thus, though I had grown out of the first stage of youthful enthusiasm when I revelled in squalor and discomfort, and sincerely believed myself to be one of the hubs round which the future Revolution and the redemption of mankind circled, and though experience had opened my eyes to much that was unlovely, and not a little which was despicable, in my associates, still I stuck at my post and continued my work on the paper.

On arriving at the office towards nine every morning, my first task was to get Short out of pawn in the neighbouring coffee-shop, where he retired — regardless of the fact that his pockets were but capacious vacuums—in order to regale himself on shop eggs and fly-blown pastry, and where his person was detained as a pledge till my purse redeemed him.

I would then work away, "dissing" or "comping," "locking up forms," or writing a "leader," till some of the Italians, keenly alive to their ownership of stomachs, would call me off to partake of a Milanese *minestra*, or to pronounce on the excellencies of a mess of *polenta*. Then would follow an hour devoted to digestion and talk, when Short, if in a bad temper, would smoke abominable shag, and raise the bowl of his clay pipe into quite perilous proximity with his eyebrows, and if genially inclined, would entertain some one member of the company to dark tales and fearsome hints as to the depraved habits and questionable sincerity of his or her dearest friend.

He had of late developed a great interest in my welfare, and Kosinski had been his special butt. He had always hated the latter on account of his vast moral superiority to himself, and seemed specially desirous of discrediting him in my eyes. The Russian came pretty frequently to the office during the months following on Giannoli's disappearance. He was always singularly uncommunicative about his own concerns ; his intimate friends were not aware of his address; how he lived or what his home life was none seemed to know; and, indeed, he was one of those men who, without ever saying a word to that effect, make one feel that their private life is no concern of any one but themselves. Short, however, hinted at things he *could* say if he *would*, spoke in general terms of the disgracefulness of exploiting the affections of women, referred in an undertone to "that Kosinski's" luck, adding that, of course, one had a right to act according to one's inclination, still Anarchists should set an example, &c., &c. I, of course, took such observations at their true value; I knew Short and Kosinski too well to give two thoughts to the matter. Still when, on top of all this mysterious talk, I received Giannoli's letter, in which he spoke of his folly in trusting his supposed friend, and accused him of being neither more nor less than an agent in the hands of the International police, I felt my brain whirl, and really wondered whether I was the sole sane person in a mad world, or whether the reverse were not the case.

It was now some weeks since I had last seen Dr. Armitage. He had written to explain his absence, alleging stress of work, in which I readily believed; for though I knew his regular practice had been much neglected during the preceding year, I also knew that there was not an Anarchist within twenty miles who did not expect him to attend on himself and family when in illness or trouble, an obligation with which the doctor willingly complied, though not only did he take no fees, but generally had to provide the patients with all their creature comforts. No sort of change had occurred in our relations to each other, but lately he had seemed more than ever preoccupied, absorbed in the propaganda, ever devising new plans for spreading the "movement." He seemed less and less inclined to keep up his West End connection, and confessed that he had but scant patience wherewith to listen to the polite ailments and sentimental troubles of fashionable ladies. He had given much time to the *Tocsin,* writing many really remarkable papers for it, but lately, since Kosinski had come more to the front, and I had been so much taken up with Giannoli's affairs, he had, perhaps intentionally, kept more away from the office.

It was with a feeling of real pleasure that I saw him enter at last one Saturday evening early in April. I had been feeling tired and depressed, and only by an effort of will had I kept myself at my work. I was struck at the change that a few weeks had wrought in the doctor's appearance. His hair had grown unusually long, quite noticeably so, his tall figure was somewhat bent, and there was an unusual appearance about his dress. He had not yet cast aside the garb of civilisation, but his trousers evinced a tendency to shrink, and he appeared to contemplate affecting low necks in the matter of shirts. His feet were shod in sandals of a peculiar make, and there was a feverish look in his eyes. As he came towards me his characteristic kindly smile lit up his drawn features, and he grasped my hand with friendly warmth. I was delighted to see him, but somewhat shocked at the alteration in his looks. In answer to my inquiries as to his prolonged absence, he explained that he had been very busy for one thing, and that he had also been much preoccupied with his own thoughts on questions of principle and propaganda.

"You know, Isabel," he said, "my habit of silence when confronted by mental problems. I think I must belong to the race of ruminating animals, and it is only by quietly chewing the cud of my ideas that I can digest and assimilate them. It used to be just the same in my student days, and doubtless the habit will stick to me through life. When I have once thought out a point, and settled in my own mind on the right course of action, I am not as a rule troubled by hesitation or doubts, and then I like to talk and discuss, but the initial stage seems to need solitude. Besides, I know you have been very much taken up of late months. I have seen Kosinski sometimes, and had your news from him. You are not looking well; you must have been overtaxing your strength, and need a rest."

"Doctor, cure yourself, I might well say," I

rejoined. "There is nothing much amiss with me. I am a little fagged perhaps, nothing more. But you look very much run down. I am sure you have been neglecting yourself very much of late."

"Oh, no, on the contrary," replied the doctor, "I have been giving much thought lately to food and dress reform in their bearings on the social question, and I have been putting some of my ideas into practice in my own person. I have never felt in better health. All superfluous fat has been got rid of, and my mind feels singularly lucid and clear. I have been going on quite long rounds propagandising, often walking as much as twenty and thirty miles a day, and, thanks to my somewhat more rational dress and to my diet of raw oatmeal and fresh fruit, I have found no difficulty in so doing. But will you not come for a walk with me ? It is a beautiful evening, and here the atmosphere is so close and stuffy. Do come, I should so enjoy a quiet talk with you. I have much I want to say to you, and I have come this evening in the hope of an opportunity to say it."

I agreed, and we sallied forth. At the entrance to the courtyard we encountered Mrs. Wattles holding forth to a group of gossips amongst whom stood Short (for no scandal-mongering was too trivial to interest him), on the disappearance of Giannoli from her house and her suppositions as to his fate—a theme of which she never wearied.

I managed to slip by without attracting her attention, so absorbed was she with the enthralling
mystery, only to find myself in for another almost worse danger. For there at the corner of
P. Street and the Euston Road stood the Bleeding Lamb, surrounded by a hooting and uproari-
ous crowd. He had, it appeared, interrupted the
Gospel-preaching of the Rev. Melchisedek Hicks
with some inappropriate inquiry as to the probable whereabouts of Nelson on the resurrection
day. This was considered irreverent by the admirers of the Rev. Hicks, who forthwith began
to jibe and jeer at the Bleeding Lamb, who, in
his turn, exchanging the meekness of the traditional victim for the righteous indignation of a
prophet misjudged, had volleyed a torrent of abuse
on all present, consigning them unconditionally
to hell-fire. As Armitage and I neared the scene
a constable was taking the names and addresses
of all concerned, and was manifesting his intention of marching off the poor Lamb to durance
vile.

Armitage took in the situation at a glance, and,
hurrying up, addressed the man in blue. "I
know this man very well, officer," he said in an
authoritative voice. "I can answer that he gives
his name and address correctly ; there is no need
to arrest him."

"And who are *you* ? I should like to know,"

inquired the irate policeman; "I think I can answer for your address, Colney Hatch ain't far off the mark."

"This is my card," answered the doctor, handing one over to the constable with a dignified gesture. The latter seemed somewhat impressed and taken aback, and after grumbling some remarks in an undertone and eyeing the Lamb in a suspicious and unconvinced manner, he told him to be off sharp if he did not wish to find himself in the cells, and then vented his spleen and unappeased zeal on behalf of his country by cuffing, shoving and abusing the corner-boys who had assembled to witness the fun. We availed ourselves of the consequent confusion to make good our escape, dodging the Lamb, who manifested an intention of coming along with us; and soon we found ourselves, thanks to a penny tram fare, in fresher, cleaner quarters. We got down at the corner of Parliament Hill. The sun had just set and the clear spring twilight lent a wonderful charm of serene peace to the scene. The undulating expanse of Heath was growing darker and darker; in the west still lingered the last sunset hues of pink and saffron and green; and overhead in the deep blackening blue of night the stars were just becoming visible. We had strolled on in silence for some time, hushed by the solemn stillness of the evening. At last Dr. Armitage exclaimed, "Ah,

Isabel, how I sometimes long for rest and peace, and sweet wholesome surroundings! How beautiful life might be passed with a companion such as you. The earth is beautiful, man is naturally good; why cannot we all be happy?"

I was a little taken aback at the doctor's remark, though I had half expected something of the sort. During the early months of my Anarchist career, when battling with the first difficulties of starting the *Tocsin*, we had been so constantly together that we had got into a way of divining each other's thoughts and feelings almost without the need of words. We never thought or talked of anything but abstract questions of principle or the immediate needs of the propaganda, yet, as was only natural, an undercurrent of personal sympathy had sprung up between us which I had felt to be somewhat more pronounced on the doctor's side than on my own. However, with him, excess of emotion always manifested itself in renewed and redoubled zeal for the propaganda, leading him to elaborate some quite extraordinary schemes for advancing the Cause, such as, for instance, supplementing his daily work by keeping a coffee-stall at night, as he considered that such a plan would afford an excellent opportunity for quiet personal argument and for the distribution of literature to probable converts; so that he had never broached personalities in any defi-

nite style. Then events had followed on one
another with surprising rapidity; the advent of
the Italian refugees had contributed to change
the *personnel* if not the principles of the *Tocsin;*
a common friendship for Giannoli had brought
Kosinski and myself more together and I had
always had a decided sympathy for the Russian,
increased perhaps by the instinctive feeling that
if there were one man who would refuse to budge
one inch from his principles for a woman that
man was he. I seemed to have lived ages, my
character was developing, a sense of humour was
gradually modifying my views of many ·matters,
and during these last few months Armitage and
I had drifted somewhat apart.

There was something pathetic in his voice that
night as he spoke. His whole appearance told
me that he had been passing through an acute
mental and moral crisis, and a queer feeling came
over me which seemed to warn me that something irreparable was about to take place between
us. I felt deep sympathy for this noble nature
struggling for the ideal in a world all out of
gear; so thoroughly unselfish and self-sacrificing
as hardly to grasp clearly the personal side of
its sufferings, and slowly and unconsciously, in its
very effort to free itself from material trammels,
falling a victim to monomania—striving too high
only to fall in a world where the sublime is divided

by but a step from the ridiculous, and where all are capable of laughing and sneering, but few indeed of appreciating qualities such as Armitage possessed.

"We might well ask 'what is happiness?'" I rejoined in answer to his remark, anxious to steer the conversation clear of personalities. "How vain and trivial all our struggles seem whenever we find ourselves face to face with the serene indifference of Nature. What are we, after all, but fretful midges whizzing out our brief hour?"

"Ah, one is often tempted to think so," answered Armitage—and I confess that I gave vent to a sigh of relief as I realised that he was now started on a discussion—"but as long as injustice prevails we must continue the struggle. I often long for rest, silence, oblivion; but the mood passes and I awake more keenly alive than ever to the greatness of our Cause, and our duty toward the propaganda. Nothing must be allowed to interfere with our devotion to it, and, what is more, Isabel, we must strive to live in such a way as to free ourselves from all considerations that might hamper our action on its behalf. We must simplify our lives; we must not neglect to set an example even in small matters. The material claims of life absorb far too much of our time. We are constantly selling our birthright for a mess of pottage. We shall never be truly devoted propagandists till we have freed ourselves from all care for the morrow."

" You are right," said I, " but such ideas may be carried to an excess. We must live our lives ; and as that is so we must attend more or less to our personal wants."

" That I do not deny, Isabel," answered the doctor ; " what I aim at is to simplify them as much as possible. Thanks to my new diet I shall never have to waste time to procure the wherewithal to fill my stomach. Nuts and raw fruit are easily procured, and contain all the elements essential to physical health. I am sure you will agree with me on this point when you have considered it at length. Then again in the matter of dress, what could be more hateful or harmful than our modern costume ? It is awful to think of the lives wasted in useless toil to produce the means by which a so-called man of fashion contrives to make himself hideous and ridiculous in the eyes of all sensible people. Besides there is no doubt that we are all the creatures of our surroundings, and so the influence of food and dress on character must be inestimable."

" Oh, doctor, do not harp so on this dress and food question !" I could not help exclaiming. " Really, seriously, I think you have let your mind run somewhat too much in a groove lately. Talk of vegetarianism and dress reform ! why, what you need, it seems to me, is a steak at the Holborn and a starched shirt collar! Seriously, it grieves me to think that you should be giving yourself up so entirely to such notions. I consider you could do far more good to the Cause by keeping up your practice, pursuing your studies, and working on the lines you used to be so successful in."

Hardly had I spoken than I regretted the hastiness of my remark. I could see at a glance that my friend was pained, more at feeling that I was out of sympathy with him than at my actual words. He suggested that we should turn homewards. We were nearing Fitzroy Square when he exclaimed—

"You know, Isabel, that I have always had a great admiration for you. I have thought you would prove one of the great figures of the coming Revolution; I still think so, but I see that our ways are parting. You laugh at me; yet I feel sure that my position is right. I am sorry I have not your sympathy in my work. I had counted on it; I had come this evening to tell you so. Perhaps some day you will understand my views and agree with them. Till then, good-bye. I am due at a comrade's house at Willesden; he is going in for the No Rent Campaign, and I have promised to help him move to-night, but first I must go home and get out of these cumbersome clothes into a more rational dress; coats and trousers impede one's every thought and movement. Good-bye," and he grasped my hand and was off, walking with a rapid, almost feverish stride.

On reaching home the servant informed me that a gentleman had called for me, and that on hearing I was out he had expressed his intention of returning. The girl could not remember his name, but I gathered from her description that he was a foreigner.

Just then a ring at the door interrupted her remarks, and I was surprised to see Kosinski enter the room. He walked straight up to me with an unwonted look of perturbation about him.

"Could you come with me at once?" he said in low, hurried tones.

"Where?" said I, feeling quite alarmed. "What is the matter?"

"With me, to my room. I need the help of some woman, but there is no time to waste. I will explain *en route*. Will you come?"

"Certainly, at once," and I walked out with him.

I had not chanced to see him since Giannoli's last letter in which he was denounced as belonging to the ranks of the Italian's false friends, since when I had only heard the insinuations of Short, which, as can easily be imagined, had not deeply impressed me, coming from such a quarter. Still I should not have been surprised had I felt a momentary embarrassment at finding myself suddenly in his company, and under such decidedly unusual circumstances, but such was not the case. No one could look into Kosinski's steady grey eyes and earnest face, pale with the inward fire of enthusiasm, and not feel conscious of standing face to face with one of those rare natures who have dedicated themselves, body and soul, to the service of an ideal. I walked on hurriedly, keeping up with his swinging stride, wondering where we were going, but not liking to break in on his reserve by probing questions. Suddenly he seemed to wake to a sense of reality, and turned sharply round to me.

"We are going to my room in Hammersmith," he said. "I want your assistance, if you care to come; there is a woman there dying, a friend of mine. You are the only person of whom I should care to ask such a favour. Will you come? I hardly think it will be for many hours."

So then Short was right; there was a woman at the bottom of Kosinski's life; and simultaneously with this idea there flashed across my brain a feeling of shame at having for one instant entertained a mean thought of my friend. "I will come," I answered; "you did well to count on my friendship." We hurried on for several minutes in silence. Then again Kosinski spoke:

"I had best tell you a little how matters stand," he said. "I am not fond of talking about private concerns, but you have a right to know. Eudoxia has lived with me for the past two years. I brought her over with me from America. She has been suffering with consumption all this while, and I do not think she will last the night."

" Is she a comrade? " I ventured to inquire.

" Oh, no. She hates Anarchists; she hates me. It will be a blessing to herself when she is laid to rest at last. She was the wife of my dearest friend, perhaps my only friend outside the Cause. Vassili had a great intellect, but his character was weak in some respects. He was full of noble ambitions; he had one of the most powerful minds I have known, a quite extraordinary faculty for grasping abstract ideas. I was first drawn towards him by hearing him argue at a students' meeting. He was maintaining a fatalistic paradox : the total useless-ness of effort, and the vanity of all our distinctions between good and bad. All our acts, he argued, are the outcome of circumstances over which we have no control ; consequently the man who betrays his best friend for interested motives, and the patriot who sacrifices happiness and life for an idea are morally on the same footing—both seek their own satisfaction, aiming at that goal by different paths ; both by so doing obey a blind impulse. I joined in the argument, opposing him, and we kept the ball going till 4 A.M. He walked with me to my lodgings and slept on a rug on the floor, and we became fast friends. But though

R

his mind was strong, he was swayed by sensual
passions. He married young, burdening himself
with the responsibility of a woman and family,
and went the way of all who do so. He would
have lost himself entirely in the meshes of a
merely animal life ; he seemed even to contemplate with satisfaction the prospect of begetting
children ! But I could not stand by and witness
the moral degradation of my poor friend. I kept
him intellectually alive, and when once stimulated
to mental activity, no one was ever more logical,
more uncompromising than he. Soon after my
imprisonment he got implicated in a conspiracy
and had to flee to America. When I arrived there
after my escape I found him in the most abject
condition. His wife, Eudoxia, was ill with the
germs of the disease which is now killing her, and
was constantly railing at him as the cause of their
misfortune, urging him to make a full confession
and throw himself on the mercy of the Russian
authorities. Poor thing ! she was ill ; she had had
to leave behind her only child, and news had
come of its death. Vassili would never have done
anything base, but he had not sufficient strength
of character to rise superior to circumstances.
Another weak trait in him was his keen sensibility
to beauty. It was not so much the discomfort as
the ugliness of poverty which irked him. I have
always noted the deteriorating effect art has on

the character in such respects. He was grieved
at his wife's illness, goaded to desperation by her
reproaches, sickened by the squalor of his surroundings, and instead of turning his thoughts
inwards and drawing renewed strength and resolution from the spectacle of the sufferings caused
by our false morality and false society, he gave
way completely and took to drink. When I found
him in New York he was indeed a wreck. He
and his wife were living in a filthy garret in
the Bowery; he had nothing to do, and had
retired permanently on to a rotten old paillasse
which lay in a corner; his clothes were in pawn;
he could not go out. Eudoxia earned a few
cents daily by slaving at the wash-tub, and most
of this he spent in getting drunk on vile, cheap
spirits. When he saw me arrive he railed at me
as the cause of all his woes; blamed me for having
dragged him on to actions he should never have
done if left to himself; and pointing to his wife
and to the squalid room, he exclaimed, 'See the
results of struggling for a higher life.' Eudoxia,
for her part, hated me, declaring that I was
responsible for her husband's ruin, and that, not
content with making his life a hell on earth, I was
consigning his soul to eternal perdition. Then
Vassili would burst into maudlin tears and weep
over his own degeneracy, saying that I was his
only true friend. I grieved at the decay of a fine

mind; there was no hope now for him; I could only wish that his body might soon too dissolve. I gave him what little help I could, and he soon drank himself to death. I was with him at the last. He seemed overcome by a great wave of pity for himself, spoke tearfully of the might-have-beens, blamed me for having urged him to deeds beyond his strength, and ended by exclaiming that he could not even die in peace, as he did not know what would become of his poor wife, whose strength was already rapidly failing. ' I am leaving her friendless and penniless. I dragged her away from a comfortable home, promising her happiness. She has had to sacrifice her only child to my safety, and now, prematurely old, soured by misfortune and illness, I am abandoning her to fight for herself. She is my victim and yours, the victim of our ideas; it is your duty to look after her.' I promised him so to do, and she has been with me ever since."

I had walked on, absorbed in the interest of his tale, heedless of the distance we were covering, and now I noticed that we were already skirting Hyde Park, and reflected that our destination must still be far ahead.

"As your friend is so ill had we not better take the 'bus? You said we were going to Hammersmith, and there is still quite a long walk ahead of us," I suggested after a few minutes.

"Oh, are you tired?" he inquired; "I ought to have thought of it. I always walk." I noticed that his hand strayed into the obviously empty pocket of his inseparable blue overcoat, and a worried look came into his face. I at once realised that he had not a penny on him, and deeply regretted my remark. Not for worlds would I have suggested to him paying the fares myself, which I should have thought nothing of doing with most of the others.

"Oh, it was not for me," I hastened to rejoin, "I am not in the least tired; I only thought it would be quicker, but after all we must now be near," and I brisked up my pace, though I felt, I confess, more than a little fagged.

Again we trudged on, absorbed in our thoughts. At last, to break the silence I inquired of him if he had seen Armitage lately.

"It must be quite ten days now since I last saw him at a group-meeting of the Jewish Comrades. I fear he is developing a failing common to many of you English Anarchists; he is becoming something of a crank. He talked to me a lot about vegetarianism and such matters. It would be a thousand pities were he to lose himself on such a track, for he has both intellect and character. He is unswerving where principle is at stake; let's trust he will not lose sight of large aims to strive at minor details."

Again a silence fell on us. My companion was

evidently reviewing his past; my brain was occupied in blindly searching the future; what would become of us all? Kosinski, Armitage, myself? Vassili's words, "This is the result of struggling for a higher life," haunted me. Should we after all only succeed in making our own unhappiness, in sacrificing the weak to our uncompromising theories, and all this without advancing the cause of humanity one jot? The vague doubts and hesitations of the past few weeks seemed crystallising. I was beginning to mount the Calvary of doubt.

After a quarter of an hour Kosinski exclaimed: "Here we are. You must not be taken aback, Isabel, if you get but scant thanks for your kindness. Eudoxia is not well disposed towards our ideas; she looks upon her life with me as the last and bitterest act in the tragedy of her existence. Poor thing, I have done what I could for her, but I understand her point of view."

Without further ado we proceeded along the passage and up the mean wooden staircase of a third-rate suburban house, pushing past a litter of nondescript infancy, till we stopped before a back room on the top floor. As Kosinski turned the door handle a woman stepped forward with her finger to her lips. "Oh, thank Gawd, you're here at last," she said in a whisper, "your sister's been awful bad, but she's just dozed off now. I'll go to my husband; he'll be in soon now."

"Thanks, Mrs. Day. I need not trouble you further. My friend has come to help me."

The landlady eyed me with scant favour and walked off, bidding us good-night.

The room was of a fair size for the style of dwelling and was divided in two by a long paper screen. The first half was evidently Kosinski's, and as far as I could see by the dim light, was one litter of papers, with a mattress on the floor in a corner. We walked past the screen ; and the guttering candle, stuck in an old ginger-beer bottle, allowed me to see a bed in which lay the dying woman. There was also a table on which stood some medicine bottles, a jug of milk, and a glass ; an armchair of frowsy aspect, and two cane chairs. The unwashed boards were bare, the room unattractive to a degree, still an awkward attempt at order was noticeable. I stepped over to the bed and gazed on its occupant. Eudoxia was a thin gaunt woman of some thirty-five years of age. Her clustering golden hair streaked with grey ; small, plaintive mouth, and clear skin showed that she might have been pretty ; but the drawn features and closed eyelids bore the stamp of unutterable weariness, and a querulous expression hovered round her mouth. The rigid folds of the scanty bedclothes told of her woeful thinness, and the frail transparent hands grasped convulsively at the coverlet. As I gazed at her, tears welled into my eyes. She

looked so small, so transient, yet bore the traces of
such mental and physical anguish. After a moment
or two she slowly opened her eyes, gazed vacantly
at me without apparently realising my presence,
and in a feeble, plaintive voice made some remark
in Russian. Kosinski was at her side immediately
and answered her in soothing tones, evidently
pointing out my presence. The woman fixed on
me her large eyes, luminous with fever. I stepped
nearer. "Is there anything I can do for you?" I
inquired in French. "No one can do anything for
me except God and the blessed Virgin," she replied
peevishly, "and they are punishing me for my sins.
Yes, for my sins," she went on, raising her voice and
speaking in a rambling delirious way, "because
I have consorted with infidels and blasphemers.
Vassili was good to me; we were happy with our
little Ivan, till that devil came along. He ruined
Vassili, body and soul; he killed our child; he has
lost me. I have sold myself to the devil, for have I
not lived for the past two years on his charity?
And you," she continued, turning her glittering
eyes on me, "beware, he will ruin you too; he has
no heart, no religion; he cares for nothing, for
nobody, except his cruel principles. You love
him, I see you do; it is in your every movement,
but beware; he will trample on your heart, he will
sacrifice you, throw you aside as worthless, as he
did with Vassili, who looked upon him as his dearest

friend. Beware!" and she sank back exhausted on the pillows, her eyes turned up under her eyelids, a slight froth tinged with blood trickling down the corners of her mouth.

I was transfixed with horror; I knew not what to say, what to do. I put my hand soothingly on her poor fevered brow, and held a little water to her lips. Then my eyes sought Kosinski. He was standing in the shadow, a look of intense pain in his eyes and on his brow, and I knew what he must be suffering at that moment. I walked up to him and grasped his hand in silent sympathy; he returned the pressure, and for a moment I felt almost happy in sharing his sorrow. We stood watching in silence; at regular intervals the church chimes told us that the hours were passing and the long night gradually drawing to its close. Half-past three, a quarter to four, four; still the heavy rattling breath told us that the struggle between life and death had not yet ceased. At last the dying woman heaved a deep sigh, she opened her wide, staring eyes and raised her hand as if to summon some one. Kosinski stepped forward, but she waved him off and looked at me. "I have not a friend in the world," she gasped; "you shall be my friend. Hold my hand and pray for me." I knelt by her side and did as I was bid. Never had I prayed since I could remember, but at that supreme moment a Latin prayer learned in my infancy at my mother's knee came back to me; Kosinski turned his face to the wall and stood with bowed shoulders. As the words fell from my lips the dying woman clutched my hand convulsively and murmured some words in Russian. Then her grasp loosened. I raised my eyes to her face, and saw that all was over. My strained nerves gave way, and I sobbed convulsively. Kosinski was at my side.

"Poor thing, poor thing!" I heard him murmur. He laid his hand caressingly on my shoulder. The candle was flaring itself out, and everything assumed a ghastly blue tint as the first chill light of dawn, previous to sunrise, stole into the room. I rose to my feet and went over to the window. How cold and unsympathetic everything looked! I felt chilly, and a cold shudder ran down my limbs. Absolute silence prevailed, in the street, in the house, in the room, where lay the dead woman staring fixedly before her. Kosinski had sunk into a chair, his head between his hands. I looked at him in silence and bit my lip. An unaccustomed feeling of revolt was springing up in me. I could not and did not attempt to analyse my feelings, only I felt a blind unreasoning anger with exist-ence. How stupid, how objectless it all seemed! The church clock rung out the hour, five o'clock. Kosinski rose, he walked to the bedside, and closed poor Eudoxia's staring eyes, and drew

the sheet over her face. Then he came over
to me.

"I shall never forget your kindness, Isabel.
There is yet one thing I will ask of you; I know
that Eudoxia wanted a mass to be said for her
and Vassili; will you see about carrying out this
wish of hers? I cannot give you the money to
pay for it; I have not got it."

I nodded in silent consent.

He paused a few minutes. He seemed anxious
to speak, yet hesitated; at last he said, "I am
leaving London, Isabel, I can do nothing here,
and I have received letters from comrades in
Austria telling me that there things are ripe for
the Revolution."

I started violently: "You are leaving! Leaving
London?" I stammered.

"Yes, I shall be able to do better work elsewhere."

I turned suddenly on him.

"And so you mean to say that we are to part?
Thus? now? for ever?" A pained look came
into his eyes. He seemed to shrink from personalities. "No," I continued rapidly, "I will,
I must speak. Why should we ruin our lives?
To what idol of our own creation are we sacrificing our happiness? We Anarchists are always
talking of the rights of the individual, why are
you deliberately sacrificing your personal happi-

ness, and mine ? The dead woman was right; I
love you, and I *know* that you love me. Our
future shall not be ruined by a misunderstanding.
Now I have spoken, you must answer, and your
answer must be final."

I looked at him whilst the words involuntarily
rushed from my lips, and even before I had
finished speaking, I knew what his answer would
be.

"An Anarchist's life is not his own. Friendship,
comradeship may be helpful, but family ties are
fatal; you have seen what they did for my poor
friend. Ever since I was fifteen I have lived
solely for the Cause; you are mistaken in thinking that I love you in the way you imply. I
thought of you as a comrade, and loved you as
such."

I had quite regained my self-possession.
"Enough," I said, interrupting him. "I do not
regret my words; they have made everything clear
to me. You are of the invincibles, Kosinski;
you are strong with the strength of the fanatic;
and I think you will be happy too. *You* will
never turn to contemplate regretfully the ashes
of your existence and say as did your friend,
'See the result of struggling for a higher life!'
You do not, you cannot see that you are a slave
to your conception of freedom, more prejudiced
in your lack of prejudice than the veriest bour-

geois; that is your strength, and it is well. Good-bye."

He grasped my proffered hand with warmth.

"Good-bye, Isabel. I knew you were not like other women; that *you* could understand."

"I can understand," I replied, "and admire, even if I deplore. Good-bye."

Slowly I moved towards the door, my eyes fascinated by the rigid lines of the sheet covering the dead woman; slowly I turned the handle and walked down the mean wooden staircase into the mean suburban street.

CHAPTER XII

THE *TOCSIN'S* LAST TOLL

As I walked home from Kosinski's in the early morning I felt profoundly depressed. The weather had turned quite chilly and a fine drizzling rain began to fall, promising one of those dull, wet days of which we experience so many in the English spring. The streets were deserted but for the milkmen going their rounds, and the tired-looking policemen waiting to be relieved on their beats. I felt that feeling of physical exhaustion which one experiences after being up all night, when one has not had the opportunity for a wash and change of clothes. I was not sleepy, but my eyes were hot and dry under their heavy eyelids, my bones ached, my muscles felt stiff; I had the uncomfortable consciousness that my hair was disordered and whispy, my hat awry, my skin shiny; and this sub-consciousness of physical unattractiveness heightened the sense of moral degradation.

I felt weary and disgusted, and it was not only, nor even principally, the knowledge that Kosinski had gone out of my life which accounted for this. I felt strangely numbed and dull, curiously able to look back on that incident as if it had occurred to some one else. Every detail, every word, was vividly stamped on my brain : I kept recurring to them as I trudged along, but in a critical spirit, smiling every now and again as the humour of some strangely incongruous detail flashed across my brain.

What really weighed me down was a sense of the futility, not only of Anarchist propaganda but of things in general. What were we striving for ? Happiness, justice ? And the history of the world shows that man has striven for these since the dawn of humanity without ever getting much nearer the goal. The few crumbs of personal happiness which one might hope for in life were despised and rejected by men like Armitage, Kosinski, and Bonafede, yet all three were alike powerless to bring about the larger happiness they dreamed of.

I had acquired a keener sense of proportion since the days when I had first climbed the break-neck ladder of Slater's Mews, and I now realised that the great mass of toiling humanity ignored our existence, and that the slow, patient work of the ages was hardly likely to be helped or hindered by our efforts. I did not depreciate the value of thought, of the effort made by the human mind

to free itself from the shackles of superstition and
slavery; of that glorious unrest which spurs men
on to scrutinise the inscrutable, ever baffled yet
ever returning to the struggle, which alone raises
him above the brute creation and which, after all,
constitutes the value of all philosophy quite apart
from the special creed each school may teach;
and I doubted not for a moment that the yeast
of Anarchist thought was leavening the social
conceptions of our day.

But I had come to see the almost ludicrous
side of the Anarchist party, especially in England,
considered as a practical force in politics. Short
and Simpkins were typical figures—M'Dermott,
an exceptionally good one—of the rank and file
of the English party. They used long words
they barely understood, considered that equality
justified presumption, and contempt or envy of
everything they felt to be superior to themselves.
Communism, as they conceived it, amounted pretty
nearly to living at other people's expense, and
they believed in revenging the wrongs of their
classes by exploiting and expropriating the bourgeois whenever such action was possible without
incurring personal risk. Of course I was not
blind to the fact that there were a few earnest
and noble men among them, men who had educated themselves, curtailing their food and sleep
to do so, men of original ideas and fine inde-

pendent character, but I had found that with the
Anarchist, as with the Socialist party, and indeed
all parties, such were not those who came to the
surface, or who gave the *ton* to the movement.
Then, of course, there were noble dreamers,
incorrigible idealists, like Armitage, men whom
experience could not teach nor disappointment
sour. Men gifted with eternal youth, victimised
and sacrificed by others, yet sifting and purifying
the vilest waste in the crucible of their imagina-
tions, so that no meanness, nor the sorrow born of
the knowledge of meanness in others, ever darkens
their path. Men who live in a pure atmosphere of their own creation, whom the worldly-
wise pity as deluded fools, but who are perhaps the only really enviable people in the world.
Notable, too, were the fanatics of the Kosinski
type, stern heroic figures who seem strangely out of
place in our humdrum world, whose practical work
often strikes us as useless when it is not harmful,
yet without whom the world would settle down
into deadly lethargy and stagnation. Then in
England came a whole host of cranks who, without being Anarchists in any real sense of the
word, seemed drawn towards our ranks, which
they swelled and not infrequently brought into
ridicule. The "Bleeding Lamb" and his atheist
opponent Gresham, the Polish Countess Vera
Voblinska with her unhappy husband who looked

S

like an out-at-elbows mute attached to a third-rate
undertaker's business, a dress-reforming lady disciple of Armitage, a queer figure, not more than
four feet in height, who looked like a little boy
in her knickers and jersey, till you caught sight
of the short grizzled hair and wrinkled face, who
confided to me that she was "quite in love with
the doctor, he was so *quaint;*" and numerous others
belonged to that class; and finally a considerable
sprinkling of the really criminal classes who seemed
to find in the Anarchist doctrine of "Fais ce que
veux" that salve to their conscience for which even
the worst scoundrels seem to crave, and which, at
worst, permitted them to justify their existences
in their own eyes as being the "rotten products
of a decaying society." Such were the heterogeneous elements composing the Anarchist party
with which I had set out to reform the world.

The neighbouring church chimes rang out half-
past six as I approached home, and on reaching
the doorstep of the Fitzroy Square house I found
my brother Raymond just letting himself in. On
seeing me he exclaimed, "Oh, Isabel, where have
you been so early?—though really your appearance suggests the idea that you have never been
to bed rather than that you have just risen!" I
confirmed his suspicion and together we entered
his study.

"Well, where have you been? Is there some-

thing new on with the Anarchists ?   I have seen
so little of you for the past six months that I feel
quite out of the world—your world at least."

It was a great relief to me to find my brother so
conversable. We had both been so occupied of
late in our respective ways that we had had but
scant opportunity for talk or companionship. Raymond had now started practising on his own
account; he was popular with his poor patients
in the crowded slums round King's Cross, amongst
whom his work chiefly lay, and day and night he
toiled in their midst. Certainly the sights he saw
there were not calculated to destroy his revolutionary longings, though they were often such as
might well have made him doubt of the ultimate
perfectibility of the human race.

"Oh, I am so glad to find you, Raymond, and I
should enjoy a nice long talk together ; but you
must be tired ; you have, I suppose, only just come
in after working all night ? "

He explained to me that he had been summoned
after midnight to attend a poor woman's confinement, and had stayed with her till past four, when,
feeling more inclined for a walk than for his bed,
he had wandered off in the direction of Highgate
and had only just got home.

"By the way, Isabel," he said, " as I was coming
down the Caledonian Road I met your friend
Armitage. He is a good fellow whom I have

always liked, so I stopped him and we had a chat.
He explained to me that he was attired in his new
pedestrian costume, which indeed struck me as
almost pre-Adamite in its simplicity. He had been
helping some of his friends to move—to shoot the
moon, I fancy, would describe the situation. He
inquired of me what I was doing, and we got
talking on all sorts of scientific and philosophic
problems. It is extraordinary what an intellect
that man has. Only he lives too much in a world
of his own creation ; he seems absolutely oblivious of self, and I feel sure his hygiene and vegetarianism are simply the outcome of his desire to
free himself from all worldly cares which might
impede his absolute devotion to his Cause. He
seems to have practically abandoned his practice.
As we were wandering on rather aimlessly, I suggested accompanying him home, but he did not
appear to jump at the idea, and as I know that it
is not considered etiquette amongst you folk to
press inquiries as to address and so on, I was going
to drop the subject ; but Armitage, after a short
silence, explained that the fact was he had not
exactly got a home to go to. I concluded that he
was in for the bother of changing diggings, and
made some sympathetic remark to that effect ; but
he said that was not exactly the case—that, in fact,
he had given up having a fixed abode altogether.
As you can imagine, Isabel," continued my brother,

"this information somewhat staggered me. I knew
through you that he had long ago given up his
Harley Street establishment and moved into more
populous quarters, where I quite supposed him
still to be residing. But he calmly went on to
explain, as though it were the most natural thing
in the world, that he had been in need of a rather
considerable sum of money some weeks back for
purposes of propaganda, and that, not knowing
where else to obtain the money, he had sold up
all his belongings and cleared out of his lodgings
without paying his rent, 'by way of an example.'
All this he explained with the air of a man ad-
ducing an unanswerable argument, and as his
manner did not admit of remonstrance, I simply
asked him what he thought of doing now, which
started him off on a long account of the opportunities for propaganda afforded by such estab-
lishments as Rowton House, the casual wards, and
the Salvation Army Shelters. 'We want to get
at the oppressed, to rouse them from their lethargy
of ages, to show them that they too have rights,
and that it is cowardly and wicked to starve in the
midst of plenty ; we want to come amongst them,
not as preachers and dilettantists, but as workers
like themselves, and how can this be done better
than by going in their midst and sharing their
life ? ' I could not but feel amazement and admiration at the enthusiasm and sincerity of this man,

mingled with sorrow at the thought that such an intellect as his should be thus wasted. He is a man who might have done almost anything in the scientific world, and now he seems destined to waste his life, a dreamer of dreams, a sort of modern St. Francis in a world lacking in idealism, and where he will be looked upon as a wandering lunatic rather than a saint."

I sat silent for a few minutes. I had not quite realised that poor Armitage had come to this—a frequenter of casual wards, a homeless and wandering lunatic ; my brother was right, the world would judge him as such. I was not, however, in the least surprised at the news.

The servants had by now come down and we had breakfast brought to the study, and I gave Raymond an account of my night's proceedings. When I concluded my brother said,

" Well, Isabel, you will remain almost alone at the *Tocsin*. Kosinski is leaving, Giannoli is gone, Armitage is otherwise occupied. Will you be able to keep it going ? "

"Oh, I could keep it going," I replied. " There are still a lot of comrades hanging on to it ; new ones are constantly turning up. The work can be done between us, there is no doubt of that. It is rather of myself that I doubt. I begin to feel isolated in the midst of the others ; I cannot believe that people like Short and Simpkins can change

Society ; they would have to begin reforming themselves, and that they are incapable of. I can admire a man like Kosinski : I cannot exactly sympathise with him. As to Armitage, I can only grieve that he should thus waste his life and talents. Probably, had he thought a little more of his personal happiness, he would have avoided falling a victim to monomania, for such he is in part. And then—and then—it is not only of others that I doubt, but of myself. Am I really doing any good ? Can I sincerely believe that the *Tocsin* will help towards the regeneration of mankind ? Can mankind be regenerated ? When such questions never occurred to me, or, if they did, were answered by my brain with an unhesitating affirmative, then it was easy to work. No difficulties could daunt me ; everything seemed easy, straightforward. But now—but now. . . ."

"Well, then, why don't you give it up, Isabel ? "

"Give it up ? Oh, how could I ? I have never really thought of that. Oh no ; the paper must come out. I have undertaken it. I must go on with it."

"And you an Anarchist ! Why, I always thought you believed in the absolute freedom of the individual, and here you are saying that you must go on with a work in which you no longer feel the requisite confidence, for the mere reason that you once, under other circumstances, started it."

"You are right, Raymond, logically right, but life is not ruled by logic, whether we be Anarchists or Reactionaries. I feel that I could not give up the *Tocsin*, my interests centre round it; besides, I do not say that I have altered my ideas; I am still an Anarchist, I can honestly work for the Cause; I only said that I doubt. I feel depressed. Who has not had at times periods of depression and doubt?"

"Well, we shall see," replied Raymond. "I got a letter from Caroline last night which I wanted to show you. She says she will be home in another three months, as she has accepted a further engagement for the States now that her tour is nearly over. When she comes home it will be a little company for you in the house. She has friends, and she is sure to be much sought after now, as she seems fairly on the road to becoming a celebrity in the musical world."

I read the long letter, written in the brilliant style which characterised everything about Caroline. She described her triumphs in the various cities of the Argentine and Brazil, the receptions given in her honour, the life and society of these far-away countries, with a brightness and humour which brought home to me the whole atmosphere of the places and people she described. Caroline had always been fond of society, and even before leaving England had become quite a favourite in musical circles; but her quick, bright intelligence had never allowed her to be blind to much that was vulgar and ludicrous in her surroundings. I was truly glad to think that we should meet again before long. The common memories and affections of our childhood formed a solid basis for our mutual friendship, but I could not help smiling as I read the last paragraph of her long epistle: "I expect by now Isabel has had time to grow out of her enthusiasm for revolutions and economics, and will feel less drawn towards baggy-trousered democrats and unwashed philosophers than when I left. Perhaps she may even have come round to my view of life, *i.e.*, that it is really not worth while taking things too tragically, and that it is best to take the few good things life brings us without worrying one's brains about humanity. Selfish, is it not? But I have generally noticed that it is your stern moralists and humanitarians who cause the most unhappiness in the world. Anyhow, if Isabel is less wrapped up in Socialism and Anarchy we shall be able to have a good time when I come home. I am sure to be asked out a good deal, and if the fashionable people who patronise musical celebrities are not free from their foibles and ridicules we shall anyhow be able to amuse ourselves and laugh at them up our sleeves."

So Caroline already counted on my having outgrown Anarchy and unwashed philosophy, as she

phrased it, and grown into drawing-room etiquette!
But she was wrong! I should go on with the
Tocsin. I should still work in the Cause; I had
done so till then, and what had happened since
yesterday to alter my intentions? Nothing, or at
least nothing of outward importance. Only, since
my last interview with Armitage and my parting
with Kosinski, I had begun to formulate to myself
many questions which till then I had only vaguely
felt. Still I repeated to myself that I should go on
with the paper, that I should continue to lead the
same life. Of course I should! How could I do
otherwise? And even if I had changed somewhat
in my ideas and my outlook on life, I certainly did
not feel even remotely attracted towards the sort
of society Caroline referred to. I had a vivid
recollection of once accompanying her to an *at
home,* given in a crowded drawing-room, where the
heavily-gilded Louis XV. mirrors and Sèvres vases
and ornaments, with their scrolls and flourishes, all
seemed to have developed the flowing wigs which
characterised the Roi Soleil, and where the arm-
chairs and divans were upholstered in yellow and
pink satin, and decked out with ribbon bows to
resemble Watteau sheep. Oh no; certainly I
should not exchange the low living and high thinking of my Anarchist days for such artificiality and
vulgar display.

Sunday was generally a very busy day with me,

almost more so than week-days, for there were meetings to be held, literature to be sold and distributed, and lectures and discussions to be attended. I was in the habit of rising rather late, as very often Saturday night was an all-night sitting at the office of the *Tocsin*, and Sunday morning was the only time I found it convenient to pay a little attention to the toilet. But I used generally to manage to be by twelve in some public place, and help Short and M'Dermott to start a meeting. Short, influenced by his inherent laziness, had succeeded in persuading the Italians that he was a great orator, and that they could not better forward the Cause in their new country than by carrying for him the movable platform from which he delivered his spirited harangues; so that one or two of them were generally present helping to form the nucleus of an audience, and ready to lend their valid support should any drunken loafer or top-hatted bourgeois, outraged in his feelings, attempt to disturb the proceedings. Hyde Park was generally my destination in the afternoon, and in the evening we used to repair in force to the hall of the Social Democrats, there to take part in the discussion which followed the lectures, or else some meeting in Deptford, Canning Town, or Stratford would claim my attendance. But on this particular Sunday I felt too tired and despondent to think of rushing out in my usual style.

I shut myself in my room and tried to rest, but
I could not free myself from the sights and thoughts
which had beset me during the night. The words
of Kosinski's friend, "And this is what comes of
struggling for the higher life," still haunted me;
the dead woman, staring blindly into space rose
before me, an image of the suffering forced on the
weak by the strong. Then my thoughts reverted
to Giannoli. What was he doing? I had not
heard from him for over a month, and his last
letter had been far from reassuring. He hinted at
some desperate enterprise he was engaged on, and
as I had no further news of him from any quarter
I thought it not unlikely that he had been arrested,
and was, even then perhaps, suffering unknown
tortures in one of those dreaded Spanish prisons,
where the old systems of the Inquisition still prevail, though modern hypocrisy requires that all
should pass in silence and darkness, content on
these conditions never to push too closely its inquiries, even though some crippled victim who may
escape should rouse for a moment a spasmodic
outburst of indignation in the civilised world. And
even were this not his fate, it was a sad enough
one in all conscience: to rush all over the world,
wrecked in health, driven from place to place by his
wild suspicions, th offspring of a diseased imagina-
tion; deprived of friends, for his mania of persecution drove them off; deprived of means, for

he had sacrificed his all to the propaganda, and his health and mode of life did not permit of any settled occupation.   I felt strangely anxious about him, and this led my thoughts back once more to Kosinski, with whom I had been brought so closely into contact through our relations with Giannoli.   I should never see him again in all probability.   He had told me he was going to Austria.   He too belonged to the *knights of death*, as an Italian comrade had named a certain section of the Anarchists ; and he was working out his inevitable destiny.   I wondered now how I had ever allowed myself to conceive of him otherwise.   I had always known it was impossible, and I felt that it was only an impulse of rebellion against fate which had led me to speak.

Finding sleep out of the question, I got up and attempted to write an article which I had promised to bring down to the *Tocsin* the following morning. The subject I had chosen was "The Right to Happiness," and I argued that man has a right not only to daily bread, as the Socialists maintain, but also to happiness, consisting in the fullest development and exercise of all his faculties, a condition only possible when the individual shall be perfectly free, living in a harmonious society of free men, untrammelled by artificial economic difficulties, and by superstitions inherited from the past.   Some days previously we had had a dis-

cussion on the subject at the office of the *Tocsin*,
and I had maintained my views victoriously against
the pessimistic dogmatism of a German comrade.
But now my arguments seemed hollow to myself,
mere rhetoric, and even that of third-rate quality.
Happiness ! Did not the mere fact of attaining
our desires deprive them of their charm ? Life
was an alternating of longing and regret. I pushed
paper and pen aside, and began roaming aimlessly
about the house. The large old-fashioned rooms
impressed me as strangely silent and forlorn. I
wandered up to the attic which our father had
used as a laboratory, and which had always struck
us children as a mysterious apartment, where he
did wonderful things with strange-shaped instru-
ments and bottles which we were told contained
deadly poison. His apparatus was still ranged on
the shelves, thick in dust, and the air was heavy
with the pungent smell of acids. The large
drawing-rooms with their heavy hangings looked
shabbier and dingier than of old ; I could not help
noticing the neglected look of everything. I had
hardly entered them during the past year, and now
I vaguely wondered whether Caroline on her return would wish to have them renovated. Then I
remembered how I had received there for the first
time, some four years ago, my brother's Socialist
friend, and I could not help smiling as I recollected
my excitement on that occasion. I was indeed

young in those days! I picked up a book
which was lying on a table thick in dust, and sat
down listlessly in the roomy arm-chair by the
fireside, which had been my father's favourite seat.
I began turning the pages of a volume, "The
Thoughts of Marcus Aurelius," and gradually I
became absorbed in its contents.   Here was a man
who had known how to create for himself in his
own soul an oasis of rest, not by practising a selfish
indifference to, and isolation from, public matters
—not by placing his hopes in some future paradise,
the compensation of terrestrial suffering, but by
rising superior to external events, and, whilst ful-
filling his duty as emperor and man, not allowing
himself to be flustered or perturbed by the inevitable.   "Abolish opinion, you have abolished this
complaint, 'Some one has harmed me.' Suppress the
complaint, 'Some one has harmed me,' and the harm
itself is suppressed."   What wisdom in these words!

It was a long while since I had thus enjoyed
a quiet read. For several months past my life
had been a ceaseless round of feverish activity.
Looking back, it seemed to me that I had allowed
myself to be strangely preoccupied and flustered
by trifles.   What were these important duties
which had so absorbed me as to leave me no
time for thought, for study, no time to live my
own life ? How had I come to give such undue
importance to the publication of a paper which,

after all, was read by a very few, and those few
for the most part already blind believers in the
ideas it advocated? Yet I told myself that the
Tocsin had done good work, and could yet
do much. Besides, I had undertaken it, I must
go on with it; life without an object would be
intolerable. The slow hours passed, and when
night came I felt thoroughly worn out and exhausted, and soon got to sleep.

I awoke on Monday morning with a sense of
impending misfortune hovering over me. I had
taken refuge in sleep the previous night from a
host of troublesome thoughts and perplexing
doubts, and I now experienced the hateful sensation of returning consciousness, when one does
not yet recollect fully the past, yet realises vaguely
the re-awakening to suffering and action. I wanted
to get to the office early that morning, for publishing day was near at hand and there was a lot of
work to be finished. I felt that the drudgery of
composing would be a relief to my over-strained
nerves; so, without waiting for breakfast and the
morning paper which I generally scanned before
leaving home, I dressed rapidly and set out for
the *Tocsin*. I had not gone many yards when
my attention was attracted by the large placards
pasted on the boards outside a newspaper
shop :—

" Shocking outrage in Madrid.   Attempt on the life of Spanish Prime-Minister — Many victims. Arrest of Anarchist Assassin.   London Police on scent."

Giannoli !   The name flashed across my brain as I rushed into the shop and purchased the paper.   My heart thumped with excitement as, standing in the shadow of some houses at the corner of the street, I hastily opened and folded the sheet and ran my eyes down the long column, freely interspersed with headlines.

" On Sunday evening, at half-past six, when the fashionable crowd which throngs the Prado at Madrid was at its thickest, and just as the Minister Fernandez was driving by in his carriage, a man pushed his way through the crowd, and shouting 'Long live Anarchy,' discharged at him three shots from a revolver ; the aim, however, was not precise, and one of the bullets wounded, it is feared mortally, the secretary, Señor Esperandez, who was seated beside his chief, whilst the Minister was shot in the arm.   Several people rushed forward to seize the miscreant, who defended himself desperately, discharging the remaining chambers of the revolver amidst his assailants, two of whom have sustained serious injuries.   He was, however, overcome and taken, handcuffed and bound, to the nearest police station.   On being interrogated he refused his name and all particu-

T

lars as to himself, only declaring that he attempted
the life of the Minister Fernandez on his own
individual responsibility, that he had no accomplices, and that his object was to revenge his
comrades who had been persecuted by order of
the Minister. When informed that he had missed
his aim, and that Fernandez had escaped with a
broken arm, whilst his secretary was in danger of
death, he expressed his regret at not having succeeded in his object, saying that this was due to his
wretched health, which rendered his aim unsteady ;
but as to Señor Esperandez, he declared that he
considered him also responsible, inasmuch as he
was willing to associate himself with the oppressor
of the people. Neither threats nor persuasion
could induce him to say more. The police, however, are making active inquiries, and have ascertained so far (midnight of Sunday) that the prisoner
is an Italian Anarchist recently landed at Barcelona
from America, passing under the name of Paolo
Costa. This name, however, is considered to be
false. He is a tall man, of rather distinguished
appearance. The police do not credit the idea that
he has no accomplices, and during the evening
extensive arrests have been made in Madrid and
Barcelona. Over a hundred of the most noted
Anarchists and Socialists in these cities are now in
prison."

Such was the brief outline of facts as given by the *Morning Post.* Of course I had not the slightest doubt as to the identity of the prisoner; the state of weakness and ill-health which had caused him to miss his aim was conclusive, added to the many other reasons I had for supposing him to be Giannoli. This, then, was the deed he had been contemplating! Only the day before I had been wondering why I had no news of him; but a few hours previously he went forth to his death. For it meant death, of course; of that I had no doubt. He would be garotted; I only hoped that he might not be tortured first. I gave a hasty glance at the other details given by the paper. A column was dedicated to the virtues of the prime-minister. He was upheld as a model of the domestic virtues (a few months back Continental papers had been full of a scandalous trial in which Fernandez had been involved), and was represented as the man who had saved Spain from ruin and disaster by his firm repression of the revolutionary parties: by which euphonious phrase the papers referred to the massacres of strikers which had taken place at Barcelona and Valladolid, and the wholesale arrest and imprisonment of Anarchists and Socialists in connection with a recent anti-clerical movement which had convulsed the Peninsula.

These arrests had given rise to a great political

trial for conspiracy before a court-martial, which
had ended in a sentence of death passed on five of
the prisoners, whilst the others were sentenced to
terms of imprisonment varying from thirty to five
years. It was to revenge the injustice and the
sufferings caused by this policy that Giannoli had
attempted the life of the Spanish minister.

Another paragraph caught my eye :—

"London police hot on scent : raids and arrests.

"Our correspondent has interviewed a leading
detective at Scotland Yard who for some years past
has been charged with the surveillance of suspicious
foreign Anarchists. This clever officer informs our
correspondent that he has no doubt the plot was
hatched in London, and thinks that he could name
the author, an Italian Anarchist of desperate ante-
cedents who disappeared from London under
mysterious circumstances nearly seven months ago.
London is a centre of Anarchist propaganda, and
foreign desperadoes of all nationalities flock hither
to abuse the hospitality and freedom which this
government too rashly concedes them. Englishmen
will one day be roused from their fool's paradise to
find that too long have they nursed a viper in their
bosom. We trust that this lesson will not be wasted,
and that the police will see to closing without delay
certain self-styled clubs and 'printing-offices' which

are in reality nothing but hotbeds of conspiracy
and murder."

I hurried along as I read these last words. We
were evidently once more in for troublous times.
The office of the *Tocsin* was clearly designated in
the paragraph I have quoted ; perhaps the office
would be raided ; perhaps the Italian comrades
who were staying there would be arrested. I rapidly
reviewed in my mind's eye the papers and letters
which were in the office, wondering whether anything incriminating would be found ; but I did
not feel much perturbed on that score, as it was my
invariable custom to burn all papers of importance,
and I felt certain that nothing more compromising
would be found than the Bleeding Lamb's tract on
the Seven-headed Beast, which, according to its
author, would "make the old Queen sit up a bit,"
and Gresham's treatise on the persecutions of the
Early Christians. I was glad to think that Kosinski
had settled to leave the country. I knew that
Giannoli had left with him much of his correspondence, and I trusted that this would not
fall into the hands of the police.

I had now nearly reached my destination and, as
I turned up the corner of Lysander Grove, I at once
realised that something unusual had taken place at
the office. The shutters were still up at Mrs.

Wattles's green-grocer's shop, and that lady herself
loomed large at the entrance to the courtyard
leading to the *Tocsin*, surrounded by her chief
gossips and by a dozen or two of dirty matrons.
Several windows were up in the houses opposite
and slatternly-looking women were craning out and
exchanging observations. I hurried on and, pushing
my way past Mrs. Wattles, who I could see at a
glance was in liquor, and heedless of her remarks,
I ran down the narrow courtyard to the office door
which I found shut. I knocked impatiently and
loudly; the door opened and I was confronted by
a detective.

What I had expected had happened. The office had
been raided, and was now in the hands of the police.

In answer to my inquiring look, the detective
requested me to come in and speak to the inspector.
In the ground-floor room three or four Italian
comrades were gathered together. The one-eyed
baker, Beppe, was addressing the others in a loud
voice; as far as I could gather from the few words
I caught, he was relating some prison experiences.
The group looked unusually animated and jolly;
the incident evidently reminded them of their own
country. As soon as they saw me enter they interrupted their talk, and Beppe stepped forward to
shake hands, but the officer of the law interposed:
" Now, you fellows, stay there; the young lady is

going to speak to the inspector." I told Beppe I
should soon be down, and he retired, pulling a wry
face at the detective, and making some observation
to his friends which made them all roar with
laughter. Upstairs a scene of wild disorder greeted
my eye. Four or five policemen were turning
over heaps of old papers, searching through dusty
cupboards and shelves ; heaps of pie lay about
the floor—evidently some one had put a foot
through the form of type ready set for the forthcoming issue of the *Tocsin ;* on the "composing
surface" stood a formidable array of pint pots,
with the contents of which the men in blue had
been refreshing themselves. On a packing-case in
the middle of the room sat Short, his billycock hat
set far back on his long, greasy hair, smoking a
clay pipe with imperturbable calm ; whilst little
M'Dermott, spry as ever, watched the proceedings,
pulling faces at the policemen behind their backs,
and "kidding" them with extraordinary tales as to
the fearful explosive qualities of certain ginger-beer
bottles which were ranged on a shelf. At the
editorial table, which was generally covered with
a litter of proofs and manuscript, more or less
greasy and jammy, owing to our habit of feeding
in the office, sat the inspector, going through the
heaps of papers, pamphlets, and manuscript articles
which were submitted to his scrutiny by his

satellites.   I took in all this at a glance, and walking straight up to the inspector, I demanded of
him an explanation of this unwarranted invasion
of the office.

His first answer was an interrogation.

" You are Isabel Meredith, are you not ? "

This opened up an explanation which was brief
and conclusive.   The inspector showed me a
search-warrant, duly signed by a magistrate, and
another warrant for the arrest of Kosinski, and
informed me that the office had been opened to
him by Short, who had represented himself as
one of the proprietors.   The primary object of
the search was to see if Kosinski, who was wanted
by the police in connection with the Madrid outrage, were not on the premises, and also to see
if there were no incriminating documents or
explosive materials concealed there.

" And have you found anything very alarming ? "
I inquired sarcastically.

" No, miss," the inspector replied in the same
tone ; " the most dangerous object in this place
seems to be your printer " (he pointed at Short),
" and we have kept at a fairly safe distance from
him.   Still, of course, I have to go through all
these papers ; they may yet give us a clue to the
whereabouts of Kosinski or your friend Giannoli ; "
and here he looked me straight in the face,

" Maybe," I simply replied with a shrug.   I felt perfectly tranquil on that score, and had but small doubt that Kosinski was by now already on his way out of the country, as he would judge from the papers that the police would be on his track.

"And when will this search be over?" I inquired.

"Oh, I cannot exactly tell you.   It will take me some days to go all through these papers. We shall probably be here for two or three days."

I looked around me.   Everything was disorganised.   The type cases had all been emptied into a heap in the middle of the room, the forms ready locked up had been pied, the MSS. and papers sequestered.   It was utterly hopeless to think of bringing out the *Tocsin*.   The scene reminded me of my first experience of an Anarchist printing-office after the police raid on the *Bomb;* but now I no longer had Armitage to encourage me with his unswerving optimism and untiring energy, nor Kosinski to urge me on with his contempt of dilettantism and half-hearted enthusiasm.   True, Short was there, much the same as in the old days; even his dog could be heard snarling and growling when the policemen administered to him some sly kick; but as I looked at the squalid and lethargic figure with its sallow, unhealthy, repulsive face, I was overcome by a feeling of almost physical nausea. I realised fully how loathsome this gutter Iago had become to me during the past few months, during which I had had ample opportunity to note his pettifogging envy and jealousy, his almost simian inquisitiveness and prying curiosity. I felt I could not work with him; his presence had become intolerable to me. I realised that this was the *finale*, the destined end of the *Tocsin* and of my active revolutionary propaganda. I had changed. Why not let the dead bury their dead?

At this moment the policeman who had opened the office door to me came up bringing a letter, which he handed to the inspector.

"It is for you, miss," that functionary said, reading the address, "but I have orders to open all correspondence. You will excuse my complying with them."

My heart stood still. Could it be from Kosinski or Giannoli? After a moment the inspector handed the note to me. It was from the landlord—a notice to quit. I walked up and showed it to Short.

"Well, what will you do?" he inquired. They were the first words we had exchanged that morning.

"I shall leave," I replied.

"And how about the paper? Do you think of starting it again?"

"No, I do not think so; not for the present at any rate."

"And the 'plant'?"

"I shall leave that too. You can look after it, you and the comrades!"

"Oh, the comrades!" sneered Short, and returned to his pipe.

I turned once more to the inspector. "I am free to leave, I suppose?" I inquired. "I cannot see that my presence here serves any purpose."

"Oh yes, miss, you can go if you like. The presence of the printer is sufficient for us. I understand he is one of the proprietors?"

"Oh yes, he is a proprietor," I replied, and turned on my heel. M'Dermott came up to me.

"Well, my dear," he said, "so you are leaving. Well, I don't blame you, nor wish you to remain. After all, it is no use trying to tinker up our rotten system, or to prop up society with such wretched supports as our friend here," and he pointed at Short. "What we need is to get round them by our insidious means, and then go in for wholesale assassination!"

I could not help smiling as the little man gave vent to this bloodthirsty sentiment in an undertone; he wrung my hand warmly, and we parted.

"What do you intend doing with those Italians who stay here?" I inquired of the inspector as the sound of a guitar proceeding from downstairs recalled my thoughts to them.

"I think it best to detain them here until I have finished searching the place thoroughly; then if I find nothing to incriminate them, they will be free. You need not worry about them, miss, they do not seem likely to suffer from depression."

The twanging of the guitar was now accompanied by Beppe's powerful baritone voice, whilst the others joined in the chorus:

"Noi, profughi d'Italia . . ."

I walked down the stairs.

"Good-bye, Comrades!"

"Good-bye, a rivederci!" and after giving one last look at the familiar scene, I walked out.

As I made my way down the yard leading to the street, I encountered Mrs. Wattles at the back door of her shop. She had now reached the maudlin stage of intoxication. Her eyes were bleary, her mouth tremulous, her complexion bloated and inflamed. There was something indefinite in her appearance, suggesting the idea that her face had been boiled, and that the features had run, losing all sharpness of outline and expression. She fixed me with her fishy eye, and dabbing her face with the corner of her apron began to blubber.

"S'elp me Gawd, miss," she began, "I never thought as I should come to this! To have them narks under my very roof, abrazenin' it out! I always knew as there was something wrong abart pore Mr. Janly, and many's the time I've said to 'im, 'Mr. Janly, sir,' I've said, 'do take a little something, yer look so pale.' But 'e always answered, 'No, Mrs. Wattles, no; you've been a mother to me, Mrs. Wattles, and I know you're right, but I can't do it. 'Ere's for 'alf a pint to drink my health, but I can't do it.' And I dare say as it were them temp'rance scrupils like as brought 'im to 'is end."

At these tender recollections of Giannoli the good lady quite broke down.

"To think that it was I as let you that very shop two years last Christmas, and that pore Mr. Cusings, as was sweet on you then—I've not seen 'im lately—and now the coppers are under my very roof! It seems a judgment on us, it really does. But I always told Wattles that if he went on treatin' of 'is wedded wife more like a 'eathen than a Christian woman, as a judgment would come on 'im, an' now my words is proved."

She seemed by now quite oblivious of my presence: a quivering shapeless mass of gin-drenched humanity she collapsed on to the doorstep. And with this for my last sight and recollection of the place which had witnessed so much enthusiasm, so many generous hopes and aspirations, and where so many illusions lay buried, I walked forth into the London street a sadder if a wiser woman.

THE END